TEAGAN HUNTER

Editing by Editing by C. Marie

Proofreading by Judy's Proofreading & Julia Griffis

Cover Design: Emily Wittig Designs

To every Auden out there...
I hope you find your own version of home.

Chapter 1

HUTCH

Lawson: Can't believe you ditched us for a wedding, Hutch. How lame.

Fox: It was for his sister, you dick. Family over friends.

Lawson: STEPSISTER. Not even blood.

Locke: Leave him be, Lawsy.

Lawson: How about you leave ME be, old man.

Locke: Wait until we're back out on the ice.

Lawson: What are you going to do? Break a hip in my direction?

Fox: Give it a rest, Lawson.

Lawson: Bite me, Fox.

Hutch: You're all fucking annoying.

Keller: Hey, I didn't say shit.

Lawson: You never do, which is just as annoying.

Locke: I still don't know why I gave any of you my number.

Lawson: Serpents Singles, baby! That's why.

Keller: Stupid name.

Fox: It does have a nice ring to it…

Locke: No. Absolutely not.

Lawson: I'll wear you all down. Don't worry.

Keller: *out. You'll wear us all OUT. And don't worry, you already do.

I set my phone back on the bar top at the airport lounge, shaking my head at the conversation I just read. It continues to buzz, but I ignore it. My teammates will never stop bickering back and forth, so it's pointless trying to keep up.

Last year, the team I spent so many years with left me unprotected in the expansion draft. I wasn't too shocked when my name was called, but it still left a bitter taste in my mouth. I gave Nashville everything I had, and they left me out to dry. Sure, my numbers dipped during my last season with them, but I didn't think it was so bad I wouldn't be offered another contract. That's exactly what happened though, and I had to live with it.

So, I pulled myself up by the skate laces and decided to give my all to the Seattle Serpents. I was the first player to sign a multi-year deal with them, sealing my fate with the team for the next six years…probably my last six in the league.

I knew building a new team from scratch was going to be hard, but I didn't realize we would suck so bad right out of the gate. The only bright spot in the season was befriending these idiots, who, based on the way my phone keeps buzzing, are still bickering.

We didn't break off into our own little group intentionally. We all just happened to be the only single guys left on the team without interest in settling down.

I'd never, ever tell them—because they'd never shut up about it, especially Lawson—but I'm glad I have them to keep me company. Sometimes it can be lonely when you've dedicated your entire life to something in hopes of winning the ultimate prize—the Stanley Cup.

I want to lift that Cup more than anything, and I'm willing to do anything to make it happen. That's why this year, I'm focusing solely on hockey. No distractions, especially not with the captain spot up for grabs. I want to wear the C for this team almost as much as I want the Cup.

The familiar sound of *Sports Desk* hits my ears and I glance up at the TV hanging over the back of the first-class lounge bar.

"Coming up next, we'll talk more about Adam Hayes, the young star forward from the Carolina Comets who will be joining the Seattle Serpents for their upcoming season."

"You have got to be kidding me." A low groan leaves me as I slink farther into my chair as they go on and on. I'm thoroughly annoyed by the idea of being on the same team as this jackass. Sure, I've known about it for a while now, but that doesn't mean I want to be reminded of it. I guess with the new season approaching, they're ramping up and recycling their old coverage.

We played Carolina a few times last year, and they

were a good team—hell, they just won the Cup—but there is no way this kid is good enough to fill the skates of our guy who retired at the end of the season. Yes, he was getting old and slow, but this kid? After all the shit I've heard about him? All the times I've been told he's nothing but a troublemaker? No fucking thanks. I have zero interest in babysitting. I'm focused on a deep Cup run, not worrying about some young little shit who will likely cause the team much more trouble than he's worth.

"I take it you're not a Carolina fan."

I look up to find the bartender watching me with curious eyes. They've got a glass in one hand and a rag in the other.

I pinch my brows together in a silent question.

They nod toward where my hands are turning white around the glass of whiskey I'm holding. "You're squeezing that glass extra hard and glaring at the television, so I assumed it had something to do with that. By the way, you break that glass, you pay for it."

I bring the whiskey to my lips and guzzle down what's left before setting it back down and pushing it toward the bartender. "Can I get one more?"

They let out a low laugh, probably at my non-answer. "Sure thing."

They turn to grab me another whiskey with precisely two ice cubes—the perfect number to open the flavor while not watering down the booze—and I turn my attention back to the television.

"Hayes was part of the incredible history-making Stanley Cup run the Comets had last season." The commentator turns to the man next to him. "So, what do you think, Jonesy? Think he'll add something to the Seattle Serpents that they're missing?"

Jonesy laughs obnoxiously. "Well, Chuck, the addition of him certainly couldn't hurt. They have these big stars on the team, you know? And I don't want to mention any names, but they know who they are. They aren't showing up like they need to, so maybe a younger guy is just what they need."

I gnash my teeth.

Fuck Jonesy. Fuck him and fuck Chuck and fuck all of them sitting at that desk with those smug smiles, but especially Jonesy because I know—*I know*—it's me he's referring to. Have I been up to par out on the ice lately? No. This was my worst season in the NHL by far. That said, do I need it constantly thrown in my face, especially during the off-season? Fuck no.

The bartender slides a new whiskey in front of me at the right moment, and I waste no time snapping it up and tossing it to the back of my throat.

I use two fingers to shove the empty glass back their way. "Another."

They look down at the glass, then at me, brows

furrowed tightly. I raise one of my own, begging them to challenge me. I'm not drunk—not even fucking close. I'm well within my rights for another drink, and right now, I could really use another drink.

Finally, after several beats, they nod and turn to grab the bottle. This time when they push the glass back my way, I take my time sipping on it, trying my best to tune out the bullshit being spewed on the television.

"Right, Jonesy, but even though things didn't pan out for them last season, they still have some incredible veteran players on their team. That's got to count for something."

All right. I take back all the bad things I said about Chuck. He can stay.

"It does, but only if those guys step up. If their veteran guys or Vezina-finalist goalie aren't doing what they're usually pretty dang good at to close out games, it doesn't matter, Chuck. Especially not when you have Vegas, who went all the way to the Final their first year. It just looks bad all around."

Yep, *fuck Jonesy*.

My phone buzzes against the counter, and I glance down at the screen.

"Wow. You really aren't a Carolina fan, huh?"

I peer to my right where the voice came from. There's a woman who looks at least a few years younger than me sitting two chairs down. She swirls the wine in her glass, and her other arm is slung across the back of her chair, her body angled my way. Her eyes flick between my face and my hand wrapped around my whiskey.

I loosen my grip, not missing how the corner of her plump pink lips twitches like she's trying to hold back her laughter at my clear discomfort.

Tugging my hat down lower just in case, I rest my forearms on the bar top and tell her, "Don't have much of an opinion on Carolina."

She snorts out a laugh. It's loud and pulls the attention of several people, especially since the bar is quiet, but if the new eyes on her bother her, she doesn't show it.

"Strike one," she mutters.

"Strike one?"

She shoves her shoulders back and sits up straight, tipping her chin up. "You lied. You look like you're about to Hulk out every time someone says something about Carolina. That proves you have an opinion about the team, even though you claim otherwise. So…" She lifts a shoulder. "Strike one."

She's not wrong, but I sure as hell don't appreciate being called out on it. I don't want to talk about it, but she's either not picking up on that or doesn't care.

"And you're keeping score because…?"

Ever so slowly, she drags her eyes from my own where they're hidden beneath the brim of my hat, down my face, throat, chest, body, and all the way to my feet tangled up with the barstool I'm sitting on. Her stare isn't intrusive and there's nothing overtly sexual about it, but it still has me shifting in my seat. I just can't decide why.

When she shifts her eyes back to mine, there's a hint of a smile on her lips. It's unsettling, but only because I *liked* how she looked me over. I swear I could *feel* her touching me…and I didn't hate it.

"No reason." The words come out sing-songy as she continues swirling her wine, never looking away from me once.

I narrow my eyes. "Strike one."

"Excuse me?"

"I think you heard me."

"I did. I'm just unsure why *you're* keeping score."

I lift one corner of my mouth and tell her, "No reason."

Now it's her turn to narrow her eyes at me, and the gesture sends a short rumble of laughter through my chest. It's unexpected, and based on how the woman's eyes widen, I'm not the only one surprised by it.

While she's busy being stunned, it's my turn to get a good look at her. Her chestnut hair is thrown into a chaotic bun that's sitting atop her head. I can't tell if the look is intentional or if she really doesn't care. Either way, it matches her relaxed look—black leggings and an oversized gray sweater that reads *Crazy Cat Lady* and keeps slipping down on one side, exposing a pale shoulder that looks soft to the touch.

She doesn't belong here.

It's the only thought running through my head as I examine her appearance. We're sitting in the first-class lounge, for fuck's sake. There's no way this is where she's supposed to be, not dressed like that.

"See something you like?"

I lift my eyes from the pair of plain white sneakers on her feet to her face. Two dark brows are raised high, and a slight smirk plays on her lips.

"Nice outfit," I tell her, giving her my shoulder and lifting my whiskey back to my lips. I take a sip, holding the biting alcohol in my mouth for several seconds before swallowing.

Fuck me. Nothing like a glass of good whiskey to help me ease my nerves before a flight. You'd think being a pro hockey player who flies a good chunk of the year, I wouldn't be bothered by flying, but that's not my luck. I loathe being cooped up in a plane where I have no control over what will happen to me. If there's one thing I like, it's having control.

"Thanks!" she retorts with false cheerfulness. "Picked it out myself and everything."

I hate the way my lips twitch at her sarcasm. I hate even more the way my hands shake as I lower my emptied glass.

"Nervous flyer?" she guesses. She's clearly in the mood to chat and doesn't seem to care that I'm not.

"Yup." The word is clipped, and I hope it's enough to make her realize I don't want to be bothered.

It's not.

"You know, adding alcohol to the mix can actually exacerbate your flight anxiety."

I peek over at her. She's not looking my way. Her attention is on her drink sitting in front of her. "Is that your daily word?"

"Hmm?"

"Exacerbate? Is that your daily word or something?"

She giggles. "No. I just have this weird habit of busting out the big words when I drink too much." She takes a healthy sip of her white wine. "Nervous flyer," she tells me, setting the empty glass on the counter just as a voice comes over the intercom.

"*Flight 1027 for Seattle will begin boarding in five minutes. Please make your way to the gate.*"

I reach into my back pocket and pull my wallet out. I pluck two twenties from inside and toss them on the counter, nodding to the bartender who kept my drink refilled the entire hour I've been sitting here.

"You know," I say to the woman as I push to my feet. She turns toward me, those damn brows arched high once more. "Adding alcohol to the mix can actually *exacerbate* your flight anxiety."

Her lips inch upward in a gleeful grin. "That so?"

"Yep. Heard it firsthand from some crazy cat lady at an airport lounge."

"She sounds smart."

"She sounds drunk."

"Buzzed," she clarifies. "And only barely."

I don't know her well enough to argue that fact, so I let it go, instead grabbing my backpack from the floor next to the chair I just vacated.

"Have a good flight, Mr. Grumbles," she mutters as I walk by.

I laugh, shaking my head as I make my way from the lounge to my gate. She's right—I am grouchy today. I'm grouchy because I had to spend the last two weeks with my family, who, at times, can be wonderful, but this latest trip? It was nothing but one painful event after the next since it was my evil stepsister's wedding. She married a man who is basically the male equivalent of her, which equaled two long weeks of them being the most dramatic humans on the planet and calling off the wedding three separate times, including *on the wedding day* thirty minutes before the bride was set to walk down the aisle because she hated the first look photos—whatever the fuck those even are.

Then, just when I'm coming down from all the bullshit of the trip—including losing my luggage on the way there—I'm reminded that when I hit the ice in two weeks, I'm going to have a new teammate I'd rather not have. So yeah, I am grouchy, and I don't give a shit if a random woman in the airport lounge thinks I'm an asshole because of it.

I reach the gate just in time to hear them announce that first-class passengers can board, so I scan my ticket with the airport worker, then walk down the narrow and awful-smelling ramp to the plane I am not looking forward to sitting on for the next six hours, especially since I know I have to sit next to someone. I'd much rather have nobody next to me, but the flight I chose didn't have single-seat options, so I'm stuck trying to avoid conversation the entire ride home.

I grab my tablet from my backpack, then slide my headphones over my ears—the last thing I want is for my seatmate to think I want to talk—and load up Netflix. I connect to the in-flight Wi-Fi and queue up *Community* to continue my eighth rewatch, then I settle back into my seat, turning my head away from the aisle so I don't make eye contact with anyone that walks by. I've somehow managed to make it this far in the trip without someone recognizing me, and I'd like to keep it that way.

I keep the noise canceling off so I can hear any announcements, but it's all the same crap it usually is: the flight attendants saying things like *full flight* and reminding people not to overstuff the bins above them and asking everyone to take their seats quickly.

"Attention passengers: we're looking for an Auden Sinclair. Auden Sinclair, are you on this flight?"

The attendant repeats the name twice more before shrugging, then announcing they'll be closing the door for takeoff.

"Wait! Wait! I'm here!"

I'm sitting close to the front of the plane, and even with my headphones over my ears, I can hear the voice coming from the walkway. It's a woman, so I assume it's this Auden Sinclair person we're waiting on. She sounds panicked, and I guess I would be too if I were the idiot holding up the flight for everyone else.

"I'm here!" she repeats as her shoes slap against the airplane floor. "I'm here. So sorry. I had to pee."

The attendant gives her a tight-lipped smile. "No trouble. Next time, please remember we have lavatories on board that you're more than welcome to use."

"Sure, but those dang things are always so tiny, and I swear someone always has to take a massive shi—"

"Good morning, folks. I'm Captain Archer, and I'll be your…"

The captain cuts off whatever the woman was going to say next, which is fine by me. I'd rather not listen to her excuses and just get this damn plane off the ground.

Seconds later, a shadow falls over me, then the bin above me is pulled open. *Shit*, I curse to myself. Because why wouldn't my seatmate be the late person? Goes with the theme of the rest of my trip, I suppose.

She plops down next to me, her bag hitting the tray table as she clambers into the seat. The table falls, but it doesn't seem to bother her. She just sets her bag on top of it and begins rooting around in it. A familiar scent tickles my nose as she gets settled. I can't exactly place it, but I could swear I've smelled it recently. Today, even. It smells like—

"Oh, hey! It's you! Hi, Mr. Grumbles!"

I turn toward the cheerful voice coming from my left.

It's her. The woman from the lounge. She's smiling at me like we're old friends, like she can't wait to annoy me for the rest of the flight—like she's going to *enjoy* annoying me.

She moves her hand around, the one that's plunged deep inside the oversized black bag, then it reappears with a bag of chips. She shoves the awful-smelling things right under my nose, shaking the bag as if I can't smell the pungent foot-like stink coming off it.

"Frito?"

I want to roll my eyes or sneer at this woman because what the hell is she thinking? Could she not tell from my demeanor in the lounge that I'm in no mood to talk? If I didn't want to talk then, I sure as hell don't want to talk now.

But I don't say anything like that. I don't roll my eyes, and I don't sneer. I simply shake my head once, answering her question.

"Your loss."

She shrugs, takes the bag back, and shoves a few chips into her mouth, and even with my headphones on, the crunch is loud and obnoxious.

Fucking hell. This is going to be a long flight.

Chapter 2

AUDEN

Why are the hot guys always such assholes?

And I don't mean the good kind of asshole. I mean an *asshole* asshole. Unfortunately for me, my seatmate is of the *asshole* asshole variety, and he's stupidly hot.

I noticed him the second he walked through the doors of the airport lounge. They slid open, and he walked through the lobby like he owned the damn place. Hell, with how he carries himself, shoulders pressed back and head held high, he just might.

He breezed right past me and settled into his chair, then proceeded to toss back four drinks in the span of an hour. Unlike me, who had one drink and began feeling it not even a quarter of the way in, he didn't stumble or slur his words in the slightest. I'm sure a lot of that had to do with just how damn big the guy is.

There's no way he's anything under six foot four, which means he's a hot *and* tall asshole—my weakness.

The most infuriating part of our time in the lounge wasn't that he was being a jerk. No. It was that I felt bad for him. With the way his hands shook, it was obvious he feels uncomfortable flying. It made me want to reach over and hold my own over them to steady his movements.

Fine. Maybe I also want to know if his touch burns as hot as his stare. Because boy oh boy did it feel like flames were licking at my skin as he raked his eyes over me.

I grin to myself thinking about what must have gone through his mind as he took in my attire since I am not one of those people who dress up to go to the airport. It's the fucking airport, for crying out loud—who cares what you look like? Especially when chances are you're going to get hot and sweaty and end up smelling like an airplane wherever you land. It's pointless to get all fancy, even if you do plan to use the first-class lounge.

"Ma'am, could you please put your seat in the upright position and close your tray for takeoff?"

I glance up to find the attendant standing over me with a tight-lipped smile. She doesn't like me. That much is obvious with how her grin wobbles and how the corners of her eyes crinkle a bit too much, like her movements are exaggerated.

Good thing for her is that I'm refusing to let anyone spoil my good mood today. I just closed a major deal with yet another professional sports team—my second this year, thank you very much. There's nothing that can get me down, not the grouchy guy sitting next to me and not the flight attendant who clearly hates me.

"Sure thing." I click the button on my chair as I shove my bag between my legs and kick it until it's under the seat in front of me. I push the tray up and twist the handle, but my effort is futile because the second I remove my hand, the tray falls right back down into my lap.

"Please, ma'am. Your tray," the attendant says, appearing once more. Somehow, her already strained smile is even *more* strained.

I shoot her the biggest grin I can muster. "I'm sorry. I don't know what's wrong with it. I—"

"It's fine, Darla," a velvety smooth voice says from my right. A large hand lands on the tray, holding it in place before it can fall again. "I'll make sure she gets it back up."

The woman—Darla, I guess—peeks over at Mr. Grumbles. This time, the smile that spreads across her lips is genuine because she likes *him*. Honestly? I can't say I blame her, not with all that sweet, sweet sugar he just dumped all over his words, making him sound like a concerned gentleman and not some grumpy asshole.

"Thanks." She tucks a loose strand of hair behind her ear, batting her lashes. "I appreciate that."

"Sure thing, doll."

He sends her a wink, and I'm betting with the way Darla fans herself as she scurries off, her first stop will be the bathroom to give those wet panties of hers a check.

He loosens his grip on the tray, and it falls into my lap once again.

"It's broken," I tell him.

"I know," he responds, reaching down between his legs and pulling his backpack from under the seat in front of him. He unzips the main pocket, then shoves his hand right to the bottom, digging around for something. What? I have no clue. Unless he's MacGyver or has a spare airplane seat part in his bag, I have no idea how he's going to fix the tray.

"Then why not tell *Darla*?"

I hate how I say her name like I have some reason to hate her. I don't. I don't even know her.

"Because she can't fix it any more than you can." He says it to me like I'm ridiculous for thinking otherwise.

"And *you* can?"

"Yes." He pulls out a roll of tape, shaking it. "See?"

"You have tape in your backpack?"

He doesn't respond. Instead, he slides his bag back under the seat and rips off a few pieces of tape before sticking them to the tray, securing it like nothing happened.

When he's finished—and he double-checks to make sure it's not going anywhere—he slides the empty roll of tape into the pocket attached to the chairs in front of us, then he settles back into his spot and turns to face the window.

What the...

"Um...thank you?" It comes out as a question because I'm not entirely sure if I *should* thank him. What kind of weirdo walks around with tape in their backpack? Is he *really* MacGyver, then? Like a super-duper hot MacGyver?

"Hmm."

That's his only response, which doesn't surprise me.

The plane begins moving, and I hold my breath as it does. I hate flying, hate it so dang much. Unfortunately, my job requires me to do it multiple times a month. You'd think I'd be used to it by now, but I'm not, especially not taking off and landing. Those are the two worst parts for me. My anxiety always spikes and makes me want to scratch and claw my way from the aircraft.

I grip my armrest tightly and gulp in several breaths as the plane makes its way to the runway.

In. Out.

One. Two.

In. Out.

One. Two.

I repeat it over and over, and just as I think I have it all under control, the engine really fires up, and so does our speed. Much like how my seatmate's knuckles turned white against his whiskey glass, so do mine around the armrest. I wonder how he's holding up, being a nervous flyer and all. I'd peek over at him, but I can't for the life of me convince myself to open my eyes. My breaths grow more and more ragged as our speed increases, and my body tingles from all the panic racing through me.

That's when I feel it.

I peel my eyes open and look to the right just as Mr. Grumbles finishes slipping his headphones over my ears.

"It helps."

Two words. That's all he says—or mouths—before turning to look out the window like nothing happened.

I don't take my eyes off him for a second, not even when the wheels of the plane leave the tarmac. Not when the plane tips back and we're at that angle I dread so damn much, and not when we hit some turbulence as we soar up, up, up and through the clouds. I don't even pay attention to the country music —the one genre I can't stand—filling my ears.

Instead, I watch him. I count the few freckles scattered over his cheeks. I look at his eyelashes, the ones that are long and dark and cast a shadow across his face. I trace the length of his nose over and over again, noticing on my third pass how it hooks just slightly to the right, like maybe once upon a time it was hit.

I watch him as he watches the clouds pass by until the captain comes over the intercom and announces we have reached cruising altitude but are expecting a bumpy ride. His shoulders tense at the announcement as my stomach begins to do flips.

"A bumpy ride? God, I hope that's not true."

He finally looks back over at me, and our eyes collide, his blue-gray gaze with my own hazel one. It's not a heated stare. It's not an annoyed stare. It's simply two strangers who hate flying catching eyes.

I reach for his headphones to give them back, but he shakes his head. Ignoring him—because I'm not going to commandeer his headphones for the entire flight—I pull them free anyway and hold them out his way. He stares at them for a few seconds before reaching out and grabbing them.

"Thank you," I tell him. "You didn't have to do that."

"It was either that or having to deal with Darla being pissed the whole flight because you ripped off the armrest." He nods toward where my hands were previously wrapped around the piece of plastic. "Your nails already left marks."

I wince. "Oops."

He shakes his head, slipping his headphones back over his head. He doesn't pull them over his ears, instead letting them rest around his neck. I'm surprised. I thought for certain he'd go back to his show and ignore me for the rest of the flight, but I'm not about to point that little fact out to him. I like his company entirely too much, even if he is kind of a dick.

I'm sure most people find me annoying on flights, but if I don't talk throughout the duration, I'll get all gross and gaggy and want to vomit. Talking is my comfort, my way of keeping my mind off the sky and focused on the here and now. I've tried reading—it makes me more nauseated. I've tried watching something—the same as reading. Sleeping is a no-go, too, mostly because I'm terrified I'll snore or fart and someone will record me and put me on blast on the internet, where I'll become a viral sensation for all the wrong reasons. They may say all press is good press, but I highly doubt they mean *that*.

"Soooo…" I start, and slowly, *very* slowly, he turns back my way. I gulp when his eyes connect with mine. He's still wearing that stained baseball cap—something that doesn't really go with his pressed jeans and Armani sweater—so it's not like I'm getting the full effect of his gaze, but even with the shadow cast across his face, it's obvious his eyes are beautiful.

"So?" he prompts when I don't speak. It's another surprise. I thought for certain he'd turn away again when I didn't continue.

"So, *Mr. Grumbles*, is Seattle your destination or just a stop along the way?"

"Hutch."

I tip my head to the side. "Excuse me?"

"Hutch," he repeats. "My name is Hutch, not Mr. Grumbles." He narrows his eyes just slightly when the moniker rolls off his tongue, but it's not a mean kind of narrowing. It's almost like he…*likes* it.

Huh.

"Are you sure?" I ask him. "Mr. Grumbles has such a nice ring to it, and it seems to fit you oh so perfectly."

His lips twitch, but just as quickly as it happens, he's back to frowning. "I'm sure."

"Ah." I nod a few times. "I get it now. Well, *Hutch*, it's nice to meet you. I'm—"

"Auden Sinclair," he interrupts. "I'm aware."

He's aware? As in, he knows who I am? Like he knows the Sinclair name or knows *me* specifically?

"They called your name over the intercom," he explains before I can ask him to clarify. "When you were holding up the plane and Darla was looking for you."

This time when he stares at me, his look *is* mean.

"What? Can you blame me? The bathrooms on planes are so tiny and gross. There's always somebody who stinks it up." I scrunch my nose up. "No, thanks."

"You didn't think when they announced our flight was boarding soon you should have used the restroom then instead of waiting until they were almost done boarding?"

"And follow you out of the lounge like some crazed stalker? Not a chance."

"Yet here you are anyway." He picks up his tablet and closes out the app he had pulled up. He grabs his backpack from under the seat, slips his device back into it, and sits back, resting his hands in his lap. "Yes, Seattle is my final destination."

"Hey, whoa! Don't say that!"

His dark brows shoot up. "Say what?"

"You know...FD."

"I'm not following."

I look around, making sure nobody else is paying us any attention. They aren't. They're all completely absorbed in their own lives.

I lean into him, trying hard to ignore how my senses feel like they're on overload when the cedar and sandalwood of his cologne hit me as he meets my movements. Our heads are close, nearly touching, and I'm doing my absolute best not to lose myself in his blueish-gray eyes.

"Final destination," I whisper.

He tips his head to the side in a silent question.

"The movie," I explain. "It all started with a flight to Paris that exploded in the sky. I don't like uttering those words on a flight. Just in case, you know?"

Those damn full lips of his twitch once more. I want to reach over and wipe the smirk off his face.

"That makes complete and total sense." His words drip with pure sarcasm, and his eyes spark with mischief. "Not at all crazy-sounding."

"Don't mock."

"I would never mock you, Auden Sinclair."

"Oh, I have a feeling you definitely would…Mr. Grumbles."

Another lip twitch, another urge to reach over to him. It's the second time in just a minute, which is two times too many, so I sit back, putting distance between us once more.

"Are you superstitious?" I ask.

He laughs lightly, the quick sound somehow still deep and rumbly. "You could say that."

He doesn't offer anything else, and as much as I want to ask him about it, it doesn't seem like my place, so I drop it.

"Is Seattle yours?" he asks. "Your…" I widen my eyes, begging him silently not to say the phrase I hate so much. "Destination," he finishes.

I exhale slowly. "It is. I'm born and raised in the PNW. You?"

"Upstate New York."

"But you live in Seattle now?" He nods in response. "Wow. That's quite the distance to cover. How'd that come to be?"

"Work."

One word. That's the only answer I get. Again, as much as I want to, I don't press.

"Were you visiting family in New York, then?"

"Unfortunately."

"Uh-oh. Family drama?"

He laughs derisively. "Usually, no, but this was my stepsister's wedding. Easily the worst bridezilla I've ever seen, and I've been in a lot of weddings over the years."

"Always the groomsman, never the groom?" I tease.

"Is that your not-so-subtle way of asking if I'm married?"

Oh. Well, that wasn't my intention, but now that he's mentioned it...

"No," he states before I can say anything else. "I'm not married, nor do I ever *want* to be married."

"*That's* the vibe I've been getting from you!" I slap the armrest, then snap my fingers. "You're a jerk with a chip on his shoulder because he got dumped, and now, he's heartbroken and refuses to ever be in love again."

He laughs, and this time, it's a full-body laugh, the kind that draws the attention of everyone around you. And yep, there's the guy in front of us turning around to glare.

I wave at him, then turn back to a still-laughing Hutch.

"What's so funny?"

"You've got me pegged, huh?" He shakes his head, grinning down at me because even seated, he's still that much taller than me. I have no idea how he's not feeling cramped in these seats. Even in first class, it's not like there's an abundance of room on the plane.

"Am I wrong?" I tip my chin up, already feeling victorious in our little verbal sparring match.

His grin slips just a bit. "Not entirely."

"Uh-oh. Was it recent?"

"Was what recent?"

"The heartbreak. Is that why you frown so much?"

"I frown a lot?"

I slide my eyes to the wrinkles between his eyebrows, caused by how tightly they're crushed together. "You're frowning as we speak."

I laugh as he tries his hardest to get his lips to turn up and his brows to relax. It's a futile attempt because no matter what he does, he's still frowning.

"So, is it fresh?"

"No. It's not fresh." His eyes drift away from mine, looking over my shoulder like he's being taken back to better days. When he finally returns his gaze to mine, he says, "And yours? Was your heartbreak recent?"

"My heartbreak? What makes you think I had my heart broken?"

He casts his eyes downward, tracing the length of my body. It's as heated as the first once-over he gave me. If he was trying to be subtle about it in the lounge, he failed. He was as subtle then as he's being now, which is to say—not at all. "Well, for starters, you're a crazy cat lady."

I drop my head, looking down at my most favorite sweater, and grin. "I don't have any cats."

His head tips sideways again. "Then…"

"It was a gift from my sister, an inside joke between

the two of us. We're twins, so naturally, our parents used to dress us in the same outfits. Every year for our birthday since we were eighteen, one of us has overseen buying matching shirts. Five years ago, she got me this. *She's* the crazy cat lady, so *I* had to be a crazy cat lady too." I shrug. "I'm fine with it. It works as a great deterrent for creepy guys in airport lounges."

That mischievous spark that dwindled out of his eyes when I mentioned his past heartbreak reappears. "I'm not the one who wouldn't leave me alone."

I point to my chest. "Nervous flyer, remember? Talking helps calm my nerves."

"Have you tried—"

My gasp cuts off his words as the plane hits turbulence, and I'm back to clutching the armrests like a lifeboat. My back is pressed straight against the seat, and I slam my eyes closed, hoping and praying the rest of this flight goes by quickly and with no more bumps and this is the only turbulence we experience. I really don't want a bad flight to be the thing that ruins my day.

Static over the intercom hits my ears.

"Good afternoon, everyone. This is your captain. I just wanted to let you know some rough weather has popped up, and we're in for a bit of a bumpy ride. I won't be turning that seatbelt sign off anytime soon, and the beverage cart won't be run. We apologize for any inconvenience and hope to get through the worst of it quickly."

"Crap, crap, crap," I mutter.

That's when I feel it—*him*. Hutch closes his hand around mine, peeling the fingers clutching the seat free and wrapping his hand around them. It's a soft hold, but it's comforting all the same, warm. It feels familiar and not at all foreign. It's enough to pull me from my panic, and I gulp in several breaths for what feels like the first time in minutes.

I have no idea how long passes until the bumps subside, but when they do, I finally pry my eyes open and look over at Hutch. His eyes are already on me. If he's scared too, I can't tell. He's not giving anything away other than pure sympathy that's directed at me. I want to hate it so much, but I don't, not with his hand still wrapped around mine.

I slide my eyes down to where our hands are still clasped together, then look back up at Hutch. He gives me a soft smile before removing his touch, and I miss it the second it's gone. His tongue darts out to wet his lips, then he blows out a heavy breath, running his hands over his thighs a few times, his own nerves finally showing through.

"It was eight years ago." He looks up at me. "Eight years ago, I was stood up at the altar."

My jaw slackens at his words, surprised he

confessed something so personal and important to some random woman he's just met, but my shock is momentary. I realize *why* he's just confessed this to me —he's trying to distract me. He's *talking*.

I like that he's talking.

"It was for the best," he continues like my mouth isn't still hanging open. "I know that now, but back then, it sucked. Either way, it's in the past. Besides, I'm married to my job, and that's all the commitment I can manage."

His words don't surprise me. Based on how finely he's dressed, I assumed he was on a business trip. Those of us obsessed with work can usually pick out the others.

"You too, huh?"

He does that little head tip again. "You're married to your job?"

"According to my father, yes."

And my sister and my best friend and just about everyone who knows me. It's no secret that I love to work. I've never hidden that fact. But lately…lately I've been starting to see the merits of all their protesting, though I'm not ready to fully confront that truth just yet.

"Is that why you're traveling?" Hutch interrupts my thoughts. "For work?"

"Yes, and wouldn't you know, for someone who

hates flying so dang much, I do it at least three times a month."

"Three times? That's it? Those are rookie numbers, Sinclair. Gotta beef those stats up."

Sinclair.

I don't know why, but I like that he called me by my last name. Nobody ever calls me that, which is ironic since it sits on the side of every building I own.

"Do you often travel for work, then?"

"Too often, if you ask me." He smiles fondly. "But I wouldn't trade it for the world. I love my job."

"And what is it you do for a living, Hutch?"

He opens his mouth, but nothing comes out as the lights go out, a baby starts to cry, and all hell breaks loose around us. An overwhelming sense of dread hits me, and there is no doubt in my mind that the plane is about to crash.

I'm about to die. I'm about to die sitting next to the hottest jerk on earth, and I never even got to see if his lips taste as good as they look. I guess this day can be ruined after all.

Chapter 3

HUTCH

"There are no other flights out tonight?"

"For the third time, sir, no. The weather out there is too bad, and no planes are allowed to leave." Almost like the weather can hear the woman deliver the shitty news, a loud clap of thunder shakes the walls of the airport. "See? Nobody is flying in that. You're stuck for the night. We've already rebooked you for the first flight out in the morning, Mr. Hutchinson."

I repress my sigh and give her a tight smile before muttering a quick *thanks* and turning on my heel. Fucking great. Just awesome. This is exactly what I wanted to happen today. Just when I thought this trip couldn't get any worse, I'm proven wrong.

"Hey."

The voice is quiet and shaken, and I know who it is before I even turn.

Auden lifts her hand, the same one I held until the flight finally landed here in Chicago, and she gives me a small wave with a wobbly smile. Her bun is gone, and her dark brown hair is now spilling around her shoulders. It's still messy, like she's run her fingers through it a thousand times, and I wouldn't be surprised if that were true.

When the lights went down and we hit the worst turbulence I've ever experienced, I thought for certain she was never going to breathe again, but here she is. She made it through. *We* made it through.

At least I have that going for me today.

"How are you?" I cross the distance between us, stopping a few feet away from her. "Are you all right?"

"I'm feeling better," she claims, even though she doesn't look it. Her complexion is still pale, and the quake in her voice that wasn't there before remains. "I'm a bit shaky and queasy, though."

"Have you eaten anything?" I ask when her stomach rumbles loud enough for me to hear. We landed about an hour ago, and they've been working their way through the passengers, getting us rebooked for tomorrow. Auden disappeared as soon as we got off the plane, and this is the first I've seen her since.

She shakes her head. "Just those few Fritos. I thought I'd grab something in Seattle, but…"

"Do you want to get something here? Looks like we're stranded in Chicago for the night."

"So I've heard." She rolls her eyes. "Stupid storms. I've always hated them, but now I hate them even more. I was really looking forward to sleeping in my own bed."

She's telling me. I've been missing my California king for weeks now and had grand plans of spending a solid twelve hours in it tonight. That plan is now thrown out the window.

"Anyway," she says, "thanks for the offer on food, but I'm going to grab a room at the hotel down the way, then catch a flight out tomorrow." She exhales heavily, then takes a step closer.

Then another. And one more. We're only inches apart now, so close I can *feel* the heat radiating off her. She tips her head back to look up at me.

"I'm not sure I would have survived that flight if you weren't there." Her soft pink lips turn upward. "So, thanks, Hutch. For *everything*."

She wraps her hand around mine, giving it a gentle squeeze before pressing up on her tiptoes and letting her lips rest against my cheek so quickly it almost feels like nothing at all, even when it's definitely something. She drops back down to her heels, sends me another smile, then walks away from me. I watch her go with her big black bag hauled up on her shoulder, those damn Fritos hanging out the top.

Stop her.

The words tumble around in my mind, but I do my best to shove them away. I have no reason to stop her. Hell, I shouldn't even want to because I don't know her. I think it's my subconscious wanting to ensure she's okay, especially after how shaken she was on the flight, but she's fine now. She's okay, and so am I. We should go our separate ways and put this awful day behind us.

I chuckle, shaking my head at the ridiculousness of this whole goddamn experience. I hike my backpack up higher, then hit the bathroom before making my way to the exit. I'm not going to sleep in an airport overnight. No way, no fucking how.

I pull my phone from my pocket and find the highest-rated hotel nearby: The Sinclair. I recognize the name, and not just because of it being Auden's last name. We stay in those hotels all the time. They're my favorites, so I hit book on the app without thinking twice.

Ten minutes later, I'm sitting in the back of a cramped Toyota, wishing like hell I'd never gone to the wedding. I could have spent that time—and this time —at home working on conditioning for the upcoming season. I *should* have done that. Hockey is important to me, and that's where my focus should have been. But *no.* I just had to be back in New York.

The Uber drops me off and I get checked in, then drop my bag in my room before heading right back down to the hotel bar. A drink is exactly what I need after this long day.

"What can I get for you?" the bartender asks the second my ass hits the stool.

"Whiskey, two cubes."

"Preference?"

"Whatever's strong."

He laughs. "Sure thing."

He turns to make my drink, and I lift my hat, running a hand through my hair before tugging it back down.

"Strike two."

No fucking way...

I turn on my stool to find Auden sitting at the opposite end of the bar. Her hair is wet and she's changed clothes, but it's her. I'm certain of it.

She lifts her drink—another white wine—to her lips and takes a sip, never breaking eye contact with me.

"I think we may need a new nickname soon with you racking up all these strikes. Hope you weren't a baseball player in another lifetime. It would be really embarrassing for your stats."

Joke or not, the reminder of how my stats are in fact sitting in the toilet doesn't feel good. It has my jaw tightening just thinking about how damn badly I need to fix things, but I try to shove the thoughts aside. That's not a *me* problem right now. Right now, I want to have a drink to unwind and then get to bed. That's it. No dwelling on anything else.

The bartender slides my drink in front of me, and I reach for it like it's the last beverage I'll ever consume, slamming it back in one go. He lifts his brows but doesn't say anything. Instead, he grabs the bottle of whiskey and refills my glass, then walks away.

I wipe my mouth with the back of my hand, then turn back to Auden. "What was my infraction this time?"

"Stalking. It's never an attractive look."

I lift my brows. "Who says *you're* not stalking *me*?"

"I was here first. I can't be the stalker if I'm here first."

"Or"—I hold a finger up—"you're just *saying* you were here first to throw me off."

She clutches her chest. "Why, Hutch, I would *never* do such a thing." I roll my eyes at her terrible attempt at a Southern accent. "Besides, we just shared a near-death experience—I think we're bonded for life or something."

"You do realize the plane didn't go down, right? It was just an emergency landing."

She waves off my words. "It was as close to near-death as I ever want to get."

"I hear that."

I tried to stay calm and collected for her sake—and I'd never admit it out loud to anyone—but that was easily one of the scariest experiences of my lifetime, and I'd like to never, ever endure a repeat of it.

There's a soft creak from my right, and Auden slides off her stool, sashaying my way. She takes the spot next to me, then lifts her glass in the air.

"To near-death experiences and new friends."

I tap my whiskey to her wine, then we take a drink at the same time, but like me only moments ago, she doesn't stop at a sip, instead emptying her entire glass.

"Another one, please, Jon. A fresh bottle this time, will you?"

Jon nods and hurries off for another bottle of wine.

"First-name basis with the bartender, huh?"

"First-name basis with the stewardess, huh?" She lifts a brow, begging me to challenge her.

I roll my lips together, fighting a smile. "That's fair."

Jon comes back with a new bottle, pulls out the cork, and refills Auden's glass. He watches as she takes a sip. When she shoots him an appreciative wink, his ears burn red, and he ducks his face, clearly smitten with her.

"So..." she begins, angling her body toward mine. I match her movements, noting how our knees bump together and how she leans into the touch like she leans into me. That same orange-honey scent from before hits my nostrils, and I inhale heavily. It's unique and somehow familiar already. "Of all the hotels in the area, you picked this one, the same one I'm staying at. What a strange coincidence, huh?"

I crowd closer to her, watching as her pupils grow to twice their size with our proximity. "Or, like me, you just Googled the highest-rated hotel in the area and booked a room. Not really a coincidence if you think about it."

Her lips curl up in a grin. "I don't know, Hutch. It sounds like fate to me."

She was cheery on the plane, at least when she wasn't clutching the chair and begging for the plane to stop descending. But now? Now she looks playful, maybe even a little devious.

I like devious.

"Are you telling me you think the universe is trying to throw us together? You think meeting in the lounge, then being seated next to one another and meeting here is all because fate has bigger plans for us?"

"Of course. How else would you explain it?"

"Coincidence."

"You don't really believe that, do you?" Another spark in her eye. Another playful grin as she inches closer, her knee slipping in between my legs, pressing against my thigh more and more firmly as the seconds pass.

I know what she's doing. I know what she wants, and fuck me if I don't want it too. After the day I've had, I could use this. I could use *her*—and that's what I would be doing: using. Just for one night. Just a little fun.

"I guess for just one night, I can suspend my disbelief."

That damn spark again.

"Just one night," she counters, her hazel eyes dropping to my lips. It takes effort for her to drag them back to my gaze, and when she does, it's clear where this is leading, clear how badly she wants it too.

I've heard near-death experiences can bring about a rush of desire, the adrenaline from it all sending your sex drive off the charts. I'd say that's what's happening now, but that was nearly two hours ago. This is just two strangers meeting. Two people who agreed to one night of fun. Two people who need the other in a carnal way. And I'm more than willing to see how this plays out.

"I think I may be ready to turn in for the night,"

she says, her pretense so damn false it may as well be a veil I can see through it so clearly.

She digs into her small clutch and retrieves a familiar-looking card. She slides it my way before grabbing her wineglass and finishing off what's left like nothing just happened.

"Just charge it to my room, Jon. His drinks too."

"Sure thing, Ms. Sinclair," the bartender says. He shifts his eyes to me, and jealousy burns in them. He knows exactly what's happening, just like I do.

Auden turns back my way, giving me a saucy grin before saying, "Have a good night, Hutch."

See you soon, Hutch. That's what she really meant.

She slips away from me, rounding the corner to the elevators. I listen as the car arrives and the doors *whoosh* closed behind her.

It's just me and Jon now, and that's the way it stays for the next fifteen minutes. He busies himself with cleaning glasses between shooting daggers my way, and I sip on my whiskey. After he sets his eighth glass in a row onto the counter with a thud, I chuckle. I've overstayed my welcome, and that's fine. I have someone waiting for me anyway.

I knock back the rest of my whiskey before reaching into my back pocket and grabbing some cash. I slide a hundred-dollar bill across the counter for Jon to piss him off even more, then grab the room key Auden left behind.

"Have a good night, Jon." I smirk. "I know I'm going to."

I don't stick around to watch him seethe, instead heading for the elevator. When it arrives, I step inside, pressing the button for the twenty-seventh floor. I try not to let that number—the same one I wear on the back of my jersey—get to me as the elevator climbs the floors.

This is probably reckless. Completely stupid.

But right now, I don't care.

Hockey season starts soon. Once my skates hit the ice, I won't have time for things like this. I'll be engrossed in the game with no time for any extracurriculars. I'll have to focus on one thing —winning.

But that's not for another two weeks. Right now, none of that matters. All that matters is this, Auden. I could tell down at the bar that she needs this as much as I do, that she wants this as much as I do. So why not give in?

The doors slide open, and I step out. There are only two rooms on the floor, and I let out a low whistle. How the hell did she get a room up here? I'm still trying to figure out how she was even in first class, and now this? Maybe she's just really good at sweet-talking and got a deal.

I press the card against the reader, and the machine lights up green, giving me the go-ahead to enter. I grip the handle and turn it, but I don't push the door open quite yet.

This could be a mistake, Hutch. She lives in Seattle too. You could run into her there. She could be some crazed fan for all you know. Do you really want to do this?

That's ridiculous. I'm being ridiculous. I'm damn good at reading people, and my alarm bells don't go off around Auden. This is fine. This will be fine.

I shove the thoughts away, then swing the door open, stepping inside. A soft *click* sounds as the door finds the latch, and I'm bathed in darkness. I blink a few times, letting my eyes adjust to the room. With the curtains open, the space isn't entirely dark, so I can still find my way around when I walk farther into the room.

The suite is quiet, so the running water is quick to draw my attention. I make my way across the room toward the sound. The bathroom door is slightly ajar, and just as I'm about to push it open, it's yanked open.

"Holy shit!"

Auden smacks at my chest, a reflex likely, and I grab her wrist in the process, holding her still and to me.

She jerks her head back, peering up at me with wide eyes. "Hutch."

It's just one word. Whispered. Hushed. Soft.

But it feels so much louder, feels like so much more.

"You scared the crap out of me," she says just as quietly. "I didn't think you were coming."

"I can see that." I rake my eyes over her. She's wearing a big, white, puffy robe and her hair is back up in that damn messy bun. I want to reach over and pluck her hair free so I can watch it cascade around her shoulders as badly as I want to undo her robe and see what she's wearing underneath.

But I don't do either. I catch her gaze with mine, not missing how ragged her breaths are or how that fear in her eyes has turned into something else.

Lust.

I release her hand, letting it fall fully onto my chest, then I grab her waist with my other hand and tug her closer. She falls into me with ease, like it's the most natural thing in the world to her. I slide my fingers up her sides, loving the shiver that runs through her, and keep going until I reach her face. There's a hitch to her breath when I cup her cheek, letting my thumb run over the softness of her skin.

"Going to bed, Auden?"

Her tongue rolls across her bottom lip, and she swallows once. "Maybe."

"Would you like some company?"

Another swallow. A soft sigh.

"Hutch…"

It's not a protest; it's a plea.

And it's all I need.

I crush my mouth to hers and discover I was right —her pink lips are soft, soft and sweet and so fucking delicious. Her hands bunch into fists, clasping my shirt, and though I should probably care since the damn thing was expensive, I don't have it in me. Not right now. Not when she's rising up on her tiptoes and trying to gain the upper hand.

I pull away, chuckling when she groans at the loss. I slip a finger under her chin, tipping her head back so I can peer down into her lust-filled eyes.

"I'll be the one calling the shots here, sweetheart. Understood?"

Her tongue rolls across her lips again, and I follow the path with my thumb, feeling the warmth of her breath on my digit.

"Understood," she whispers.

"Very good," I mutter before taking her mouth with mine again.

When I slide my tongue against the seam of her lips, she moans, granting me the access I want as I gather her into my arms and press her back against the wall. I shove my knee between her legs as I devour her mouth and her chin and her cheek. I kiss every inch of her face before dragging my lips downward and over the column of her neck, loving the choppy sounds that leave her with every gentle touch, loving how she tries to grind down on my knee but can't because my other hand is preoccupied with holding her still.

She lets out another moan when I drag my teeth over the spot just below her ear. I clamp down on the skin, applying light pressure before running my tongue over the spot to soothe it. She's practically wiggling against me at this point, and I laugh darkly.

"You're being mean. I knew you'd be mean."

"I think you like me being mean."

"Shut up," she says, but the *up* comes out a pleased rumble when I nibble on her again.

I drag the hand on her waist inward, toward the front of her loosely tied robe. Fuck me, I am dying to know what's underneath.

"Tell me, Auden." I kiss her lips softly again. "When I peel this robe open, what will I see? Hmm?"

Another kiss.

"Are you naked under this?"

Kiss.

"Will your tits spill out?"

I give the thick belt a gentle tug.

"Will I get a glimpse of your pussy?"

She sucks in several heavy breaths, and I'm not

sure if it's my words making her sweat or the fact that the material begins to give beneath my hands, opening just wide enough for me to slip inside. I do so, and then it's me doing the heavy breathing.

I snap my gaze to hers. "You're naked."

She nods.

"Fucking hell," I mutter, releasing her so I can step back to admire her properly as I peel the robe open all the way.

She wasn't lying; she is naked, completely fucking bare except for the soft patch of dark curls on her mound. Her body is speckled with little dots of sweat, and goose bumps rise along her skin as I take in my fill of her. Her thighs rub together, her hips are full, her stomach is not completely flat, and her tits are just what I like—more than a handful.

She grabs the edges of the robe, pushing the material back until it slides over her shoulders and down her arms all the way to the floor, where it pools at her bare feet. She goes to take a step toward me, but I shake my head, stopping her movements.

She obeys.

I like that she obeys.

But I see the fight in her eyes, and I have a distinct feeling she's not used to someone else taking charge like this. She rests back against the wall, and I step into her, crowding against her, loving her softness against my hard body. I drag my fingertips lightly over her skin, loving how with every inch I cover, her breaths grow harsher.

When I finally reach my destination, I grab the clip that's holding her hair up and tug it free, watching as her brown locks fall around her shoulders like a halo. Funny because I have every intention of behaving sinfully tonight.

"You're fucking perfect, sweetheart," I mutter, unable to stop myself from reaching out and touching her. I trace a single finger between her breasts, dragging it down, down, down until I find just what I'm looking for.

"Oh god," she groans when my knuckle grazes over her soaked slit. "Hutch…please…"

I don't know what possesses me to do it. I usually don't fall to my knees for such a small plea, but I can't help it—I drop. I kiss her soft belly, then her thighs. I kiss her everywhere but where I want to kiss her most. I do it until she's bucking off the wall, begging for me to taste her properly. I hook one leg over my shoulder, and I smile at the strangled cry that leaves her.

"You know, Auden…" I kiss her mound, the tuft of curls tickling my lips in the most delightful way. "I never did eat dinner."

A stuttered breath. Another kiss, this one closer to the meal I'm so looking forward to.

I peek up at her, loving how she's watching me with hazy eyes. She wants this as badly as I do.

"And I'm fucking starving."

Her eyes drift closed as I drag my tongue over her slit, burying it deep, groaning when the sweetness of her cunt hits my tongue. She tastes just as good as I hoped.

No—*better*.

"Holy hell," she mutters as I give her another swipe. "That feels so—*ahhh*…"

I laugh as her words turn into a garbled mess when I suck her clit between my lips, apparently applying just the right amount of pressure. I alternate between that and rolling my tongue against her, not leaving a single part untouched.

Her hand lands on my head, and it's only then that I realize I'm still wearing my ballcap. She rips it off, tossing it I don't even know where, and even though it's my favorite hat, I don't care, not when her fingers are curling into my hair in the most delightful of ways and she's tugging me closer to her.

"Right there. Don't you dare stop," she instructs.

Normally, I'd fight her. I'd stop just because I could. But now that I've had a taste, I can't.

I don't stop at all until she's falling apart around me, her legs shaking, her thighs jiggling, her entire body taut as her orgasm races through her. It's just as perfect as she is.

When her shakes subside, I shove up to my feet, yanking her to me and pressing my mouth to hers so she can see just how good she tastes. I slide my hands under her ass, then she wraps her legs around my waist, and I carry her to the bed, dropping her softly onto the mattress. I wrench my mouth from hers, my hands going to the back of my shirt. I yank it over my head and toss it aside and then move on to my belt. I toe off my shoes as I undo my jeans and shove them down my legs along with my boxer briefs, but not before plucking a condom out of my wallet.

Man am I fucking glad I tucked a few in there just in case I met someone at the wedding, and man am I fucking glad I never got the chance to use them. It's like I knew I'd meet Auden.

I use my teeth to open it, then roll it on, giving my cock a few strokes because I can't help it. The taste of her still lingering on my lips, her looking at me like she is…

I meet her eyes, and a slow smile curves her lips.

"On your knees, sweetheart."

Slowly, she rolls over, then pushes up so her ass is in the air.

Fuck. I'd wager she looks even better like this.

I run my hands over her cheeks, giving them a light

pinch. She groans when I do it, so I test the waters and give them a gentle smack. Another groan. I slap at her again, this time a little harder. The sounds that leave her are carnal, and I fucking love them.

I land another blow as I climb onto the bed behind her. She fists the silk sheets beneath her, wiggling her ass in the air, searching for my touch. I slip a hand between her legs, loving how wet she is for me. She cries out when I slide a single finger into her, then another.

A shout when I wrench them out of her and slide my cock home without warning.

"Holyfuckshitohmygodyes."

I don't know where one word ends and the next begins. It's all a mess, just like she is as she comes for the second time tonight. It's sudden and out of nowhere, neither of us expecting it. I don't let it stop me, though. I grip her hips tightly, slamming into her again and again, her body giving way to every rough movement.

"Yes, yes, yes. More," she chants. "More, Hutch."

I give her more, pulling out until just the tip of me is inside her before sliding home again. I do it over and over until we're both sweaty messes and she's literally shaking from holding herself up. I wrap my arms around her waist, pulling her up to give her arms a break.

"You're doing such a good job." I press a kiss to the spot on her neck that I'm quickly learning drives her wild. I curl my hand around her throat, applying soft pressure. It's not enough to restrict her airway, but enough that she knows I'm the one in control. "You take me so well, sweetheart. This cunt was made for my cock. You know that?"

"Yes." She moans, nodding lazily. "So good."

"Think you can give me one more?"

She shakes her head, and I laugh.

"Strike two, Auden. Don't lie."

"I'm not. I can't, Hutch. I can't."

"You can. You will. Touch yourself. Get there."

Just as I expect, she listens to me. She slips her hand between her legs, playing with her clit as I continue to fuck into her.

It's not long until I hear her mutter, "I'm so close."

I apply just the slightest bit of additional pressure to her throat, then rut into her twice more, and she squeezes me tightly, her orgasm hitting her for the third time tonight. It's just enough to send me over the edge, and I fill the condom with my cum.

I slow my movements as she sucks in breath after breath, my own chest heaving against her back. I let her slide out of my arms and to the bed as I pull out of her, and she makes a noise as I crawl off the mattress.

"Bathroom," I tell her, and she nods, rolling over to her other side.

I dispose of the condom, then wash my hands before making my way back to the bedroom. She's curled up on her side, already snoring softly; I should go. We both got what we wanted out of this. There's no reason for me to stick around.

But that doesn't stop me from slipping back into bed. It doesn't stop me from fitting my body around hers. It doesn't stop me from wrapping my arm around her, tugging her as close to me as possible.

And it doesn't stop me from falling into the most peaceful sleep I've gotten in weeks, making this awful trip not seem so bad after all.

Chapter 4

AUDEN

You take me so well, sweetheart. This cunt was made for my cock. You know that?

"Auden?"

I snap my head up, surprised to find three sets of concerned eyes on me.

"Huh?"

Lilah, my best friend and executive assistant, gives me one of those *Are you serious right now?* looks. She rolls her eyes, then mouths, *"Color scheme."*

I shove my shoulders back, then look right at the man with his arms crossed, lips pinched tightly together.

"Mr. Barnhart, I've told you the color scheme I want for the hotel. I am not wavering on it. You either get me the Deep Sea Blue, or I'll find someone else who will."

It's a threat, and a thinly veiled one. Mr. Barnhart knows it as well as I do, just like he knows I am serious. I've been doing this for too many years to bend at the will of some man who won't get me what I paid for.

He nods once and gives me a gruff "Fine, I'll find it."

I know it's not an issue of finding it. He's mad because he wanted to use a different color so it would match better with some leftover wood he wanted to use, but I *know* what I want my hotel to look like, and it's not what he's trying to do.

"Thank you. Now, anything else?"

Nobody on the video chat says anything. "Great. We'll catch up again on Friday."

I close my laptop and exhale heavily, resting back in my oversized chair.

"I don't think Mr. Barnhart Sr. is going to like you yelling at his son," Lilah says.

"And I don't think he'll like it when I take my contract elsewhere." I lift a brow. "Besides, I didn't yell. I threatened him."

Lilah laughs. "You did, and it was amazing." She picks up her coffee and takes a healthy drink before cutting her blue eyes my way. "So, were you thinking about *him* again?"

"Who?"

"Don't play dumb, Auden. It's unbecoming. You

know exactly who I'm referring to—the mystery man who dicked you down so good you're still thinking about it weeks later."

Heat courses through me at her words, and the face of said man flashes through my head.

Hutch.

After our first time together, I fell asleep, only to be woken back up a few hours later for another go. Luckily, I had a few condoms stashed in my purse, and we made good use of them for rounds three and four.

The sun was just beginning to peek through the curtains when I was drifting back off to sleep. That's the last thing I remember before waking up to someone pounding on my door at noon. I'd missed my checkout—not that it really mattered—and my flight.

But most of all, I missed Hutch. I had no idea when he'd snuck out of the room, but I know it was entirely too soon.

God, the way he handled me. The way he talked to me. The way every touch made my body light up. It was unlike anything I'd ever experienced before, and although it was just supposed to be a one-night stand, I wanted more.

A month later…I still do.

"Maybe," I tell Lilah, even though it's a full-blown lie.

"Ugh," she groans. "I'm jealous. Sooooo jealous. I

haven't been laid in...well, an embarrassingly long amount of time. Like since-last-month kind of long."

I snort at her idea of a long time. Before Hutch, I hadn't had sex since last year...and it's October. It's safe to say my love life hasn't been a priority for me. I've been so focused on getting my two new hotels done that, until I felt that tingle between my legs for Hutch, I hadn't even realized it had been so long.

Now that I know what I've been missing? I want more.

"Why can't I meet some handsome stranger at the airport and have him whisk me away to a hotel where he ravages me like a madman?"

I want to tell her it's because that stuff only happens in movies or romance novels, but clearly, I'm wrong. I still can't believe the coincidence of us ending up together so many times. When Hutch walked into the bar at The Sinclair in Chicago, I nearly toppled my wine. Out of all the hotels in the area, he had to choose the one I went to? How was that even possible?

Then he said he searched for the highest-rated place, and it all made sense. I mean, he was wearing an Armani sweater like a second skin. He clearly had taste and wanted the best of the best, and I was thrilled to know *I* was that best.

Well, not me, but my hotel. It wasn't the first time

I'd heard the compliment, but it sure as hell felt like it was as it fell off his lips.

God, his lips... I swear I can still feel them on my skin.

"You're doing it again," Lilah accuses, and I doubt it's a false accusation.

For the past month, I've been walking around in a daze. I can't tell if it's because it was the best sex of my life or if I'm just still mystified by how it all came to be.

"Sorry," I tell her, and I really am. I shouldn't be daydreaming about some man I'll never see again. I should be focusing on all the great things I have coming up.

I clear my throat, then sit forward, holding my hand out. "Give me the file, will you?"

She shoves a huge black folder into my hand. "Here it is, the entire team roster for the Seattle Serpents, including the new guy on their team. His name is—"

"Hayes," I tell her, that name sending all sorts of goose bumps over my body, not because of him, but because of Hutch. The people of *Sports Desk* talking about the new trade to the local hockey team was what introduced us. "I've heard about him. I hope he doesn't cause any trouble like he did for The Grandview in Vegas."

It was all over the news for weeks. Rising NHL star

makes a splash—literally. He threw not one, but two huge garden statues into the rooftop pool, causing a crack in the concrete. It ended up causing over fifty thousand dollars in damage. I'm not saying it's the reason he was traded to Seattle…but it just might be.

"I think he'll calm down. At least, I hope so." She adds that last part under her breath.

I peel open the folder and scan the first page. It's a quick rundown of the contract The Sinclair signed with the team earlier this year. Starting this season, The Sinclair is the official partner of the Seattle Serpents. If the team travels to a city where we have a hotel, that's where they'll stay, and any team who plays in Seattle will stay right here in the very first Sinclair property. It's an incredible deal, a once-in-a-lifetime sort of a thing. I know I'm damn lucky to get this opportunity, and there is no way in hell I'm going to screw it up.

Which is why I plan to do as much research as possible on the team I've partnered with. I've met with and looked into everyone else in the organization and the NHL, but I haven't yet given my focus to the players themselves. I knew they'd be moving around during the summer, so I kept pushing it off, but with hockey season officially underway, it's time to do my homework.

"And this is everything?"

"It's as much as Sadie could find," Lilah tells me, referring to *her* executive assistant. She was so excited last year when I told her she could hire anyone she wanted. I didn't expect her to bring her little sister on and was honestly not thrilled about it at first, but seeing how hard Sadie works, I think it ended up being a good fit.

I nod, closing the folder. I grab it and my laptop, then rise from my chair. Lilah follows my lead, waiting for me to come up beside her before going anywhere. I told her from day one that if she were going to work for me, we would always walk side by side. I'd never lead her anywhere. I might technically be her boss, but we're equals.

"I'll take this with me and look over it while I'm on the way to Denver." I trap my bottom lip between my teeth, worrying it back and forth as we walk from the conference room.

"Just say what you're going to say, Auden."

I grin over at Lilah. She's known me too long. She knows my tells. Sometimes it's a good thing, and sometimes it's annoying.

Right now, I consider it good.

"It's not weird I'm going to the game, right?"

"What? No! I think it'll be good for you. Get a little experience in the hockey world. I mean, you're an official partner now—you need to know what you've invested your resources into." She gives me a stern look, warning me not to argue, so I don't.

She's probably right. It's not weird to want to see what I've gotten myself involved with, and the only reason I'm going to the game in Denver is because I have a meeting there with my general manager. We've had some small issues pop up, and I want to nip them in the bud before they get out of hand.

"I just wish I could go with you. Some of those guys on that team?" She fans herself. "Oh, mama. I likey." She bounces her brows up and down a few times.

I point a serious finger at her. "Don't even think about it, Lilah Jane."

"Buzzkill." She juts her bottom lip out. "You're no fun when you get bossy."

"And it's no fun when there's some scandal because The Sinclair's mixed business with pleasure and I have to fire you because I lost all my money."

"I don't know…based off some of those photos I saw, those guys can give *a lot* of pleasure."

I shake my head at her. "You're ridiculous."

"Yeah, but you totally love me."

"I'm *obligated* to love you. We've been friends for too long."

"Don't remind me." She playfully bumps her shoulder against mine.

I've known Lilah since I was ten years old. We met on the playground, both of us uninterested in the usual like monkey bars or playing ball. All we wanted to do was build. We'd pull four boxes of plastic bricks outside every day, then construct the most elaborate buildings just to tear them down twenty minutes later. It was the greatest fun I'd ever had.

Throughout the years, my obsession with building things grew, but Lilah's waned. She was more interested in keeping everything organized while all I wanted to do was tear it apart a thousand times. So, when I realized if I was going to make a real go at building my own company, I needed someone I knew was going to be able to handle all the fine details. Lilah was my first and only choice.

She bet on me, and I bet on her. I haven't regretted it once, which is why I know the warning I'm giving her about not hooking up with the players will be heeded. She'd never mess this up for me.

Her phone buzzes in her pocket at the same time mine goes off against my laptop.

"That would be your reminder to not miss your flight this time." She gives me a sticky-sweet smile, but I see the threat underneath it: *Don't you dare make me have to rebook you again.* "You have thirty minutes to get to the airport or I'll put you on that plane myself."

"Yes, Mom." I roll my eyes, then wrap her in a

quick hug. "I'll be back in two days. Try to keep things running smoothly around here, would you?" I wink at her when I pull away, knowing full well I'm leaving the place in capable hands.

"You got it. And, hey, maybe try not to sleep with the guy sitting next to you this time?"

"Lilah!" I hiss, looking around to make sure nobody overheard that. When I see I'm in the clear, I laugh, shaking my head at her. "You're so bad."

"You love it." She curtseys. "Now go. Have a safe flight."

A shiver runs through me at her words, and I do my best not to let my smile wobble. Ever since my trip back from New York, I've been even more anxious about flying. I downplayed how bad the flight was to Lilah to hide my nerves, but now that today is here, my stomach is already doing flips just thinking about getting on a plane again. I hate flying now more than I ever did.

Ugh. I hope this doesn't end in disaster like the last trip.

Or maybe I hope it does…because I sure as hell wouldn't mind another tumble in the sheets with Hutch.

"Well, folks, we made it safely to Denver. On behalf of me and the rest of my staff, we want to thank you for flying with us and wish you a good rest of your trip."

I wake up just in time to hear the tail end of the announcement from the pilot. I never sleep on planes, like *ever*, but I guess my anxiety about the flight was so bad I zonked out from the stress of it all. Which, hey, I'm totally fine with, though it does mean I didn't get a chance to look over the Serpents file like I wanted.

Oh well, I can do that after the game. I grab my oversized black bag, stuffing the unread file inside, then rise from my seat.

"Oh, miss." I turn toward the old man sitting next to me. "You dropped this."

I look down at what he's holding out and swallow thickly as I grab it from his hand.

"Thank you."

I give him a small smile, then turn back around. My fingers run over the brim of the stained ballcap Hutch was wearing. I guess in his haste to leave, he forgot to grab it from the hotel floor. I nearly walked out of the room without seeing it myself, but it caught my eye at the last second.

I don't know why I kept it. Maybe as a reminder of the wild night, a memento. I'm not sure. I just know I like the way the old, worn-out Yankees logo feels as I run my finger over it. It's comforting and quiets my brain when things get too loud.

So that's what I do—I run my finger over the logo as I make my way from the airport and to my hotel. I only let it slip from my fingers for a moment while I change for the game tonight. Then I promptly pull it over my head when I leave.

"What the heck is that on your head?" my dad asks when I make it inside the arena after flashing my badge to security. Perk of being the daughter of a former NHL player.

After playing only five seasons, my dad retired due to a career-ending injury to his hip. He spent the next few years coasting along until he met my mother, who he fell madly in love with. She was what most people would call a free spirit, always flitting from one place to the next, so that's what they did. They bought an RV, and they traveled the world together, never settling down in one place for too long, not even when me and my twin sister, Rory, came along. We grew up in that RV for the first ten years of our lives until, eventually, we settled in Washington, but we still moved around the state a lot.

After having a stable home life for all of six months, my mother couldn't cut it and took off. She came back a few times over the years but never stuck around for long. Even now she only texts or calls on holidays and birthdays and doesn't make any effort to see us, and I've accepted that. It's just who she is.

But it's okay. I have my dad, and he's all the parent I need.

"It looks like you plucked it off the street."

He tries to steal it off my head, but I swat his hand away.

"Stop it. It's not from the streets. It's a...loan."

His brows pinch together.

"From a friend," I add.

More pinching.

"It's a good luck charm for tonight."

"You're rooting for Seattle, aren't you?"

I shrug. "What can I say? I'm dedicated to my hometown team."

He laughs because he knows I don't know a lick about the game he loves so much.

"I knew that new contract would come back to bite me in the ass."

I roll my eyes and wrap my arms around him. "It's good to see you, Dad."

He squeezes me back tightly like he hasn't seen me in months, even though I just visited in June for Father's Day.

"Missed you, kiddo. No Rory?" he asks, referring to my twin.

"Of course not. I couldn't peel her away from her clinic if I tried."

Thanks to my father setting aside all of his NHL money for us girls, Rory was able to chase her own passion—animals. I guess it's kind of fitting she's named after a Disney princess—Aurora—since she runs two clinics out of Seattle and is the top-rated veterinarian in the city.

"One day I'll get her to a game. She'll fall in love with it, just like I know you will."

My dad never pushed us into sports, something I was thankful for, but he always reminded us we wouldn't have what we do without the greatest sport of all—hockey. When the chance arose to sign with the Serpents, I couldn't say no. It felt good to give back to the game that gave me my life.

"Come on. We don't want to miss puck drop."

We weave our way through the crowd, and I laugh a few times when my dad gets recognized. He didn't have the longest or most acclaimed hockey career, but he's still a hero to Colorado fans. They'll never forget his overtime-winning goal that sent the then Quebec team to the Stanley Cup Playoffs. Sure, they didn't win, but that doesn't mean it wasn't a huge part of the team's history.

We make it up to our suite just in time for the game to start, and the teams are off to the races. My dad stands at the edge of the box looking down on the rink with a serious expression. He hasn't worn skates in at least twenty years, but he still looks at the game like it's his entire world. Well, aside from me and Rory.

The first period is uneventful, neither team scoring and not much happening, but then in the second it's like two new teams out there. They're checking each other left and right, drawing and taking penalties like mad. There are even a few scuffles thrown in. For all the fighting and effort, neither team has a point on the board heading into the third.

"Son of a bitch," my dad mutters. "These guys can't find the back of the net for shit."

The agent he's been chatting with—Shepard something or another—laughs, clapping him on the back. "You're telling me. I have two Seattle players out there who are playing for their careers right now. If they don't step it up, they're going to be sorely disappointed in the offers they get next year."

"Which boys are yours again?" Dad asks.

"Twenty-seven and ten. Talented as hell, but something's been off with them lately. It's like they lost all their hockey sense or something since the trade to Seattle." The guy shakes his head, lips downturned, and his frown reminds me of another guy who frowns entirely too much…

I shake my head, annoyed with myself for letting

my mind go there yet again. I need to stop thinking about him. It was a one-time thing. I know that...but as much as my brain is on board, my body isn't, and right now it's still ignited by anything that reminds me of Hutch.

I should have gotten his first name. It wasn't until the next morning that I realized I never even thought to ask what it was. At the time, it didn't matter, but now I wish I had it so I could return his hat to him.

There was a split second where I thought about looking him up in the system, but I quickly talked myself out of it. I pride myself on running my company on integrity, and invading someone's privacy like that isn't very honorable. If we're meant to see one another again, it will happen. I'll give him his hat then. Until that happens, I'll keep it safe.

"Do you know number twenty-seven?"

I look up at the agent. "Pardon?"

He nods toward the hat on my head, the one I'm currently rolling my fingers against without even realizing it. "He has a cap just like that. Just as gross-looking too. He's sort of famous for wearing it all the time, no matter how badly he needs to throw it out. Do you know him?"

I don't know what to say. Thanks to me falling asleep on the plane, I don't know who 27 is, but even if I did, I'm sure it's just another weird coincidence he has a hat similar to mine. Well, similar to Hutch's. That's all.

I shake my head, dropping my hand. "I don't. Sorry."

He nods a few times, never taking his eyes off the hat. "Interesting."

But he doesn't say *what's* interesting. He just turns his attention back to the game.

Three minutes later, Colorado nets their first goal of the night. Four minutes after that, Seattle gets theirs. With just thirty seconds left in the third, another goal is scored, and the entire arena goes silent except for the man standing next to me.

"Hell yeah! That's my boys!"

Seattle wins, sending Colorado skating off the ice with their heads hung low. Even though I don't really follow the sport or either team, I'm ecstatic to see Seattle pull out the win, but I try to keep my cool in front of my dad.

"Well, hell, kiddo, they did it." My dad squeezes my shoulder. "I think you may just be their lucky charm. May have to start going to all the games."

I laugh because there's no way I'd ever have the time for that. "I'm sure they'll manage to win if I'm not there."

"Hey, don't brush it off that quick. Hockey superstitions are real." Another squeeze. "Now, come on. Let's go grab some dinner back at the hotel, huh? Maybe tomorrow your old man can get you out on that golf course I've heard so much about."

One of the biggest draws of The Sinclair properties are all the amenities they provide, like full golf courses, luxury spas, and state-of-the-art rooms that include full-motion beds. I'm almost certain a big reason the Serpents were willing to sign on was the golf courses in several of our key locations. Hockey players love their golf, even old, retired ones like my father.

He turns to the agent and sticks his hand out. "It was great chatting with you, Mr. Clark. I'm sure I'll catch you at another game."

"Call me Shep—we're friends now." He turns to me. "I'll be in Seattle next week. If you're open to another game, just give me a call. I'll always make room for someone else in the suite." He looks at my hat once again. "Maybe I can introduce you to my player. He'll love your hat."

"Oh, that's not hers. She's never watched a baseball game in her life. Have you, kiddo?" Dad rubs his elbow against mine, sending me a wink. "Probably why you're not a little more starstruck in the presence of *the* Shep Clark."

My dad and Shep exchange a few more words, mostly talking about their respective sports careers, then we're finally heading back to the hotel. Dinner comes and goes quickly, and we're back in our rooms before eleven. I should probably head to bed since we have an early tee time, but after that nap on the plane, I'm not tired just yet. The folder with all the player information is peeking out of my black bag; I know just what to do to help me unwind for the night—research—and I know just the place to do it.

I grab the folder and the Yankees cap, then head for the bar downstairs. Time to find out all I can about this team I just partnered with.

Chapter 5

HUTCH

"I still don't understand how the fuck that goalie stopped that puck. It was right there on the red line, ready to slide straight to the back of the net, but nope, he saved it." The right-winger shakes his head. "Fucking goalies and their creepy flexibility."

"I've not heard any complaints about it." Fox, our number one goalie, gives a sly grin. "In fact, just last night, your mo—"

Lawson smacks the table before pointing his finger Fox's way. "Don't you dare bring my mother into this."

"To be fair, you walked right into it," I point out.

Lawson sneers at me. "You're taking his side?"

I hold my hands up. "I'm not taking any sides. Just stating facts."

The goalie leans into me. "But you're totally on my side, right?"

I ignore him, not wanting to get into it tonight...
though, if I'm being honest, I *am* on Fox's side. I'd
never tell Lawson that, though. He'd never shut up
about it.

I look around the table at the group of misfits
we've accumulated since last year.

There's Fox, our netminder who, even though he
didn't deserve it, got left out to dry by us too many
times last season. He was once Vezina-finalist-worthy,
but thanks to a crummy year in New York and us
tanking last season, there are whispers about him being
washed up.

Then a left winger and centerman: Lawson, who
almost never shuts up, and Keller, who almost never
talks. He's only said two words since the game ended.

Locke, a fellow defenseman who's been playing
since I was in high school.

And finally, Hayes and me.

It's a small group, but we're tight as hell. Well,
besides Hayes. He's not in the group; he's just here
tonight because he's new and has nowhere else to go.

I missed these guys over the last few months,
missed the camaraderie of the team. I missed
bullshitting with them and sitting around after a game,
rehashing everything like we are now. Giving this up
will be the thing I miss the most about no longer being
in the league, whenever that is.

Sooner rather than later if I keep playing the way I am.

The corners of my lips tug down at the thought. We might have walked away with two points tonight, but we got lucky. We played like crap yet again, and I really don't want to get this season off on shaky footing like we did last year. I have too much on the line for us to blow it again.

"That was a nice pass up the ice to Hayes. Gave us a good breakaway chance. Smart play," Whitlocke, or just Locke, tells me quietly as Fox and Lawson get into a heated debate about mom jokes. Hayes' eyes bounce back and forth between them, having no idea he's being discussed right beside him. "Kid just needed to slow it down a bit, bait the goalie more. He's young, but he'll learn."

"Thanks," I mutter in reply. "I'm still not sure he's a great fit, but we'll see."

"Give him time," Locke encourages.

Being that he's been in the league the longest out of anyone else on the team, I think it's safe to say he knows what he's talking about and I should trust him. I'm just not sure I'm ready to bet the rest of my career on giving Hayes time.

I lift my hat off my head, tossing it onto the table, then rake my hands through my hair. I glare down at the foreign logo on the cap. Well, not really foreign. It's the Serpents logo, but it's not *my* hat, so it feels wrong. *I* feel wrong. I've felt wrong since the second I left that hotel room with Auden. It's not because I felt bad leaving her behind—she knew the score.

It's because I left my most prized possession behind and didn't even realize it until I was on the plane to Seattle. It's not escaped me that I've been playing extra shitty to start the season. It's the missing hat. It has to be.

I can't be that bad...can I?

Hayes' laughter breaks through my morbid thoughts.

"You remind me a lot of some of the guys from the Comets," he says. "Always bickering back and forth like this." There's a longing to his look, and I get it. He's new here. He's missing his old teammates and wasn't here last year to bond with us. "But they're all boring and settled down now. They don't do after-game shit like this anymore."

"To be fair, my brother Jacob has been boring his entire life. That's not because he settled down like an idiot." Lawson shakes his head.

Fox raises his glass. "To not being an idiot!"

All of us—minus Hayes—raise our own cups and smash them together in the middle of the table. We take a swig, then bounce them on the table twice before settling back in our chairs like nothing ever happened.

"Uh...what was that?" Hayes questions, looking around like we're a bunch of morons.

We might be, but I don't care. It's our thing, and we're not changing it.

Someone bumps my foot, and I look up to find Locke giving me that damn intuitive look of his that I hate so much. I try to ignore it, looking anywhere but at him, but everyone is staring at me, each of them telling me something different with their eyes.

Fox's say, *Should we?*

Lawson's tell me, *Do it. Do it. Do it.*

Keller is impossible to read like usual.

And Locke's scream, *He's new and needs guidance. Do the right thing.*

Fuck me if his isn't the loudest.

I slide my hand through my hair again, then clear my throat. "We're sort of..."

"Single. We're all single," Lawson supplies.

Hayes nods. "I can get on board with that."

"Yeah, but can you get on board with *staying* single?" Keller finally speaks up, resting his elbows on the table. "Because that's kind of a requirement to be part of the club."

"Club?"

I wince. "Stop calling it that. It sounds so stupid. The only thing worse is that ridiculous name you insist on using."

"Fucking Lawsy's fault. He got it stuck in my head," Keller insists, blaming his teammate. "Just like that stupid name."

"What's the name?" Hayes asks.

"Serpents Singles." Lawson grins proudly, puffing his chest out. "I coined it."

"And I fucking hate it," I tell him, taking another hefty drink from my non-alcoholic beer. I try not to drink much during the season, but I still like the taste. It's like having a drink but without the crappy side effects. "We don't need a name."

"Sure we do. And besides, it sounds badass."

Keller points at me. "I'm with Hutch. It's lame."

"As much as I hate to say it," Fox says, "I'm with Lawsy. I kind of like it."

"Two votes for me and two for Hutch." Lawson points to himself, then across the table to the older man with graying temples. "Locke?"

He shakes his head. "I'm staying out of this."

Lawson zeroes in on Hayes. "Are you single?"

The kid snorts. "Oh, hell yeah. Ain't no way I'm getting tied down."

"Do you like the name?"

"If it gets me in the club, I *love* the name."

Lawson smacks the table again—a favorite move of his—and lets out a loud whoop. "Then you're in." He looks at me. "I win. Rules are rules."

I laugh because there are no rules. We're just a group of single guys who want to stay single and focus on nothing but hockey and winning the Cup. That's it. That's the whole thing.

I look around the table once more.

Just let him in, Fox's gaze says.

Haha, I won, says Lawson's.

Keller is indifferent.

Do the right thing, Locke encourages once more.

I sigh, then look at Hayes. "Fine. You're in."

"Yes!" He pumps his fist in the air.

I glower at him. "Don't make me regret this."

I regret it.

Hayes hasn't even been in the club for an hour, and he's already on my last damn nerve. We haven't spent too much time together over the last few weeks, but so far, everything I've heard about the guy in recent years rings true.

He's too damn much.

Too wild. Too rowdy. Too impossible to tame.

He's gone up to the bar no less than four times, coming back with a different phone number each time…and a new drink. Sure, we just played tonight and are off tomorrow, but it doesn't matter. There's no reason he should be knocking back so many during the season.

I should say something, should step in, but it's almost impossible with Lawson encouraging him every step of the way. These two together are going to be more trouble than I anticipated.

"Hey, do you know that woman?"

I look behind me to where Lawson is pointing. There's a woman sitting at the bar with her head bent and shoulders slumped forward as she looks over the huge stack of papers in front of her. Even from behind, there's something familiar about her...

"Isn't that your hat?" my teammate asks.

No.

Absolutely not.

There is no fucking way it's possible.

I blink once. Twice. Then a third time just for good measure, but it's pointless.

I know what I'm looking at. I know *who* I'm looking at.

I rise from my chair, ignoring the questions the guys are throwing my way, and make my way to the bar. The closer I get, the surer I am about what I'm seeing. There is no denying it when that all-too-fucking-familiar scent of orange and honey hits me.

"Strike three."

She whirls around on her stool, her hazel eyes bright and wide.

"Hutch."

My name comes out a whisper, and it takes me right back to that hotel room in Chicago where I heard her call it out over and over as she fell apart under and on top of and beside me.

"Auden," I say, taking another step closer. She doesn't shrink back or look scared. She's still too shocked.

Her eyes dart around the bar, no doubt looking for a camera hidden somewhere, something to tell her this is all a setup and there is no way we've run into one another again. It's just not possible.

But she doesn't find anything because it *is* possible, and it's happening right now.

"Why strike three?" she asks.

"Stalking. It's never an attractive look," I murmur, repeating her words from Chicago back to her.

Her lips curve upward, but it doesn't last long, unlike the silence that washes over us. I don't know how long it stretches, but it's too long. I hate it for so many reasons.

Auden rolls her tongue over her lips, those same fucking lips I haven't been able to stop thinking about. "I...I didn't think I'd ever see you again."

"That makes two of us." My eyes drift upward. "Nice hat."

Her cheeks pinken. "I'm sorry. You left it behind, and I just…"

I watch as she reaches up, tracing her fingers over the logo. It's the same thing I do whenever I feel anxious, just run my fingers back and forth over the letters.

"I swear I didn't steal it," she says, drawing my attention back to her face.

"Just like you swear you're not stalking me?"

Another grin. "I *was* here first."

She's teasing. I like that she's teasing. It helps soothe the unease that's rolling through me. What the hell are the chances that I run into her again? In Colorado, of all places?

I nod toward the empty stool beside her. "Mind if I sit?"

"Oh, no. Of course not. Let me just…" She scrambles to move her things around, but not before I see it.

It's a folder. No—a fucking book.

And right there staring back at me is a picture.

"Auden…"

She stops mid-scramble to peek up at me. "Hmm?"

"Why in the hell do you have a photo of me?"

Chapter 6

AUDEN

I don't know how it's possible, but Hutch is standing beside me. More than that, I don't know how it's possible that I missed the most important detail of all: Hutch plays for the Seattle Serpents, the team I just partnered with.

And now he's right here in this bar, looking down at the same folder I was poring over, the same folder that held the missing puzzle piece of why Hutch keeps popping up in my life, of who he is.

Off-limits.

"Auden," he says, and my brain snaps back to reality.

"Hmm?"

He nods at the papers in my hands, the ones I'm desperately trying to hide away.

"Why in the hell do you have a photo of me?" he repeats, this time his eyes narrowing tightly.

"It's nothing," I tell him as I continue trying to clear away the evidence of our connection.

A hand lands firmly on my arm, and the heat that moves through my entire body is enough to stop me. I look at the hand—the one I know is soft but can be brutal in the best of ways—then at Hutch himself. He's staring down at me with hard eyes, that ever-present frown of his marring his lips.

I swallow the lump that's taken up residence in my throat. "I can explain."

One brow hitches up. "Oh, you'd better."

He releases my arm, and I miss his touch the second he does. He slips onto the stool next to me, pulling it closer until we're touching. He crowds against me, invading every ounce of personal space I've ever had. His eyes are dark and serious, his body language full of anger, and I can *feel* the heat rolling off him.

But I'm not scared. Not of him.

"Tell me, Auden, is this some sort of game to you?"

I tip my head sideways. "What?"

"Don't do that cute shit with me." He laughs darkly. "Is this what you get off on? Acting all sweet and innocent? Stalking hockey players and seducing them? To...what, trap me? Go to the media with all my dark and dirty secrets?" Another inch closer, so damn close I can feel his breath fanning my face. "What's your end game here? Where does this stop?"

A throat clears.

"Is there a problem here, Ms. Sinclair?"

I turn to the bartender, Keith. He's a big man with heavy arms crossed over his chest, and he's glaring at Hutch.

"We're fine," Hutch snaps.

"Wasn't asking you," Keith says just as menacingly. "Ms. Sinclair?"

I shake my head once. "No problem, Keith. Everything's fine."

He looks like he wants to question me, wants to push. He doesn't like Hutch, and I don't blame him. To anyone on the outside, I'm sure the man who's all up in my face looks like a threat, but he's not. I know he's not.

"I promise," I tell Keith.

It takes another few seconds before he finally nods, then walks off. He doesn't go too far, though, just a few feet down the bar, never taking his eyes off me.

I turn back to Hutch. He's still staring at me with heated eyes, though it's not the kind I'd hoped to see from him. He's seething, and I can't say I blame him.

"I know how this looks, but it's not that."

Another dark chuckle. "Then what, huh? What is it? Because I've been down this road with crazed fans before. I can have security over here in a flash to get rid of you, so whatever excuse you're about to give me, it better be a damn good one."

Now I'm the one laughing. It surprises Hutch, and he finally backs off, giving me breathing room for what feels like the first time in hours when really, it's likely only been a minute. The laughs keep on coming, bubbling out of me like I'm a madwoman. He's looking at me like I'm crazy, and maybe I am, but I can't seem to stop. This is just too insane for it not to be funny.

"Why are you laughing?" he asks through clenched teeth. "Stop it," he commands when I don't answer him. "*Auden.*"

My name rolling off his lips has my laughter dying, and I swipe at my eyes, drying the tears that have formed.

"What's so funny?"

"This!" I wave my hand around us. "This whole damn mess."

"You mean you stalking me?"

I roll my eyes, shaking my head. "I'm not stalking you, Hutch. I'm partnered with you."

He leans back, his brows tightening. "Excuse me?"

"I'm partnered with you. Well, not with *you* you, but your team."

"I'm not following…"

I sigh, then reach to the stack of papers sitting on the countertop. I shove them into the folder haphazardly, sending a silent sorry to Lilah for messing up all her hard work, and I slide the information on the Serpents into my bag before hitching it over my shoulder. I turn to Hutch, who is watching me with tight eyes. I hop off my seat, then extend my hand his way.

"Hi, I'm Auden Sinclair."

He glances down at my hand, then back up at my face. "I know who you are. What I don't know is *why*— why are you here?"

"I own this hotel."

His jaw slackens, and his eyes grow wide. "You… You…"

"Welcome to The Sinclair, Mr. Hutchinson."

This is all my fault. I should have never given Hutch my room key that night. I should have never invited him to my room. I should have known better than to give in to my urges.

But I did it. I gave in, and now I'm going to have to live with the consequences.

"Hey! Stop!"

I lift my head to see Hutch running my way just as the doors of the elevator slide open. I step inside and press the *Close Doors* button several times, but it's pointless. Hutch's arm slides between them, stopping the steel from fully closing. His eyes are still dark and wild as he steps in and reaches down for the button I was pressing so desperately. This time, there's nobody there to stop the doors, and they close, trapping us inside.

Alone.

I both hate and love the idea of being alone with him. Hate it because I know what he can do to my body, and love it because…well, I know what he can do to my body. I shouldn't and can't want him anymore. It's wrong on too many levels. I just wish my body would get that message.

Hutch doesn't say anything, just moves to the other side of the elevator and rests his back against the wall. He crosses his arms over his chest, his eyes never wavering from me. I hate how he's looking at me, like I'm the one who's betrayed him, but I didn't know. If I had, Chicago would have *never* happened. Ever. I keep my personal life and business life separate. I would never do anything to put my company at risk.

What happened with Hutch? It jeopardizes everything. I have a contract with his team, for crying out loud. We're coworkers, in a way. We have no business having a personal anything together.

I meet his heated stare with one of my own, tipping my chin up, not backing down.

"What?" I snap. "Are you here to accuse me of stalking you some more?"

He doesn't answer. He just stares.

I scoff, annoyed with his silence. "You know, Hutch, just because you're some big hotshot hockey player doesn't mean every woman who talks to you wants to sleep with you."

A laugh rumbles out of him. It's that same dark and sultry one from before, the one that tells me I'm not going to like what he says next...the one that sends a zing right between my legs. I try to ignore that, but it's hard.

It's even harder when he shoves off the wall, and it's nearly impossible when he crosses the small space, heading right for me and not stopping until it's *my* back pressed against the wall, until he's boxed me in and he's peering down at me with those blueish-gray eyes I've been seeing in my dreams for weeks now.

"Oh, but you already did that, huh, sweetheart?"

One word.

One word is all it takes for all my defenses to drop.

I have no clue who moves first, but suddenly my lips are pressed against his and I'm lost in him all over again. He feels different than I remember. Harder. Rougher. But I like it all the same.

I grip his shirt—a simple tee this time—tugging him closer. He slides his hands over my waist, hauling me up into his arms. I hook my legs around his waist, loving how perfectly he fits between them, loving the friction we create. I've been craving it since he slipped out of my bed and disappeared without a word.

I knew the score going in. I guess I just didn't realize I'd want to keep playing the game anyway.

A throaty growl leaves him when I move my hands under his shirt. He grabs my wrists, pinning them to the wall with one hand, and just like that, he has the upper hand again. I don't like giving up control. It's not really my thing, but with Hutch? It doesn't feel like giving up control; it feels like leveling the playing field.

He gives, and I take.

I give, and he takes.

It's a full team effort.

He slides his free hand over my side, across my belly, and goes right for the button on my jeans. He undoes them deftly, pulling the zipper down just enough for him to reach his hand inside. He doesn't even bother with pretenses; he slips right into my panties, cupping my pussy like he owns it—and right now, he does.

He dips a finger into my slit, the tip of it brushing against my throbbing clit. It's a simple touch, one that shouldn't ignite my body the way it does, but *of course* it does. I shouldn't be surprised by it, but I am. He rubs short circles over me and I'm so fucking embarrassed by the sounds he's swallowing when he slips a single finger inside of me. I can't help it—my hips move of their own accord.

"That's it. Ride my hand. Pretend it's my cock," he tells me before taking my mouth again.

And I do. I fuck myself on his finger, loving it and hating myself all at the same time. Just when I'm so damn sure I'm about to come, the elevator comes to a soft stop, pulling us both from the moment. Hutch wrenches his mouth from mine, and our chests brush together with how hard we're both breathing.

The doors slide open and cool air hits us. It's just the wake-up I needed.

"Let me go."

He does instantly. He frees my wrists, pulls his hand from my pants, and drops me back to my feet. We stand there for several seconds, and I watch as a slow, cocky grin takes over those same sweet lips that were just on mine.

"I'll be taking this." He rips the hat off my head

and disappears through the doors like nothing ever happened.

Not until I'm heading back down do I realize it was my floor he got off on, and I have to start my journey up all over again.

Chapter 7

HUTCH

Lawson: HUTCH

Lawson: HUUUUUTCH

Lawson: Here, Hutchy Hutchy.

Fox: He's not a damn dog, asswipe.

Lawson: Then why is he in the doghouse?

Fox: Aww, are you mad he didn't come home last night?

Lawson: Fuck you.

Fox: No, fuck YOU.

Keller: Fuck both of you. Some of us are trying to sleep.

Lawson: How can you sleep when your captain-to-be is missing?

Locke: He's not missing. He's down in the lobby.

Lawson: What? Why? It's like the asscrack of dawn.

Keller: Exactly. So shut the fuck up, Lawsy.

Hayes: This is one active group chat.

Lawson: Who the hell said that?

Lawson: Oh, wait—Hayes.

Lawson: I forgot about the new guy.

Hayes: Thank you?

Lawson: Don't mention it.

Lawson: But seriously...don't mention it. This group is secret, got it?

Hayes: So, like Fight Club?

Lawson: What's Fight Club?

Hayes: You know the movie? The book?

Lawson: READ THE ROOM, HAYES.

Hayes: Oh. I get it now.

Lawson: Now come on. Where are you, Hutchy?

Hutch: Avoiding all of you.

Lawson: HE'S ALIVE.

Locke: Leave him be, Lawsy.

Lawson: You're no fun, Gramps.

Keller: Jesus fuck, SHUT UP, LAWSON.

I put my phone on silent just as another message from Lawson comes in. I'm too tired to deal with this crap.

I didn't sleep a fucking wink. In fact, I'm so awake I've been sitting down in the lobby all damn night. I didn't even head up to my room. I've been sitting here watching the elevators just in case Auden comes back down.

She hasn't.

Not yet, at least, but I'm betting she will soon. She can't hide in her room forever.

I wish she'd come down. All I want to do is talk, sitting far apart from one another so nothing like what happened in the elevator happens again.

Talking *only*.

"Have you seen my daughter?"

"Sorry, Mr. Sinclair. I haven't."

My ears perk up at this, and I sit up straighter on the couch I've occupied for the last six hours.

"Would you mind calling her room? I've tried her cell a few times, but no luck. I assume it's on silent."

"Sure thing, sir."

The older man—Auden's father, apparently— turns, looking out across the lobby. Our eyes collide for a moment, and he moves on, only to snap his gaze back to mine.

"Well, well, well." He shoves off the front desk and strolls my way, a grin eating up his face. "Reed Hutchinson, right?"

I rise from my spot on the couch and stuff the hat I've been holding on to all night into my back pocket, then extend my hand the man's way. "Sure am. And you?"

"Jackson Sinclair." He gives my hand a hard shake. "I used to—"

"Play for Quebec. I remember, sir. I've seen you play many times. You had some slick hands. Plus, you can't forget *The Goal*."

Jackson laughs. "Thanks. I appreciate that. We were at your game last night. Congrats on the win."

"We?"

He nods. "My daughter and me." He waves his hand around the lobby. "This is her hotel. Incredible, huh?" The pride in his voice is evident. "She's got a gift."

"Dad, stop."

I whirl around to find Auden standing just a few feet away. She's wearing a golf skirt and a matching top. Her hair is back in that messy bun she loves so much, and a visor sits perfectly on her head. She looks nothing like the Auden I know, but I guess that's fitting since I don't really know her at all.

After I walked away last night, I immediately pulled my phone out and Googled her. It was only fair since she apparently had a file on me. I found article after article about how this twenty-nine-year-old woman built a hotel empire. She became a billionaire last year thanks not only to her luxury hotels doing so well but also the multiple deals she's made—including the one with my team.

She's a powerhouse.

"What?" Jackson wraps his arm around his daughter's shoulders and hugs her to him. "I'm just proud is all."

Auden grins up at her father with nothing but love.

I have to look away. It reminds me too much of what I'm missing.

"I tried calling you. Everything all right?" he asks her, concern lacing every word.

"Yep. Just overslept a bit."

"You? Sleep past five? Is that even possible?" He looks over at me. "This one is a workaholic. It takes a lot of sweet-talking to pry her away from her company."

Auden looks sheepish at his words, and it's still so strange to me to see her as anything other than the bold woman from the airport lounge. The woman who wouldn't stop talking the entire flight because she was too nervous. The woman who slipped me her hotel room card. The same woman who rode my face with zero inhibitions, who called out my name over and over as she came all over my cock.

It's hard to see that this Auden, the one standing in front of me with pink cheeks, is that same woman.

"We'd better get going if we want to make our tee time," Auden says. That may be true, but I'm no fool —I know she's also trying to get away from me.

Her dad checks his watch. "We have time for breakfast." Jackson snaps his fingers. "Say, son, have you eaten yet?"

"Dad, don't."

I ignore her just like he does. "I haven't, and it just so happens that I'm..." I catch Auden's eyes. "*Starving*."

It's the same thing I said to her in Chicago, and based on the way she swallows slowly, she remembers.

"Join us, then. The restaurant here is incredible—really top-notch. Just another thing my little girl did right."

"*Dad.*"

Her tone is harsher as she admonishes her old man, but he doesn't seem to care. He laughs jovially and steers her toward the restaurant. Auden peeks at me over her shoulder, her eyes narrowed and her lips pinched tightly together.

Oh, she's not happy about this at all. I smile, and her eyes sharpen. I laugh and follow right behind them.

They don't stop at the hostess stand—and seeing as it's their name on the side of the building, they really don't have to—instead heading straight for a spot in the back near the window. The morning sun spills into the room, catching on the golden silverware lining each table. It's a subtle detail but a perfect one.

Jackson wasn't kidding; his daughter does know how to build a place. I've always loved staying at the Sinclairs over the years. Their attention to detail and hospitality has been impeccable.

When we approach the table, I race ahead around

Auden, pulling her chair out for her. I can't help but laugh when she doesn't take it, pointedly moving to the one next to it, making it look like I've just pulled her father's chair out.

God, I wish we were alone so I could bend her over my knee and show her how I feel about her little stunt.

If Jackson notices anything off between us, he doesn't comment on it. He just shakes his head at his daughter and accepts my chair. I take my seat, and a waiter appears out of nowhere to fill our glasses with water and sets down a pitcher of what looks like watered-down orange juice.

"I'm not big on oranges, but they have the best mimosas here," Jackson says, grabbing the pitcher and pouring himself a glass all the way to the brim. He takes a drink and smacks his lips loudly. "Wait until you get to be my age, son. You'll learn to appreciate morning booze like no other." He takes another drink, then nods toward the pitcher. "Grab yourself one."

"I'm good, thanks. I don't drink much during the season."

"Smart player. I like that." Another loud slurp and smack of his lips, then he sets his glass down. "So, Reed, tell me...how are you liking Washington so far? Anything stand out about it to you yet?"

I slide my eyes Auden's way, surprised to find her

staring at me. When she realizes I'm looking at her, she quickly shifts her gaze anywhere but at me.

My lips twitch, and I clear my throat, turning my attention back to her father.

"I love it. I was raised in upstate New York, then lived in Nashville during my stint with the team. It was wild there, but I enjoyed it. Washington, though…it's like a whole different world. Whenever I get the chance, I like to hop in my car, roll the windows down —when it's not raining, of course—and drive. It's amazing how swiftly it can change from a forested area to a city to mountains and back again."

Jackson nods. "That was always my favorite thing about it too. I wish I could have stayed longer, but I couldn't handle the weather. My old bones don't like the rain too much, especially not my hip since the surgery."

I nod. "It does rain a lot, but I think that's my favorite part. It makes everything look…"

"Brighter," Auden supplies, and I snap my eyes to hers.

"Yeah." I nod. "Brighter."

"And greener." She lifts her water and takes a sip. "If that's even possible in the evergreen state."

"I take it you like it?"

"It's my home," she says fondly. "I've been all over the world and back again. No matter where I go or how far, the PNW always calls me back. I'll never live anywhere else."

"I've tried, trust me." Jackson laughs. "I'd love to have her and her sister, Rory, in Colorado with me, but they insist on staying thousands of miles away."

"It's not thousands. Besides, you see me every other month."

"It's not enough, kiddo. Never enough." He sends her a warm wink, then turns back to me. "And playing for Seattle…how are you liking that?"

It's not the first time I've been asked this, and just like before, I find it hard to come up with an answer that doesn't make me sound like a dick.

He must sense my hesitation because he holds his hand up. "Don't mind me. I'm just being nosy. You don't need to answer if it makes you feel uncomfortable."

"No." I shake my head. "It's not that. It's just…" I blow out a heavy breath. "Well, it's pretty damn obvious we kind of suck, huh?"

"Ah, nonsense." He waves his hand. "You just need to find your hockey sense, get that chemistry built. I know a lot of people want it to happen overnight and have the new team take off like Vegas did, but it's just not always in the cards. They were an anomaly, not an example. The Serpents will get there. I know it. You have to hang on a little bit."

He sounds like Locke, who came down about an hour ago, surprised to find me sitting there. We made eye contact, but he didn't say a word. That's my favorite thing about him—if it's not his business, he stays out of it.

"Thanks, Jackson. That means something coming from a legend like you."

"Legend?" He gives me another hearty laugh. "I wouldn't go that far, but I appreciate the compliment. I like him, Auden. Good thing you just signed on to be the Serpents' liaison hotel. You'll be seeing lots more of each other, I'm sure." He hitches his thumb toward his daughter but looks at me. "This one can't seem to stay away from all her properties. Every time I talk to her, she's on another flight to check in on them. I keep saying she doesn't need to personally see to every issue that arises, but she never listens."

"And for good reason. It's worked all these years, and look at what I've built. Why change it now?" Auden challenges. There's a bite to her words, but there's something off about them. They're missing conviction. I don't think Jackson notices, but I sure do.

"I know, I know. It's just…"

"Grandchildren." She rolls her eyes. "I know the whole spiel. I've heard it many times over the years. But I've told you, Dad, you better get used to all those cats Rory has because you're not getting kids from either of us. Commitment doesn't run in our blood."

Auden's eyes catch mine, and for the first time this morning, she grins at me. It's a soft smile like we share a little secret, and I guess we do—not just about our night in Chicago, but about our desire to not be tied down too.

He makes a *harrumph* sound, then slams the rest of his mimosa. There's a story there, but neither of them offers details. The waiter reappears and we place our orders—eggs and bacon for me, a plate chock-full of meat and potatoes for Jackson, and a muffin for Auden.

"That's all you're having? A muffin?"

She glowers at me from her side of the table. "I'm not very hungry. I seem to have lost my appetite."

Translation: *It's you. I don't want you here.*

I hide my smile behind my glass of water, happy to know I've made her uncomfortable. I don't know why I like it, maybe because I enjoy seeing her all riled up. Who knows. I just know even though I should, I don't want to walk away just yet. Not until I get some answers from her.

"So, Auden…" She sits up straighter when I address her, pressing her shoulders back and tipping her chin up. She looks haughty, which I know she's not, but if that's the front she wants to put on, so be it.

"How long have you been under contract with the Serpents?"

"Since the beginning of summer, but it didn't officially kick in until the start of the season."

I nod a few times. "Are you a hockey fan? Is that why you partnered with the team?"

"I'm a fan of giving back to my community, which is what I'm doing with the Serpents. They're local to me, so I want to be there for them, to support them."

"You're a hockey fan, then?"

"No." She pauses. "Well, sort of." She looks at her father. "I guess I kind of have to be, no?"

He laughs, not at all picking up on the heat that's flowing between us. "You haven't sat through a game of hockey in your life until last night. Not even as a kid when I was more involved with the game and alumni stuff were you interested. It's never been your thing, and that's okay. Besides, you took after me in other ways."

So, she's not a fan, and from the sound of things, she really didn't have a clue who I was until last night. She looked just as surprised to see me as I was her. Could this all really be just a weird coincidence? Could it be...

I shake my head, refusing to use the same word Auden did, that *F* word. There's just no way.

Our food arrives before I have the chance to

pepper her with more questions, and I'm fine with that. Gives less room for there to be some credibility to her theory about us. We keep the conversation light as we eat, Jackson doing most of the talking. He tells me about his business ventures and brags about Auden more. She hates it, but she allows it because it makes her father happy. I like that about her.

When I offer to pay the tab, Jackson laughs at me.

"We got it, son. Don't worry about it."

He keeps calling me that.

Son.

It's not forced. It just rolls off his tongue naturally. I like it entirely too much, probably because he reminds me so much of my own father.

"Dad, we really should be going if we want to make our tee time," Auden reminds him again.

"Ah, right." Jackson settles back in his chair. "Nothing like a good round of golf, am I right?"

"Couldn't agree more."

It's a lie. I fucking hate golf. I've never understood why so many hockey players take to it during the off-season. How can they go from playing such a fast-paced game to golf? It never made sense to me.

"Care to join us out there today?"

"Dad," Auden practically hisses, throwing the sharpest daggers I've seen from her yet, and they're aimed right at her father.

I chuckle. "Thank you for the offer, but our bus for the airport actually leaves soon. I should probably head up to my room and get packed."

And maybe catch an hour of sleep if I'm lucky.

"You're playing St. Louis tomorrow, right? Man, that's a damn good club too. Always hated playing against them. Gritty."

They really are, and tomorrow night we'll have a lot to prove with Lawsy on our team. It's always hard playing against your former club, but damn does it feel good when things go right and you beat them. I want Lawsy to experience that.

"Well then." Jackson shoves his chair back and rises. I meet his height and place my hand in his extended one. "It was great meeting you, Reed. We'll have to get together next time I'm in Seattle and our schedules line up."

"Definitely, sir."

I glance down at Auden, who is still seated, not giving a shit about manners. Her dad takes notice, and I delight in the way he scolds her with just a stare, forcing her from the chair. I smirk at her as she rounds the table to stand in front of me.

"Auden," I say.

"*Reed*," she counters.

It's pointed, her saying my name like that, and I can't help but laugh, which does nothing but make her even madder. Then suddenly, she's sliding her arms around me and pressing her body against mine, reminding me how perfectly we seem to fit together. My head swims when the smell of oranges and honey hits my senses, and I'm too damn stunned to do anything but hug her back.

"Sorry," she says, stepping back. "I'm a hugger."

She lifts her shoulders like it's no big deal, but based on the look her father is giving her, this was completely outside of her normal behavior, and I have no doubt he'll have some words for her when they're in private. I have some words for her right now, but none of them are appropriate for the present company.

Instead, I shoot her that same sugary-sweet grin I give the media when they've asked me a ridiculous question.

"No problem, *sweetheart*."

She shivers, and I know in that instant I win. She tried to rattle me by pressing up against me, but it was no match for that word rolling off my tongue.

I exchange another short goodbye with Jackson before making my way from the restaurant. When I glance back over my shoulder, I'm unsurprised to find Auden watching. I send her a wave, and she gives me her shoulder.

Feeling victorious, I head for my room to gather my things, which I never really unpacked. I meet the rest of the team just in time to catch the bus, and we're on the plane to St. Louis before I know it. Not until an hour into our flight do I realize I'm missing something again—my hat.

I know then that wasn't the last I'll see of Auden Sinclair.

Chapter 8

AUDEN

I grin down at the navy Yankees hat in my hand.

What a fool.

It's been a week since I last saw Hutch, and I haven't stopped gloating about how I was able to steal his hat back. Did he really think I was willingly hugging him with no ulterior motive? With him so stunned by the move, it was easy to slip my hand into his back pocket and pluck the hat free. He didn't feel a thing, and I bet he didn't realize it was gone until later.

God, what I would pay to have been there when he discovered it was missing. I already loved the smug look on his face like he'd won; I just wish I could have been there to see it wiped off. It might be a dick move stealing his hat, but that's what he gets for what happened in the elevator—for kissing me like he did, for using me. It wasn't fair. He knew it, and I did too.

Payback's a bitch, Reed Hutchinson.

"Remind me again why you're bringing that damned thing?" Lilah says, her nose shoved in her phone as our driver breezes through Seattle traffic like a pro, weaving in and out of lanes, cutting people off like it's going out of style.

I should probably tell him not to drive like an asshole in the company car, but we're running late for the game. For the first time ever, I don't want to miss a minute of the action, and that's it…no other motive to get there on time. It's not like I'm going to watch the Serpents play to see anyone in particular. Just supporting my local team is all.

"You know that's not the same sport, right?"

I roll my eyes at my best friend. "I think the daughter of a former NHL player knows the Yankees aren't a hockey team."

Lilah shrugs. "Just checking."

Her fingers fly across the screen, moving so fast I can hardly keep up.

"Is that Dylan?"

Her eyes light up at just his name. "Yes," she answers breathily.

I shake my head, knowing full well in another week, she'll be on to someone else. We have the same philosophy when it comes to long relationships: they're pointless. While I'm a little more selective about who I spend my time with, she's fine to date around as much as possible.

"Just in case," she always tells me.

But I know it's more than that. I know the real reason she dates around like she does: she's scared to be alone.

I, on the other hand, am perfectly fine with being alone. I suppose that's expected when your mother and father's relationship was tumultuous at best. I couldn't count on one hand the number of times my mother walked out on my dad to be with someone else, only to come crawling back a few months later wanting him back.

My father, as much as I love him, is a dumb bastard for falling for it over and over. Most kids probably want their parents' relationship to succeed, but I was thrilled when my dad finally said enough was enough and divorced her when I was sixteen. Their toxic relationship is why I don't believe commitment is in the cards for me. I've had a front-row seat to seeing someone give themselves over time and time again only to get ruined.

I don't want to ever become my father, so I keep to myself. I keep my nose down and work because that's the one thing that's never failed me—my work.

"Gross."

I smile, turning toward my twin, who happens to

share the same opinion on love as I do, except for different reasons. Hers align more with Hutch's, not mine, but in the end, it's still the same general idea: love sucks.

"Hush," Lilah tells her. "Nobody asked for your opinion."

"I have an opinion to give you."

I smack away my sister's hand before she can flip Lilah the bird. I know her too well sometimes.

Their relationship has always been like this, always bickering, but deep down, they love one another. I can see why they struggle to get along sometimes, though. Lilah is all fun and chaos, and Rory isn't. She's tough, a little rough around the edges. There's not a single thing in this world that can pierce through her hard exterior except animals in need. And me, obviously.

"Promise me no bickering tonight. The last thing I need is to end up on the jumbotron because you two got into a catfight. I bet at least three drunk guys would throw beer on us and yell for a wet t-shirt contest since you're both wearing white."

Lilah sneers at Rory's outfit. "She copied my look."

"You're both wearing jerseys," I remind her.

She huffs, and I laugh. I know once we get out of this confined car, they'll be in better moods. They have to be. How can they be grumpy when there are nachos in our future?

"God, I can't wait for nachos," Rory grumbles as she looks back out the window, watching the city pass us by and unknowingly reading my mind. Or maybe knowingly…I can never tell with the Twin Thing.

A few short moments later, Jerry pulls up outside the brand-new climate-friendly arena.

"I'll be right out here at nine, Ms. Sinclair," he says as he helps us out of the car.

"Thanks, JerBear." I toss him a wink, delighting in the way he blushes. He's an older, stoic man, and any time I can get him to break character, it makes me all giddy.

Or maybe I'm just giddy because of what we're about to do—watch hockey. I'll admit that over the last week, I've snuck my tablet to bed a few times so I could watch the Serpents play while they've been on the road.

Much to my father's dismay, I'm sure, I still don't have the best grasp on the game, but I'm slowly learning—and slowly becoming addicted too. I knew hockey has a quick pace, but I didn't realize just how fast it really is. A few times during broadcasts, they'd throw up numbers of how fast the players were moving or shooting the pucks, and every time my eyes nearly popped out of my head. I'm pretty sure some of them move faster than speed limits! It's mesmerizing in a way I didn't realize.

And fine, it doesn't hurt that the players aren't so bad to look at...especially a certain player who I just happen to know looks incredible naked.

I run my finger over the faded Yankees logo again as we approach the line to get in. I could probably pull some strings and get us through the crowd faster, but tonight I wanted to experience what it was like as a fan, not a billionaire. Just as I predicted, by the time we make it through security and to our seats, Lilah and Rory are in much better moods.

"Damn, Auden." Lilah whistles. "You really sprung for the good spots, huh?"

"I better not freeze, or I'm making you buy me a jacket," Rory says. I know it's really her way of saying, *This is amazing, and I love you.*

"Pretty great, huh?" I settle into my rink-side seat and press my hand against the glass, giving it a few whacks like I've seen them do on TV so many times over the last week.

"I need nachos," Rory announces, shoving up from her seat before her ass even hits it fully.

"Me too! I'll come with." Lilah bounces on her heels and out of the aisle.

Rory stares after her with a frown, and I laugh.

"Just go. Get me some nachos too. And be nice, Aurora Rose. Don't let her get lost."

She mutters the entire time she walks away, taking

the stairs two at a time to catch up to Lilah. How I ended up with a sister and a best friend who are total opposites, I'll never know. I'm just glad they can put aside their differences so we can all hang out together.

I take in the arena around me. It looks so much bigger than it does on TV. There are thousands of seats, most of them still empty since some time remains before the game begins. The music is loud but not overbearing. The lights are bright, and if I were anywhere else, I'd probably be dying of heatstroke under the jersey and sweater I'm wearing, but not here. I'm cool, almost cold, and I like the bitterness of it. It feels good, almost welcoming.

Ten minutes pass by as I wait for the girls to return, but I don't catch a glimpse of them. I wasn't kidding when I told Rory not to let Lilah get lost. She's awful with directions.

"All right, Serpents fans. Are you ready to see your hometown team beat those pesky jungle cats? Let's give a big, warm welcome to your Seattle Serpents!"

The music swells, and when the people sprinkled around the arena start cheering all at once, I try to figure out what they're waiting for. It doesn't take long as one by one, the team begins to skate onto the ice.

People all over begin banging on the glass, trying to get the attention of the players, but not me. I'm too fascinated by how flawlessly they're moving like they aren't on a slippery surface. It's effortless, like they've been doing it their whole lives. I'm sure some of them actually have.

They look like they belong out there, one with the ice. It's crazy to watch how laser-focused most of them are, how they're able to tune out everything around them—the music, the lights, the fans. It's like they're in a whole different world.

Thwack!

"What the—"

I curl into my seat, covering my head. A few people nearby laugh, but I don't care.

I don't care because the only sound I hear is one particular laugh. One I know. One I've been dying to hear again. When I lift my head, I'm met with a stare so damn hot I'm surprised the ice doesn't melt beneath his skates.

Hutch.

He tips his head sideways, watching me with tight eyes. His mouth moves, but I don't know what he says.

I rise to my feet, pressing closer to the glass. He says it again, but again, I can't figure it out. He lifts his stick, tapping it against the glass just above my head.

That's when I know.

My hat.

A grin curls my lips, and I shrug. He shakes his head, eyes still narrowed, but I see it anyway—his lips twitch. He wants to smile at me. He's trying hard to fight it. I know it.

But then, out of nowhere, he turns on his skates and flies across the ice.

Oh. Maybe I imagined that twitch. Maybe he's not fighting anything. Maybe he really is mad I stole his stinky old hat.

He heads for the bench, saying something to the man standing behind it. I can't see what's happening, but the guy runs off, then reappears seconds later. He hands something to Hutch, then Hutch hands it right back.

He grabs his stick and he's off on his skates again. I expect him to come back over to me, but he doesn't. Instead, he takes a lap. Then another. It's not until his third time around that he stops in front of me.

He lifts his gloved hand to show me something: a puck. He holds it against the glass, and I lean in for a closer look. There are two words scribbled on it.

Strike one.

I know what it means the second I read it, and the laugh that leaves me is loud and probably annoying based on the way the people next to me glare, but I don't care. All I care about is Hutch, who is staring down at me. This time, under that familiar heat, there's that spark of mischief from the plane.

He flips the puck over, and I see there's more to his

note*: Meet tonight?* I dart my eyes back to his. He wants to meet with me tonight?

No. It's a bad idea. Absolutely awful. I shouldn't. I *can't. We* can't.

It's too risky, too stupid. I'm not putting my contract with the team at risk just because he's a damn good kisser and can get me off in under two minutes.

Please, he mouths.

I shake my head. *Bad idea.*

He shakes his head. *Please, sweetheart.*

He's pleading. Begging even. And I hate that it's working.

Another player skates up to him, tapping him on the shoulder to let him know warmups are over. Hutch looks back at me, sending me one last pleading glance, and I find myself nodding.

"Okay," I tell him, regretting it the moment I do.

But then he grins, and all those regrets fade away. He turns to skate away, and I realize something.

"Wait!" I yell to him, banging on the glass, and he presses up against it. "Where?" I ask, though I have a feeling I know what his answer will be.

The Sinclair.

I knew it. It makes sense, though, going back to the place where it all started. Well, not *the* place, but still. The Sinclair it is.

I nod, and that grin of his grows. This time, when

he turns to skate away, I let him. Even though I'm watching him leave, that giddiness from earlier rears its cheery head because I'm meeting Hutch tonight.

I can't freaking wait.

The Serpents won.

Not only did they win, it was Hutch who got the game-winning goal. I can't remember the last time I cheered so damn hard.

It's only the team's third win of the season so far—and their first home win—but you wouldn't be able to tell by how electric the crowd is as we file out of the arena. Everyone is yelling and waving around stuffed snakes. It's just as chaotic leaving as it was when we entered. The buzz is contagious, and I'm practically bouncing on my heels.

"It's official," Lilah says as she grabs my hand, tugging me through the crowd toward where Jerry said he'd be parked. "I'm a hockey fan."

"You just like the way they look in their uniforms!" Rory yells from behind me, where she's hanging on to the strap on my jersey.

"As if you don't," I counter back to my twin, feeling extra sassy for some reason.

Fine. I know the reason. It's because as much as the crowd is buzzing with energy from the high of the win, I'm humming for other reasons.

Hutch.

"Why are you smiling so much?" Rory asks, not missing a beat.

"Because we won, duh! Keep up!" Lilah answers for me, and I nod.

My sister's shrewd eyes tell me she doesn't believe it for a second, but she doesn't fight me on it. I'm grateful because I'm not sure I could lie to her, and I'll have to. I haven't even told Lilah about who Hutch is. Sure, she knows I slept with some guy in Chicago, but she has no clue it's a player on the Serpents. She'd never let me live it down if she did know.

Besides, it's not like it's going to happen again, right?

Liar.

I try to silence the voice in my head, no matter how right I fear it may be. We're just meeting tonight so I can give him his hat back. That's it. No funny stuff.

"I see Jerry!" Lilah yells, gripping my hand tighter and picking up speed. "JerBear!" She throws her arms around the older man, pressing a sloppy, slightly drunk kiss to his cheek. "You're my favorite, you know that?"

He blushes for the second time tonight, and it makes me just as happy as it did the first time.

We file into the car, and not even a mile down the road, Lilah is passed out. Rory isn't doing much better; her blinks are getting longer and longer.

"You need to get more sleep," I tell her, resting my head on her shoulder.

"I get plenty of sleep," she argues half-heartedly.

"You do not. As your big sister, I demand you get more."

"You're three minutes older than me, Auden. You're not allowed to play the big-sister card. It doesn't hold the same weight."

"Hey, I worked hard to squeeze around your big head. I'll play that card whenever I please."

She shakes her head but doesn't say anything else. A minute later, she's snoring.

I feel bad waking her up shortly after when we arrive at her apartment building, but I love the hug my sleep-deprived sister gives me. She's not big on the touchy-feely stuff, so I take her hugs where I can get them.

Next, we drop off Lilah. She tries to convince me to stay over at her place, but I manage to wave her off, telling her I have to get home to feed my pet goldfish… which I do not have. She must be really tired because she doesn't even question it.

"Where to, miss?" Jerry asks once I climb back in the car.

"The Sinclair, please."

Jerry nods, heading off in the direction of the first-ever Sinclair. I'm not surprised by the reaction of the front desk when I step into the twenty-seven-floor building ten minutes later after sending Jerry home for the night.

"Ms. Sinclair!" Betty at the front desk shoves off the countertop. She brushes her hair out of her face and not-so-subtly slides her phone out of reach. "G-Good evening."

There's no mistaking the tremble in her voice, worried she's just been caught slacking off.

I wave off her worry. "Hello, Betty. How's your night so far?"

"Good." I see her shoulders visibly relax. "Did you just come from the game?" She nods to the jersey I still haven't taken off. "I heard they won."

"They did," I reply, still feeling that high from the game running through me. "It was incredible."

"My sister loves them. She's been texting me updates all night long. I got her tickets to the game next week for her birthday. They aren't the best since we're all the way up top against the wall, but at least she'll be there."

"Guess we'll just have to fix that, then, won't we?"

I turn on my heel, surprised to find Hutch waltzing

through the door like he owns the place—which is really funny because I actually do.

"Holy shit." Betty slaps her hand over her mouth. "I mean shit. No. Shit. No." She covers her mouth again, her hand shaking as her eyes dart between me and Hutch. She gulps loudly, then removes her hand. "I'm so sorry."

I'm about to tell her it's fine when Hutch steps in.

"It's fine," he tells her. "I get it a lot."

The front desk worker slides her eyes over every inch of the man in front of her. "Oh, I bet you do."

I laugh when what she's just said out loud registers with her, and her eyes expand to twice their usual size. She buries her face in her hands, and Hutch laughs.

"How about two tickets in the lower bowl for next week, huh? It's the Edmonton game, isn't it?"

Betty peels her hands from her face and nods. "Yes. And that would be incredible. Thank you so much, Mr. Hutchinson."

"Hutch is fine. I'll make sure the tickets get to you before the game," he promises.

She looks like she's about to burst out in song, and I'm sure Hutch catches it too, because he places his hand on my lower back. I peer up at him and those damn eyes that draw me in every time. They're not as bright as they looked under the arena lights, but I don't actually think it has anything to do with the venue.

I think it has to do with me.

"I believe you owe me something."

I know he's talking about his hat, but there's something else to his words, something more, and I'm more than willing to find out just what that something more is.

Chapter 9

HUTCH

I couldn't believe my eyes when I hit the ice for warmups and skated over to my usual spot. Auden was there, like right fucking there. Right where I do my stretches. Right where I warm up my hands. She was in my spot, and I don't think she had any clue. Just another *coincidence*, just like it was a coincidence that I got my first goal since February.

It had to be, right? There's no way it was because she was there. That's just too damn ridiculous, even for us.

"Thank you, Hilda," she says to the bartender, who sends Auden a sweet smile before taking off to care for the customer down the way. Auden brings her wineglass to her lips, taking a small sip of the sweet white liquid.

"Do you know all of your employees?" I ask her.

She nods. "I do. Or at least I *try* to. There are a lot of them in various locations, but I do my best to make myself familiar with them. I know most CEOs aren't very hands-on, but I try to be. It's still a small, niche business that I run, and details like that matter to people."

"I know what you mean. I've been on teams with guys who don't even bother learning the equipment manager's name. They think they're too good for common courtesy, but they just look like dicks. They never last long in the league."

"How long have you been playing?"

"Hockey?" She nods. "All my life, it feels like. My uncle took me to a game when I was young, probably four or five. I became obsessed with it and begged my dad to let me try it. He refused at first, but my mother wore him down. I was addicted the moment my skates hit the ice, and it's a dependency I haven't been able to kick."

"You didn't fall or anything? Nothing turned you away?"

"Of course I fell. A lot, actually, but it didn't matter. I still loved the adrenaline that flowed through me even then. It was like nothing I'd ever felt before. The smell of the ice, the feeling of the frigid air against my cheeks…I felt like I was finally home."

"You talk about it like you're in love with it."

I grin. "I am. It's the only thing that's ever owned my heart entirely."

"Even more than the woman who left you at the altar?"

I wait for that old familiar feeling of coldness to flow through me at the mention of my high school sweetheart not showing up on our wedding day, but it doesn't come.

"Yes, even more than her. In fact, I should probably send her a thank-you card. I think if she hadn't left me, I wouldn't still be doing this. I'm sure she'd have talked me out of it at some point, unable to handle the travel and the grueling schedule. I would have lost my love for the game trying to make her happy. I'm glad I don't have distractions like that—even go out of my way not to. It's hockey or nothing for me."

"That's how I feel about my company."

I'm glad she gets it. It's always hard to explain to someone who doesn't understand what it's like to love something so wholly, but I can tell that's not the case with Auden. We're similar in that regard.

"These hotels…"

She looks around the bar of The Sinclair, and I follow her gaze. The lights are dimmed, but it's not so dark that you can't see the person you're sitting next to. There's soft music playing, but it never overwhelms the

4

room. Everything about the space screams modern
elegance and comfort. I don't know how she did it, but
she created the perfect atmosphere that makes you feel
like, no matter who you are, you're at home here.

"I love them," she finishes. "They feel like home
away from home. When my dad told Rory and me
he'd taken all of his NHL money and set it aside for us
to follow whatever dreams we had, I knew what I
wanted to do with it. I've loved building things for as
long as I could remember, and hotels seemed to make
the most sense. I liked the idea of offering people a
comforting place to stay, a place that felt like home and
vacation all at once. The Sinclair was born from that."

She shrugs like it's no big deal, but it is a big deal. I
know this couldn't have been easy to build, no matter
who her father is or the head start she had with her
trust fund. She did this all on her own, and she did a
damn good job at it.

"So, Hutch…" She clears her throat. "How many
teams have you played for?"

I lift a brow. "Come on. Don't act like you haven't
Googled me."

"I didn't, actually." She smiles slyly. "But my
assistant's assistant may have."

"The file?"

"The file." She nods. "I was meant to look at it
long ago, but it was something I kept putting off. I

figured I'd get to it once the season started since it would be more finalized, and I could familiarize myself with the players then." She shrugs. "I guess that's a little quirk of mine, wanting to know the people I'm associated with."

"Not a quirk, simply good business practice. And I guess it's paid off, hasn't it, Little Miss Billionaire."

Her blush deepens. "Stop it."

"What? I'm impressed. And here I thought you had just sweet-talked yourself into the first-class lounge or you were coasting on your father's money."

Her eyes sharpen on me. "I made that money all on my own."

I hold my hand up. "I don't doubt that. I'm not saying you didn't. I'm just saying you didn't look like you belonged."

"Unlike you, Mr. Armani Sweater and Dirty Yankees Cap?"

My eyes drift to the hat that's still on her head. Little thief. I still can't believe she got one over on me and stole it back. At first, I was pissed, but then I realized it gave me an excuse to see her again, and that thought rocked me to my core.

I wanted to see her again. I *never* want to see my one-night stands again.

"It was my father's."

The words slip from my mouth before I realize

what I've said. She tips her head sideways, curious hazel eyes boring into me.

"The hat," I clarify, nodding toward it. "It was my father's. He loved the Yankees and baseball more than anything. It was the only thing we ever disagreed on. He wanted me to play baseball, and I wanted to play hockey. He passed the week after I made my NHL debut." I swallow the lump in my throat. "Hit and run during his morning run."

Her hand flies to her mouth, and I try to ignore the tears that well in her eyes.

"He was wearing that hat because he was *always* wearing that hat. When I went looking for answers and walked down the road he'd been running on, I found it a few yards from where they found him. I've had it ever since."

A choked sob leaves her, tears spilling over her eyes. "Oh god. I'm so sorry, Hutch. He didn't deserve that, and neither did you."

I feel her words sink into me, wrapping around my muscles and bones and embedding themselves in my body. I don't know why I do it, but I reach over, running my thumb over her cheek to clear them away. After they're all gone, I don't stop touching her, even though I should. I have no right to do it, but I can't stop.

Just like I can't stop myself from leaning closer.

Her hazel eyes are still shining with tears, the bright greens and browns mixing together in the most unique fashion. I've never seen anything like it before.

"Hutch..." Auden whispers, and my eyes fall to her lips.

Her beautiful, *sweet* lips. The ones I know feel so damn soft. The ones that traced over every inch of my body back in Chicago.

The ones I want to taste again.

"Last call, Ms. Sinclair."

The bartender's words wash over me like a cold bucket of water, breaking the spell Auden's seemed to put me under. I drop my hand and put distance between us.

I didn't come here tonight to kiss her. I just wanted my hat back; that's all. So what if she came to my game? So what if I scored? So what if I can't stop thinking about her?

It was just one night. That's all it can be with her contract because I know for a fact there's a clause in there regarding fraternizing with the players. I know because at the beginning of every season, we're sat down and given a stern talking-to about the same thing. Don't break shit, treat everyone with respect, and most importantly: keep your hands to yourself.

There are boundaries, and Auden and I have

crossed every single one. But…is it really that bad if nobody knows?

Yes.

"We, uh, we should probably call it a night," I tell her, trying to shake away the echo of the word rattling around in my head.

"Yeah. Probably," she says softly.

She picks up her wineglass, draining the rest. I do the same with my sparkling water and rise to my feet. She meets me there, and I place my hand on the small of her back as we make our way from the bar to the lobby.

My fingers brush against something, and I look down. That's when I realize what is stitched across her back. There's no name, just a number.

"Twenty-seven."

"Hmm?" she says over her shoulder as she continues walking.

I tug on her jersey, pulling her to a stop. She spins toward me. "What?"

"The number on your back. It's twenty-seven."

She lifts a shoulder. "I've always liked that number. My assistant, who is also my best friend, got it for me because she knew that."

"That's *my* number."

"I know. I…I read it in your file. I didn't know she was getting numbers on the jerseys, I swear. I just told her I wanted one and she showed up with this and—"

I swallow the rest of her words with my lips.

It's stupid, completely fucking reckless, but in this moment, I don't care because *she's wearing my number.* Her lips are pliable under my own. It's a soft kiss, easily the softest we've shared, but it doesn't feel any less passionate than the others.

She's the first to pull away. She steps back, putting entirely too much space between us as she sucks in stuttered breaths one after the other.

"Hutch." She shakes her head. "We shouldn't. We *can't.*"

She's right. I know she is.

She clears her throat and presses her shoulders back, all business-like. As if nothing just happened between us. As if nothing *will* happen again.

I shake my head. I want to be annoyed with how she's acting, but I get it. I truly do. That doesn't mean I like it, though.

"Can I walk you out to your car?" I ask her.

"I... Jerry dropped me off. I'm staying here tonight." Auden yanks my hat off her head, her hair a mess underneath it, then hands it over to me. "Here. I'm sorry. I...I didn't know, or I wouldn't have stolen it."

I stare down at her peace offering. I want to take it.

I really do. But if I take it, I can't see her again, and I really want to do that too.

So fucking badly.

"Take it," she says quietly. "Please."

So I do. I take the hat, and I watch as she spins on her heels and rushes to the elevators. I watch as the doors close and I watch as the screen above them counts the floors. Then I leave.

I march right out to my car and get in, firing it up and loving the rumble of the engine as I rev it a few times. I even push it into drive, but that's as far as I get, unable to convince myself to do much else as I stare up at the looming building. It's dark and sleek and stands out just enough among all the other buildings around it without looking out of place. It's tall and beautiful, the perfect mixture of sharp edges and curves. It's...

It's exactly where I want to be tonight.

I throw my car into park and wrench open the door. I go right back into The Sinclair. If Betty is surprised to see me, she doesn't say so. I can feel her eyes on me as I make my way through the lobby and to the elevators. I press the *up* button and wait.

Then wait.

And wait some more.

Finally, the bell above the door dings, and the doors slide open. A soft gasp, wide eyes.

Auden.

She swallows when she sees me, then takes one step to the right. It's my invitation, and I'd be a fool not to RSVP.

So, I do.

Auden's the first to leave the elevator when we reach the twenty-seventh floor. Unlike the last Sinclair we were at, there are no other doors, just one at the end of the hall. She pulls a card from her back pocket when we approach it and holds it up to the door, shoving it open when the light turns green.

"I always keep a room open on this floor in every hotel, just in case I ever want to drop by," she says as I follow her into the suite. "Every room is themed to the property, but the layout never changes. It's a silly little thing, but it gives me comfort to know it's always there for me no matter where I go."

I glance around, and she's right; this is exactly like the room in Chicago. I never saw the one in Denver, but I have no doubt she's telling the truth.

"It smells like you," I comment.

She grins at me as she flips on a lamp. "You noticed that, huh?" She lifts a shoulder. "What can I say? I like—"

"Orange and honey." Her eyes widen, and it's my turn to shrug. "It's distinct."

"Like in a bad way?"

I shake my head, taking a step forward. "Not at all."

"Well, good." She clears her throat, then tucks an errant strand of hair behind her ear. Her long brown locks are still messy from the Yankees cap, but if she cares, it doesn't show. "So, through here, we have—"

I grab her wrist, halting her movements. She half-turns back to me, looking up with timid eyes.

"Auden."

A gulp. "Yes?"

"You don't need to give me a tour."

Her lips part just slightly, a soft "Oh" falling from them, and I give her a gentle tug, pulling her to me. She comes willingly, fitting herself against me like she's done it a thousand times before. I tuck a finger under her chin, tilting her head back.

"We both know why I'm up here."

"Well, yes, but I figured we could at least pretend it's not just about sex."

"But it is, Auden. It's just about sex. You know that as well as I do. For some reason, we're stupidly attracted to one another, and the universe keeps throwing us together. I'm tired of fighting it."

"But we should," she counters. "We should fight it.

It's not right. I'm... I have..." She exhales shakily. "This is wrong. I don't mix business with pleasure, Hutch. *Ever.*"

"Then think of this like a business transaction."

She laughs derisively. "How? How is this business?"

I search my brain, trying to come up with an excuse, any single thing, a tiny thread—*something* to tie *this* back to hockey because I'm not ready to give it up just yet.

Then it hits me.

"It's you."

A wrinkle forms between her brows. "What's me?"

"We won tonight. You came to the game, and we won."

She scoffs. "That's ridiculous."

"We *won*," I repeat. "We won in Colorado, and you were there. We won in St. Louis the night after I saw you last. And tonight, we won, and I scored. I haven't scored all season. In fact, I haven't scored since February. But tonight, you were there, and I scored."

"I..." Her words fade on her tongue as she stares up at me, her hazel eyes bouncing back and forth between mine. After several silent seconds, she says, "I was there tonight."

I nod, leaning down and pressing a kiss to the corner of her mouth. "You were there."

"And you scored."

"I scored." I place another kiss on the other side. "Remember when you asked me if I was superstitious? Back on the plane?"

She nods, her body trembling beneath me as I trace a path down her side. "I remember."

"I am, Auden. I'm superstitious as hell, and right now, it seems like *you* might be my good luck charm."

Chapter 10

I am either the most gullible person on the planet or the most desperate. I eat up Hutch's words, believe them with everything in me. It's the only thing I can do because I *have* to justify this in some way. I want him too damn badly not to.

Pressing up to my tiptoes, I say one word. "Okay."

And then we're a mess of lips and teeth and tongues, reaching for each other at the same moment.

"Same rules as before?" he asks when we come up for air. "Just tonight?"

"Yes," I tell him.

But even as he asks and I answer, we both know it's not true. It's not just tonight. We're going to want more. It's inevitable, and we both know it.

Right now, though, I don't care. I don't care

because Hutch is kissing me and it's the best damn kiss of my life. He tips my head back, taking control of my mouth, and I let him as I drop my fingers to the hem of his shirt. I didn't get a chance to properly explore his body last time, and tonight, I intend to.

I pull up, and he lets me strip the Serpents shirt from his body. I let it fall to the floor, then press my palms against his chest, loving the softness of the hair covering him. I run my fingers through it and then down. Lower and lower I go until my hands are on the button of his jeans. He catches my wrist, pulling his mouth from mine, looking down at me with a silent question in his eyes.

"It's my turn for a taste," I tell him, and I fall to my knees.

He doesn't protest.

I draw down the zipper of his jeans, then give them and his boxer briefs a tug until they're hanging around his thighs. His thick cock bobs free, hanging heavy right in my face.

I waste no time with teasing. I don't have it in me at the moment. I just want to hear him curse and moan my name for a change. I run my tongue along his length, and I'm rewarded for my efforts.

"Fuck."

I grin, then lick at him again and again, wetting his

cock until it's soaked with my spit. Only then do I cover him with my mouth, taking him to the back of my throat in an instant.

"Auden," he moans, and I know I have him right where I want him.

I release him, then suck him back down, over and over until his hands are a mess in my hair and his legs are shaking and I know he's *so damn close*. Just when I think he's about to come down my throat, he pulls me free, tugging me to my feet.

"What the…"

But the protest dies on my lips as he lifts me in his arms effortlessly. He carries me through the suite, and I assume we're going to the bedroom, but we don't.

I hiss when cool glass presses against my back.

"As much as I want to fill your throat with my cum, I want to fill your cunt even more." He cups me through my jeans, and I swear it's like there's nothing between us. "But first, I'm going to get a taste of this sweet pussy I missed so much. Then I'm going to fuck you against this window, Auden. I want all of Seattle to see who you belong to tonight, understand?"

"Yes," I moan as he takes my earlobe between his teeth, biting down with just enough pressure that it hurts but still feels good.

He drops me to my feet, his fingers going to my

jeans. He has them unzipped and around my ankles before I can even realize what's happening. Then, like before, he drops to his knees, and *holy hell* do I love the sight of it. He inches closer to my already soaked pussy, running his nose along me.

"God, I missed the taste of you."

It's the last thing he says before he slides his tongue against me, pushing through my folds until he finds just the spot he's looking for. He flattens his tongue against my clit and sucks in the sensitive button with the perfect amount of pressure and rhythm that has me bucking against him like a madwoman.

I look a mess, my jeans still wrapped around my ankles, my shoes still on, still wearing the jersey from earlier—but I don't care. Having his face between my legs feels too damn good for me to pay that any mind. I slip my hands into his hair, holding him against me as I teeter on the edge of release.

"Hutch…" I call out his name, and it spurs him on.

My orgasm races through me seconds later. I should be embarrassed that I've fallen apart so quickly, but I'm not, not when he pulls away and grins up at me like that, his face still wet from my release as he sheathes himself with a condom I never even saw him get out. He pulls off my shoes and then my jeans and rises to his feet, taking me along with him. I hook my ankles together behind his back as he slides inside of me.

"Fuck," he mutters when he's fully seated. He presses kiss after kiss against my neck, letting me adjust to his size. "You feel so good, sweetheart."

"So do you." I kiss him and tug him closer. "You can move now."

"Is that so?"

His laugh vibrates against me, but he heeds my instructions. He begins to move into me, but it's only slightly and not at all enough. I let out a frustrated groan, which causes him to laugh even harder.

"Mean."

"You love it."

"Never," I swear as he slants his mouth over mine, taking me in a hard kiss.

But it's a lie because I do love it, and I love it even more when he *finally* moves. Slowly, he drives into me, never once taking his lips off mine. It's different than how he fucked me in Chicago. It's softer and harder all at once, and I love it just as much.

His kisses match his movements. Teasing. Pleasing. And so fucking delicious. My orgasm builds slowly, then crashes into me all at once. He laughs into my mouth when I fall apart around him.

"That's two," he says when he pulls away, not stopping his slow, short thrusts. "One more."

"I can't." I shake my head, already feeling drowsy from two orgasms.

"You will," he promises.

It's a promise he keeps as he finally releases his control and fucks into me, holding nothing back. It's rough and hard and I have no doubts in my mind I'm going to have bruising from how hard he's pressing me against the glass, but I welcome it.

"Auden…" he warns, and I know he's close.

I slide my hand between us, my fingers finding my clit. As adamant as my protests were, Hutch was right, because not three strokes later, a blinding light passes behind my closed eyes, and I come harder than I did the other two times.

"Finally," he mutters, and it's the last thing he says before he pulls out of me, only to slam back home twice more before his release hits him.

He drops his head to the crook of my neck, his warm breath tickling my skin. I'm not sure how long we stand there. Hell, I'm not even sure how he's still standing after that. I guess his stamina from the ice? Either way, it's long enough for the cool air of the room to wash over me and send shivers down my spine.

Hutch doesn't miss it. He adjusts his grip and peels me from the window, carrying me through the suite and straight to the bathroom. He sets me on the countertop, then moves to the massive bathtub and turns on the water. He doesn't add anything to it, just lets the steam fill the room as he shucks off his jeans. I hadn't even realized he was still wearing them.

God, what a mess we are.

He fits himself back between my legs and grabs the hem of the jersey but doesn't strip it off immediately.

"I like you in this," he tells me as he rolls the hem of it between his fingers, his eyes tracing the Serpents logo, a mean-looking snake with a hockey puck coming from its mouth. When he drags his gaze back to mine, there's a heat to it that wasn't there before. "But I'd like it better if my name was above that number."

I don't say anything, and I don't think he expects me to. He just lifts me off the counter and carries me to the tub where he slowly settles into the water. I sigh the second it laps over my skin, covering me in its warmth like a blanket I didn't know I had such a desperate need for.

Hutch wraps his arms around me loosely, holding me against him but not keeping me trapped. That's how we stay until the water turns cold and our fingers wrinkle. We don't talk. We don't fool around. We just sit like this.

Eventually, he pulls me from the tub and wraps me in a towel. We dry off, then crawl into bed, falling fast asleep. When I wake up in the morning, I'm alone once again, but I know it's not the last I'll see of him.

Especially since he left something behind on the dresser.

His hat.

Chapter 11

HUTCH

"Whoever the fuck that is, knock it off," Keller grumbles as I pull on my skate laces, getting them just how I like them.

I'd say it isn't like Keller to be so grumpy, but that wouldn't be true. He's easily the most curmudgeonly player I've ever shared the ice with.

"Lighten up, Keller," Fox tells him.

The right winger flips off the goalie, who just laughs.

Now Fox, on the other hand, is always easygoing. He's not only completely chill in net, he's like that off the ice too. Some goalies are pretty high-strung and have very precise routines they need to follow to get in the zone, but not Fox.

"Fucking seriously," Keller growls. "Stop with the whistling."

Locke knocks his elbow against mine. "You'd better quit or he's going to get real pissed."

I tip my head at him. "Huh?"

"The whistling, man. Knock it off."

Oh, fuck. That's me?

"You're still doing it," Locke whispers, darting his eyes to Keller, who is about two seconds from flying out of his stall and knocking some heads together. Or just head—mine.

"Oops." I shrug, tugging my laces tighter.

I didn't even realize I was whistling, which is weird as hell for me. I *hate* whistling. The sound grates on my nerves. But I haven't exactly felt like myself lately, and I know it has to do with a certain brunette who kept me up half the night.

"Someone's in a good mood today," Lawson comments, his eyes bouncing back and forth between me and Locke. "You get laid or something?"

The question is directed at me, and I ignore him.

"Oooooh. You totally did. Explains why you bailed on drinks last night."

"I bailed on drinks because I don't like to drink during the season, especially not on back-to-back nights. Something you idiots should have considered as well."

Lawson shrugs. "It's called self-control. Besides, one beer isn't going to kill me."

"Beer? You had a fucking Cosmo, you loser," Keller tells him.

"Shut up!" Lawsy chucks a puck at the perpetual grump.

"Come on, guys. Let's not get into it right now, huh? We hit the ice in ten minutes." Fox attempts to placate them, but it's pointless. They're still throwing daggers at one another.

"Are they always like this?" Hayes asks.

"Yep," I answer. "But it's all part of their pregame warmup. They'll do this every game."

I'm not exaggerating. I can't recall a game where Keller and Lawsy didn't fight beforehand. I really think it's some weird mind game Keller plays with himself to get him in a checking mood. He's always ready to skate out there and demolish guys with some hard-as-hell body contact.

"Bunch of children if you ask me," Locke comments.

"And yet nobody did, Gramps."

"Shut the fuck up, Lawsy." Keller again.

Round and round they go. I tune them out, trying to get myself ready for the game tonight. I'm eager for a repeat of last night in more ways than one, starting with winning the game and continuing with seeing Auden. I left behind my hat and my number this morning, and I woke up from my pregame nap to a text that was just one word long.

27.

That was it, but she didn't have to say more. I knew, and the sooner we get this game won, the sooner I can get to Auden, no matter how wrong it is.

Sure, we didn't know who the other was when this all started, but we know now, and yet I can't seem to care—especially not when I'm winning. It felt like I was grasping at straws last night, trying to find any reason to convince her to let me stay, but when I woke up this morning, it didn't feel like I was grasping at all. I felt different. I felt like the old me again, ready to hit the ice and make plays that win us games. I missed that version of me, and it feels damn good to have it back again. There's no way in hell I'm letting it go now, particularly as the captain spot is within my grasp.

Besides, it's not like I have to worry about Auden getting attached. She knows what this is. Other than the shit with the contract, I can't see how this isn't a good idea.

"Listen up, boys."

Everyone stops talking and moving at once. Our attention is pulled to the front of the room where our coach has just entered. He's a tall man, standing a few inches above me even, and I don't think I've ever seen him smile. I wouldn't be surprised if serious was his middle name.

"We did good last night. We played hard and we got pucks in deep when we needed to. Lawson, keep your feet fast and your ass out of the box. Keller, hit 'em hard but clean. No need to take penalties or get suspended." He looks at Fox. "You good?"

"Yes, sir," our goalie answers, that same damn grin he's always sporting just as bright and cheery as usual.

"Good." Coach's eyes land on me. "Hutch, maybe don't wait until the third to score? Get on the board early, huh?"

"Yes, Coach," I tell him.

He nods. "All right." He turns on his heel and walks from the room.

I've had a few coaches over the years, but never one as direct as him. He doesn't mince his words and he doesn't waste any time trying to build us up or tear us down. He trusts us to do our jobs out there, and I appreciate that.

But sometimes…sometimes I wish he *would* give us some direction. It might help the younger guys feel a bit more confident out on the ice.

Locke jabs me with his elbow, tipping his head. He wants me to say something to the guys, and he's right, I should say something. It's no secret I want that captain spot. This is my chance to show I can lead this team.

I rise from my stall once Coach is gone and clear my throat.

"All right, boys. You heard Coach. You know what he wants to see out of us tonight, and I know what I want to see too—grit. I want you to go out there and I want you to fight for those pucks. I want you to win those board battles and I want you to give it all you got. And, uhhhh…" I pause for dramatic effect. "Win some hockey games."

Keller rolls his eyes, Fox sticks his fingers in his mouth and whistles obnoxiously, Lawson lets out a loud whoop, and Locke just shakes his head, a grin hidden behind his unruly beard. It's the same ridiculous comment we give in interviews, a little unintentional inside joke everyone in the NHL is in on. It's funny for us but frustrating for the media, I'm sure.

The clock counts down the remaining minutes until ice time and we all get on our feet, making our way to the tunnel one by one. We're bumping lids and smashing into one another, whooping and hollering and making a full-blown ruckus until we're all buzzing with excitement.

"Foxy…release the beast!" Lawsy yells, and Fox lets out a war cry before he heads out.

We all follow behind him, hitting the ice one after another. I revel in the cool air that hits me the second my skate hits the surface. I do a few laps, getting my legs warmed up, and it doesn't take long until everything inside of me quiets down and I'm at peace. I wonder briefly if other players feel this same way too but quickly push that thought out of my head because the only thing I can see is her.

Auden.

She's back in her seat against the glass. Her smile is bright and so fucking infectious I can't help but smile back. The second I do, I'm knocked on my ass.

I whip my head up to find a player from Vegas sneering down at me. I know him: Rogers. He's a known instigator and a total prick. We had issues back when I was with Nashville and he played for Chicago. Dirty player all around, so I'm not entirely surprised by this.

"Quit looking at your slutty puck bunny and watch it," he hisses, but that's all he manages to get out before three Serpents players are on him.

It's an unspoken rule of hockey: you don't fucking cross the red line. So, my team's reaction? Warranted as hell.

"You're dead, dickhead," I hear Keller yell before he slams Rogers into the boards, his forearm going to his throat as he pins him there.

"Shit-stain motherfucker," says Lawsy, jumping in on the action, giving Rogers a face wash of a lifetime.

"Hey, hey, enough!" Locke tries to break it all up,

but I can tell just from the tone of his voice that he's not happy about it either.

I know I'm sure as fuck not.

The scuffle gets broken up, but not before Keller gets his licks in. The whole thing sets the tone for the rest of the night. Right off the face-off, Keller drops his gloves and takes a fighting major. When things get settled down, it happens again; this time Lawsy is the one to start the brawl.

Finally, when I take my first shift, it's my turn. I run right to Rogers and snatch him up by his jersey, slamming him into the glass. He laughs as we drop our gloves, but his smile is wiped clean when my fist makes contact with his face and he goes down hard.

I let the linesmen pull me away because unlike him, I don't play dirty. If a player goes down, you stop hitting. He shakes his head a few times and tries to get up but fails, wobbling on his skates from the blow he just took. Then he sets his eyes on me, furious. Absolutely fuming.

"You're going to regret that," he promises.

I laugh as the linesmen tug me away. "I doubt it."

And just like that, we're not even five minutes into the game and we already have six players in the box between the two teams. It's worth every damn PIM we get, especially when at the end of the night, the tally is 3-1 us.

"Fucking pricks," Keller grumbles, tossing his helmet into his stall after the game. "God, I hate those assholes. Everyone's always comparing us to them, but we aren't like them though. We're fucking better than that cheap shit."

He's not telling us anything we don't all already know. We've been compared to that damn team since day one. It's not entirely bad, because even for all the shit they pull, they are a good club, but damn does it get tiring to constantly have to defend ourselves.

"Not the best start to the night," Coach says, and we all quiet down. "Way too many PIMs, but we managed to snag the two points, and in the end, that's what matters. Off day tomorrow, but back at it on Tuesday. Keller, Fox, you got media."

Then he's gone again. That's it. No other words of encouragement or comfort and no comment on the cheap shot from the Vegas player. I shake my head, shoving from my stall.

"Hell of a game, boys. Way to put up a fight —literally."

"Fuck yeah!" Lawsy yells.

I grin at his outburst. I usually wouldn't entertain his crap, but I'm still feeling wired from the game and the fight. I haven't been in one of those in a hot minute, and it felt good as hell to get out some of my aggression.

"You heard Coach—no skate tomorrow, but we're back on the grind after that. Get some rest."

"Heard!"

Everyone claps twice, then we all go our own ways, hitting the showers or heading out for media. Just twenty minutes later, I'm going my own way too—right to The Sinclair.

"Was that your first fight?" Auden asks. She's naked and draped over me, our legs twined together as I run my fingers through her hair.

After she inspected every inch of me the second I walked through the door, she surprised me by dropping to her knees, telling me she wanted to *"kiss it all better."* We both knew there was nothing down there that was hurt, but we played along anyway. Afterward I set her on top of the dresser and kissed *her* all better before burying myself inside of her.

What I didn't want was her to find out that I'm sore as fuck from the hit I took earlier in the night, then the fight on top of twenty-five minutes of ice time tonight. I'm definitely feeling it right now.

"No," I answer. "But it was the first one in about three years."

"Do you like it? Fighting?"

"I don't go looking for fights if that's what you mean, but sometimes it's necessary. It's hard as an older player because you want to set an example for your team by not taking any penalties, but you also don't want to be a pushover. Tonight though..."

"That guy totally deserved it. He just mowed you over for no reason."

I shake my head. "It wasn't for no reason. It was because he knew I was distracted. He knew I was looking into the stands and not paying any attention. He was sending a message that Vegas was there to play, not daydream."

She lazily runs her fingers through the hair on my chest. "What were you daydreaming about?"

I don't answer her because I'm not sure I'm ready to say it was *her* I was looking at, mostly because I'm still not sure how I feel about it. How the hell did I let an opposing player knock me on my ass on my own ice like that? I thought I was centered, cool, and calm, head totally in the game—but one look at Auden and I was somewhere else entirely.

I don't like that, but it's not something I'm willing to address right now. I just want to enjoy what I came here tonight for: her. I roll over, taking her with me until she's underneath me.

"Did *you* like it? Seeing me fight?" I ask, grabbing

her hands and lifting them over her head. I love the way she arches into me, love how she fits against me.

"Maybe."

"Just maybe?" I run my nose along the length of her neck. "That's it?"

"Yeah. It was okay. Didn't get my panties wet or anything."

"Is that because you weren't wearing any?"

She doesn't answer, and I pull back, peering down into her eyes.

"You weren't wearing any, were you?"

She shakes her head. "Nope."

"My, my, my. Auden Sinclair, you naughty little girl."

She giggles, and I love the sound of it. "Only sometimes."

"You're full of surprises, you know that?"

"Yeah? Most people call me predictable, even boring because all I do is work."

"There's nothing wrong with working hard. Don't feel ashamed of that."

She traps her bottom lip between her teeth.

"What?" I ask. Something is obviously bothering her, but I'm not sure what.

"It's nothing." She shakes her head, and the movement causes her tits to jiggle, pulling my attention. She doesn't miss it, letting out a faux-annoyed sigh. "Typical man. You see one boob jiggle and you can't help but look."

I capture a nipple in my mouth and run my tongue flat against it. She moans, and I laugh against her.

"I don't hear you complaining about me being a typical man right now."

"Shut up," she mutters, but there's no bite behind her words, especially not when I give her other nipple the same treatment.

I kiss her breasts, giving them the attention I've yet to provide them, but soon that's not enough for either of us. I find myself kissing my way down her stomach, then between her legs until she's calling out my name wildly and begging, only to kiss my way back up and start all over again. I do it twice more, licking her to the brink just to pull away.

"*Please.*" It's a desperate cry for release, and I must be a sick man because I love the way it sounds.

"Please what?" I roll my hips into her, letting my cock slide over her slick and likely oversensitive clit. "I want to hear you say it, Auden."

She whimpers when I rut against her again.

"Please...fuck me already, Hutch. I'm begging you."

"As you wish, sweetheart," I whisper against her lips. "Be right back."

"No." She shakes her head. "No condom. Just you."

"But…"

"I'm on birth control. I haven't had sex with anyone but you since last year."

Her words shock me, but I try not to let it show.

I just tell her, "I get tested regularly, and you're the only one I've been with since Chicago, I swear."

"I believe you." She kisses me again. "Now fuck me already."

And fuck her I do. It's not soft or sweet or slow. It's hard and rough and fast, over so damn fast for both of us after going to the edge and back too many times. I pull out just in time to make a mess across her belly, then I get up and grab a rag to clean away the mess. When I climb back into bed, she curls against me, but it's not enough. I drag her even closer until she's practically on top of me.

"Mmm," she purrs, half asleep. "I could get used to this."

Me too, Auden. Me too.

Chapter 12

AUDEN

"Would it be super weird to say I'm craving toast right now?" I drag my hand idly over Hutch's chest, running the tips of my nails against him, loving the way he shivers every so often at the soft touch.

"Toast, huh?"

"I *love* toast. It's my favorite."

"Do you love toast, or do you just love butter?"

I turn my face into his body, burying my smile. How does he know me so well already? "Both."

He laughs, having known I was going to say exactly that. How could he not know? What kind of weirdo likes toast for toast and not for the insane amounts of butter you're totally justified in adding to it?

"Come on." I shove off his chest and tug on his hand. "Let's go."

"Go?" he questions, not budging no matter how hard I pull. "Where are we going?"

"The kitchen. I'm hungry." *Starving* really. Despite my short nap, I feel like I just ran about four miles, all thanks to Hutch and his ability to render me completely useless with his cock alone. Not that I'm complaining or anything. Sex with him is easily some of the best I've ever had, and I already can't wait for more.

"It's late. The kitchen's closed," he tells me.

I let out a rather unattractive snort-laugh because *Is he for real?* "I'm the owner, Hutch. The kitchen is *never* closed for me."

I tug on him again, and this time he lets me pull him. I crawl out of bed as he scoots to the edge behind me. I grab my robe off the back of the chair, slip it on, and slide my feet into a pair of slippers by the stool.

"Up," I instruct when I see he's still sitting on the bed like I'm not completely famished right now.

"I'm coming, I'm coming."

"You can be if you get up." I smile at him sweetly, like my words didn't contain a double meaning.

He groans when he moves, and my brows crush together at the sound. He's in pain, that much is obvious. I hate it. I want to crawl back to him and make him feel all better.

But also…toast.

I settle on asking, "Are you okay?"

He shoots me a smile, but it's not his usual smile. It's a little more forced, likely because he's holding back his pain. "Nothing a little kitchen sex can't fix."

"Kitchen sex, huh?"

He shrugs. "If you insist."

I laugh, loudly and obnoxiously, which has Hutch grinning too. The familiar expression is back, warm and real and just so...*him.*

He goes to grab his shorts to pull them on over his boxer briefs, but I stop him before he can get too far.

"What are you doing? Just throw on a robe and let's roll. Robes and rolling—that's what we're doing."

He looks at me like he wants to argue but thinks better of it. Probably smart because the longer we stand here, the hungrier I'm getting, and I usually have about two minutes before I turn into Hungry Bitch from the Abyss Auden and let the hunger-rage consume me.

He abandons his shorts in favor of his robe then slips on his shoes.

"I look ridiculous," he complains, glancing down at his outfit.

"You don't," I lie; he totally does. "Let's go."

I lead him out of the room and to the elevator. We don't talk as it takes us down to the first floor.

"First floor?" he questions when the doors slide open.

I don't answer, instead just shooting him a *Don't test me right now* look.

He's smart enough to pick up on what it means, raising his hands in defeat before following me out of the elevator. The hotel is fairly quiet, though I can still hear a bit of ruckus coming from the bar. It strikes me that maybe this wasn't such a good idea, to go such a public way, but the coast is clear and it's not like anyone on my staff would dare breathe a word if they saw us. They value their jobs entirely too much.

We sneak from the elevators to the service door then down the hall to the kitchen. It's empty, just like I knew it would be. We always close it early during the week.

"It feels wrong being in here," Hutch whispers behind me as I flick on the lights like I've done so many times before. This isn't my first time sneaking down here—far from it—but it is my first time bringing a guest.

"It's not. Owner, remember?"

"Yeah, yeah, Little Miss Billionaire." He slips his hands around my waist, pulling me backward until I fall against his chest. "I remember."

I shiver as his lips brush over my ear, loving how soft his touch is and desperately wanting more.

But not as badly as I want some toast.

"Feed me," I whisper back just as huskily as he did.

His laughter rumbles through both of us as he loosens his grip, unleashing me like the beast I'm currently resembling. I rush out of his embrace and give my hands a good wash then beeline for my precious toaster. I grab four slices of bread and deposit them into the slots.

The whole time, I can feel Hutch's eyes on me. I even dare a peek over my shoulder and find him with his arms crossed over his chest as he rests against one of the tables, his eyes never leaving me as I move around the kitchen, grabbing butter and jelly and my secret stash of grapes from the freezer.

"You weren't kidding about coming down here all the time, were you?"

"Nope." I hold up the glass container of fruit, where my name has been scrawled onto a sticky note and attached to the lid. "They take care of me here."

"I mean, it's only fair, right? You take care of them too." He pushes off the counter, stalking toward me. "You're really amazing with your staff. You know that, don't you?"

I shrug. "I just treat them like people."

"Yeah, but most places don't. I've been to my fair share of hotels, and this place...it's different. It really does feel like home away from home. Things like that stem from the top of the ladder, Auden."

Warmth spreads through me at his words, and I have to turn so he can't see the blush that's creeping into my cheeks.

"Don't hide," he says, knowing me too well again. He slides his arms around me as I begin buttering the perfectly toasted slice of sourdough. "Just take the compliment."

"Thank you," I tell him softly, and I do mean it. "I try to be a good leader."

"You are." He brushes my hair from my neck, then places a kiss against that spot he knows drives me wild. "You're the best I've seen."

"You hang out with many hotel owners?"

He smiles against me. "Don't be a smartass."

"You don't be a kiss-ass. You don't have to say nice things—I still totally plan on having kitchen sex with you."

"Is that a promise?" He presses into me, and I can feel that he *really* wants that to be a promise.

I do too.

I spin in his arms, and he doesn't waste a second of this new position, lifting me onto the counter in an instant. He steps between my legs, fitting between them perfectly. He takes the knife and toast from my hands, finishing the job of slathering on butter then holding the bread up for me.

"Eat."

I lean forward, taking a bite, enjoying the way his eyes don't seem to leave mine. It's silly he's feeding me, but also, it's kind of...hot. I'm not used to being taken care of; I've always done things by myself. This moment...this simple gesture...it feels like something I've never had before.

He hums softly, still watching as I sit back and chew. He takes a bite, right from where my mouth just was, then extends it my way again. I take another bite. Back and forth we go until the slice is gone.

Hutch then reaches for a grape. He picks it up, inspecting it with skeptical eyes. "Frozen grapes, huh?"

"You've never had them?"

He shakes his head. "Never."

"Oh, you are *so* missing out. Try it. It's one of my favorite snacks."

He gives it one last cautious glance before popping the whole grape in his mouth. The moan that leaves him suddenly has me hungry for something else entirely—him. He tosses another in, moaning once more, and I squirm against the counter, an ache like no other forming between my legs.

I swallow against the lump lodged in my throat. "Hey, Hutch?"

"Hmm?" he says, grabbing another grape, not paying me any attention.

"I think I'd like that kitchen sex now."

His gaze snaps to mine, the heat I love so much filling his gaze. "Is that so?"

I gulp, nodding a few times. "That's so."

This time, he doesn't take his eyes off me as he grabs another grape, lifting it to my lips. I reach my tongue out to taste it, purposefully rolling it along his fingers. His eyes flare, and it's the last thing I see before he crushes his mouth to mine.

He kisses me hard and rough, his hands crashing through my already-post-sex-messy hair as he drags me to the edge of the counter. I grip his shoulders, holding myself to him, not wanting to miss a second of his lips on mine. His hands move from my hair to my neck, one gripping the back possessively while the other continues a path downward. He doesn't stop until he's between my legs where, with no warning, he plunges a single finger deep inside of me.

"Fuck me," he groans. "Your cunt's already dripping, sweetheart."

"It's all you," I tell him.

"Only me. Gonna look so pretty stretched around my cock later."

I nod as he takes my mouth again, pumping his finger into me then adding another. Then a third. At this point, I'm humping his hand, wanting and craving more—craving *him*.

Suddenly my body feels empty, and it takes me a full ten seconds to realize why: he's gone.

No. Not gone. He's dropping to his knees. He's pushing mine apart. He's leaning forward and—

"Oh god." I toss my head back on a stuttered exhale. "Hutch."

"Reed," he says. "Call me Reed tonight."

"Reed," I repeat, sliding my hand through his hair and tugging his mouth back to me.

He resists the pull, and I glower down at him with a frown. He laughs, and his hot breath brushes against me, sending a shiver through every inch of me.

"Tonight, Auden," he says, and I love the way my name sounds in that deep voice of his, "tonight I'm going to taste you. For every lick, I want you to call out my name."

"Every lick?"

He nods. "Every single one. I leave for a week tomorrow. Don't want you forgetting whose pussy this is while I'm gone, now do I?"

He leans forward and runs his tongue along me. I sigh then groan when he sits back, staring up at me expectantly.

"Reed," I say, and he smirks.

Another lick, and my body heats tenfold.

"Reed."

Another taste, and it feels like I'm on fire.

"Reed."

A soft swipe, but it doesn't *feel* soft. It's just what I need.

"Reed."

A kiss, and I know there's no way I'm going to last much longer.

"Reed."

A suck—and I'm a goner.

"*Reed*," I call out, my whole body shuddering as my orgasm races through me like a wave attacking a shoreline. It's fierce and sudden and so damn beautiful.

He continues to lick at me softly, coaxing me through the aftermath. When he's wrung me completely dry, he shoves to his feet, then pushes his own robe aside to reveal his hard cock. He doesn't say a word as he slides inside of me, nor when he fucks me slowly, driving us both to orgasm once more. In fact, we don't speak again until we make it back to my room and are snuggled together in bed.

Only after he presses a kiss to my head does he whisper, "I'll miss you."

I'll miss you too, Reed.

It's the fourth week of November and hockey season is in full swing, which means I haven't seen Hutch in over a week, and I'm slowly going crazy because of it. I flip-flop between missing him and knowing I shouldn't, wanting to call him and talking myself out of it. The back and forth is exhausting, and it's making it hard to concentrate on work.

Which is why for the first time in a really long damn time, I'm hiding at my sister's clinic.

"If you're going to be here in my way, at least do something to help," Rory gripes. She nods toward a broom and dustpan in the corner. "Go take those out there to Casey."

I go to grab the broom, but I'm blocked from the mission when the door opens and in comes Casey.

"Oh. That's where I put that." She grabs them, then breezes back out of the office.

Rory groans, and I laugh.

She glowers at me over her computer. "Why are you here again?"

"Because I'm bored."

"You're never bored. You're running a billion-dollar company—how the hell can you be bored?"

I shrug. "I don't know. There's nothing to do. The build in Boston is a month ahead of schedule, and the opening in Tampa was flawless. All my properties are managing themselves. So, I'm just..."

"Bored?"

I huff. "Yep."

If this surprises Rory, she doesn't show it. "Have you thought about a vacation instead of lounging around my office?"

I laugh, which scares the little kitten curled up in my lap. I run my fingers over its head, trying to soothe it back to sleep.

"Yeah, right. I never take vacations. There's always too much to do. I either need to oversee a new build or help manage an emergency. A vacation is out of the question."

Rory rolls her chair to the right, her piercing green eyes boring directly into me, her full eyebrows lifted high.

"What?" I ask when she doesn't say anything.

"You just heard yourself, right?"

"Umm…yes? No? I have no idea what you're talking about."

She rolls her eyes. "You *just* said everything was fine and you're bored. There's nothing for you to do, so how exactly is a vacation out of the question?"

"Because something could come up. The build could go south in a flash. A pipe could explode in one of the properties. Literally anything could happen."

"Any of those things could happen any day, either with you cooped up in your office or with your feet kicked up on a beach somewhere. And you know what would happen? Your staff would handle it like they always do."

I shake my head. "It's not that easy, Rory. You don't get it. I—"

"*I* manage two clinics clear across town from one another. If an emergency comes up at the other one, I don't put my life on hold here to figure it out. I delegate, which is what you need to learn to do. Or are you too scared to discover that your company doesn't need you as much as you need it?" She arches a challenging brow, and the urge to run over and shave off the stupid perfectly shaped thing is strong.

Mostly because she's right. *Of course* she's right. Stupid Twin Thing.

"Shut up, Rory," I mumble, and she laughs.

She rolls back behind her computer, her nose back in her work, and I turn my attention to the adorable white kitten in my lap. I hate Rory's words, but most of all, I hate that she's right. That's exactly how I feel about my company.

Every time I've flown across the country to put out a fire that's popped up, it's already been taken care of by the time I get there. I realize it wasn't a fire at all, just a little spark that never even took off. If I'm being fully honest, it's been that way for some time now.

"You know, you could always just jet-set around the

country and go see that hockey player guy you're seeing."

What the...

Her words stun me, and she must know it because only seconds later she peeks her head around the computer screen, a knowing grin on her face.

"I knew it."

I abandon the sweet kitten and cross my arms over my chest. "I don't know what you're talking about."

She doesn't say anything. She just stares, and it's the annoying kind of stare—the knowing one.

After a full minute, I can't take it anymore.

I huff, throwing my arms in the air. "Fine! So you know! Big deal!"

She throws her head back on a laugh, an evil-sounding one if you ask me. When she finally calms down, I lift my middle finger, which does nothing but send her into another fit of laughter. Secretly, even though she's laughing at me, I like seeing her like this. She's so serious all the time, so it's nice to see her break loose a little.

"How do you know?" I ask when she's finally done cackling like a maniac.

She lifts a shoulder. "I figured it out a few weeks ago. You've been awful obsessed with hockey all of a sudden. Then at that game you dragged me to last Friday, you wouldn't take your eyes off him. That coupled with his number across your back really clued me in."

"Oh."

I grimace because if Rory's figured it out, then...

"I doubt Lilah knows," she says, reading my mind. "She was a little too preoccupied checking out their goalie to notice, I'm sure."

"Lilah has a thing for Fox?"

Rory shrugs. "Just an observation. I don't know whether it's true or not."

"Well, you just *observed* me and Hutch, and that turned out to be true."

She smiles. "Hutch, huh? Is that what you call him?"

I resist the urge to roll my eyes. "That's what everyone calls him. It's his name."

"No, it's his last name, and a shortened version of it at that. His real name is Reed. Do you call him that too?"

I flash back to last week when I last saw Hutch before he left for his road trip and the way he made me call out *Reed* every time he licked my pussy.

And he licked it *a lot.*

Rory chuckles. "Yeah, I thought so."

"Shut up," I grumble at her again.

"I think it's a good thing," she says like I never said a word. "You and him, I mean. You seem happy, and you're finally taking a break from work, which is a good thing."

"Says the fellow workaholic."

"Hey, I'm saving the lives of animals. They *need* me."

"And what? My company doesn't need me?"

"Doesn't look like it to me," she mumbles.

I reach for the magazine sitting next to me, ready to throw it at her.

"Don't you dare throw anything at me," she says, not bothering to look up from her computer. "If you hurt Legolas, it's your ass I'm kicking."

I set the magazine down and settle for glaring at her.

"I'm just saying, maybe it's not a bad thing that you're seeing him."

"I have a contract with his club, you know."

That pulls her attention to me. "I'm aware." Back to the computer. "And I know what a stickler for the rules you are, yet here you are anyway sitting in my office getting all blushy over him."

"I am not blushing."

That earns me a glare of my own, and we don't talk for several minutes. I think she's going to drop the subject, but then she hits me with the biggest whopper of all.

"You should go see him."

I whip my head up. "Excuse me?"

She rolls back out from behind her desk, this time not stopping until she's just a few feet away from me.

"You've built a billion-dollar empire. You've spent countless days and nights working your ass off, and I doubt you've slept more than four hours a night in I don't know how long."

She's wrong. I've been sleeping fine lately.

Because of Hutch.

I silence the voice in my head.

"You deserve time off. You deserve a vacation. And if that vacation happens to take you where your hot hockey player is, then that's where it takes you."

She says it like it's so simple, the most logical thing in the world. Maybe...just maybe...it is. I do work hard. Hell, I've been working hard for as long as I can remember. In fact, I think the last time I took consecutive days off was when my father turned fifty-five and we went to London to celebrate.

That was five years ago.

"I suppose I could use some time off," I say.

"You could," she agrees, scooting back over to her computer, her fingers already flying over the keyboard.

"And if I just happen to end up in, say, California for a few days while the Serpents play, it wouldn't be weird, right?"

"Not weird at all, especially since you love

shopping down on Rodeo and you're in dire need of some new clothes." She rakes her eyes over my worn-out shirt that has a picture of the Jonas Brothers on it from way back when.

"I guess I could check my schedule, maybe make it work…" I nod a few times, feeling more and more confident about it.

"You should definitely do that…at your own place and far away from me and these fifty emails I need to answer by five." She looks pointedly at the clock.

It's 3 PM. If I get my life together and make a plan, I could theoretically be in California by 7 and at the arena by puck drop.

She clears her throat when I don't move, and I get the message loud and clear. I scoop Legolas up and set him back on the chair. He doesn't budge, the little thing completely tuckered out. I round the desk and go to press a kiss to her head, but she shrinks away as usual.

Instead, I pat her shoulder twice before telling her, "Thanks, twin. I love you."

She huffs, then mumbles, "Yeah, yeah, love you too. Now please leave. And close the door behind you, will you?"

For the first time in at least a week, my head feels clear, and I know exactly what I want.

Hutch.

Chapter 13

HUTCH

"Anyone want to explain to me what the hell's happened over the last week? Huh? Anyone?"

Coach is fired up tonight. He's never like this, but right now, he's pissed, and I don't entirely blame him. We've been playing like ass again this last week, looking entirely too much like the team we were last year—just plain bad. Our passes aren't even kind of connecting, we're dropping pucks in the slots, we're not winning board battles, and I can't remember the last time we had a good, solid clean entry into the zone.

We suck.

"No?" Coach continues. "Not a single one of you has an answer for me? Hutchinson?" I lift my head at my name. "You want to be captain so damn bad, and you have nothing to say?"

I swallow the lump that's seemed to be lodged in

my throat for the last week. "It's on us, Coach. Our heads weren't in it. We know it, but we'll fix it. We'll be better tomorrow."

He doesn't like my answer, but it's all I have.

He shakes his head, scoffing. "You're goddamn right you will be."

He storms out of the room, leaving us to wallow in our failure, and wallow we do. Not a single guy utters a word as we strip off our gear and hit the showers. We don't let out a peep as we climb onto the bus either, ready for it to take us to The Sinclair for the night.

Sinclair.

Just thinking of it gives me pause. It doesn't escape me that the last time I played well was in Seattle…the last time I saw Auden. We've not talked since I've been on the road, and as much as I hate to admit it, it's getting to me more and more every night.

I… Fucking hell, I think I actually miss her.

I shouldn't. I shouldn't miss her. Not at all, but I do.

I fucking hate that I do.

We have two games left on the trip before we head back home for a five-game homestand, and I cannot wait. I've never craved being in Seattle so damn badly. I miss the weather. I miss that damn sourdough bread they're so obsessed with. I miss that cheese that makes everything taste better. And I fucking miss Auden.

I pull out my phone to text her but am unsurprised to see my battery is at just five percent. I'm awful at charging it on the road, and I guess this trip is no exception. Luckily the ride to the hotel is short, and we're pulling up to the luxurious building in under twenty minutes.

We file off the bus, that same quiet from the locker room lingering over us. Somehow, and I don't really know how, I end up in the bar along with the Serpents Singles. Still fucking hate the name, but I guess if I have to be around people right now, I'm glad it's them.

We grab a spot toward the back, and for the first time this season, I order a real beer. I probably shouldn't, but fuck, I need it tonight.

"That was brutal." Naturally, Lawson's the first to break the silence. "Fucking six–zero? What the hell is wrong with us?"

"I'm sorry, guys," Fox offers, his usual smile nowhere to be seen.

Locke pats him on the shoulder. "Don't, man. Just don't. It was a team effort tonight. It's not on you."

"Team effort." Keller scoffs. "If you count putting in the work toward losing, then yeah, we definitely exemplified team effort."

He's not wrong, but it doesn't make his words sting any less. It sucks that we're all feeling this way tonight. You tell the media one thing, that it's just one game and you're good, that you'll find a way to climb back in the next or that you're not worried about it and it's just on to the next one—it's all a fucking lie. Every loss hangs on your shoulders, weighing you down.

And this one? It's going to take a while to lift that weight back off.

"Hutch?"

There's no way I heard what I just did. I'm dreaming. I must be. But when I spin in my seat, I realize this isn't some trick my mind is playing on me.

"Auden."

I'm up and out of my chair before I even realize what I'm doing. I cross the short distance between us and have every intention of scooping her into my arms but pull up short at the last second when she holds her hand up. Her eyes dart beyond me to the group of guys behind me.

I want to say screw them. I don't give a shit if they see.

But I don't. I respect her wishes, shoving my hands into my pockets so I don't accidentally reach for her.

"What are you doing here?" I whisper.

She gives me a knowing smile that tells me everything I want to hear.

Me. She's here for me.

"I figured you could use some cheering up," she says quietly.

Oh, man. She doesn't know just how damn badly I need what she's offering. I'm about to grab her wrist and pull her to my room when I hear the last thing I want to hear.

"Who's your friend, Hutchy?"

Fucking Lawson.

I squeeze my eyes closed tightly. Maybe if I can't see him, he can't see me either and he'll drop it. I'm praying he'll let this one go, because I really, really don't want to play twenty questions tonight, especially not with Lawson.

"Yeah, Hutch, who's your friend?" This from Hayes. I fucking knew I wasn't going to like that guy.

I peel my eyes open to peek down at Auden. She's looking up at me with amusement, clearly loving how uncomfortable I am with the guys wanting to be all up in my business.

"They aren't going to stop," I say so low only she can hear.

"It's okay." She lifts a shoulder. "They don't need to know anything."

I nod a few times, then take a deep breath and steer us back to the table.

"Well fucking well." Lawson gives Auden a sleazy smile that has me itching to reach over and smack him. "What's your name, sweetheart?"

Auden jerks back at the pet name.

"Don't fucking call her that."

The words leave me before I even realize it, and I'm no fool—I know exactly how that sounded: possessive, like I'm staking a claim on Auden right here in front of everyone.

Lawson holds his hands up innocently. "Hey, sorry. I didn't realize she was spoken for."

I should correct him. I should tell him and the rest of the table she's nobody to me, but that wouldn't be true, would it? Although...it will be my bed she ends up in tonight, after all. For all intents and purposes, she is mine.

Auden clears her throat, stepping in front of me and extending her hand to Lawson.

"I'm Auden."

"Auden," he says, not knocking any of his signature charm off his words as he takes her hand. "It's nice to meet you, Auden. I'm Lucas Lawson."

"Lucas Lawson?" Her lips twitch as she tries to hide a smile. "That's quite the name."

He grins, stretching his arms over the back of the booth we're shoved into. "They call me Lawless Lawson because I can't be tamed."

"They call you that because you don't seem to understand there are rules and consequences for your actions, moron." Keller glares at Lawson before turning to Auden. "Keller."

"Hi," she says to him before shooting her eyes to me in a silent question.

What's his deal? her hazel gaze inquires.

I shrug. *He's always like that,* I reply with my eyes.

I turn back to the group, pointing each person out as I introduce him. "That's Hayes, Locke, and our goalie Fox."

"Fox?" She takes a special interest in him.

The man in question bounces in his seat, that ever-present smile of his shining bright. "Howdy, ma'am."

Keller rolls his eyes at Fox's slow Southern drawl, and I laugh. He only ever uses it to charm the ladies, but I know for a fact he's not going to be charming this one, not tonight or any other night.

"Would you like a drink, Auden?"

She looks up at me before answering Lawson, and I dip my head, letting her know it's her call.

She shrugs. "Sure. Why not?"

Fuck. I was hoping she'd just want to go up to my room and fuck each other's brains out, but I guess it would look a little suspicious if she just bailed right now. So, I do the gentlemanly thing and pull a chair out for her.

"Thanks," she murmurs, taking a seat. She pulls the drink menu from the middle of the table and flips it open. "Hmm." She taps her chin, the same one I've kissed so many times, and scans the list of drinks. "What's good here?"

The others may not see it, but I do—that hint of a smile in the corners of her lips. She obviously knows what's good here since it's her hotel. She's all in on the role she's playing, though, and I love her dedication to it.

"I hear they make a mean Cosmo," Hayes tells her, then a loud *oof* leaves him as Lawson punches him right in the stomach. Even Keller snickers at it.

"Just for that, you're buying the next round," Lawson tells Hayes.

"Fine." The new guy huffs. "Auden?"

"A white wine," I tell him automatically.

"How'd you know that?" Hayes questions.

Fuck. What do I say? What do I say?

"She just looks like a white wine gal, right, Hutch?"

I jerk my eyes to Locke, who is begging me with his own gaze to go along with it.

I point my finger at him. "That," I tell Hayes. "Now go. We're thirsty."

"I'm going, I'm going."

I'm pretty sure he mutters something about us being a bunch of assholes as he walks away, but I can't be certain. I'm too busy looking at Locke, whose eyes are darting back and forth between me and Auden, until finally, he settles on me and gives me a knowing smirk.

Fuck me. He knows.

How the hell does he know?

I don't know, but I guess I shouldn't be surprised by it. He's always been too damn intuitive for his own good. Even back when I played a few years with him in Nashville before he went to Toronto, he was the same way, always watching and always knowing.

I never found it annoying until now. I avert my eyes, looking anywhere but at his knowing gaze.

"So, Auden, how do you know Hutch?" Fox asks.

"Well, um, it's kind of a funny story." She tucks a strand of her hair behind her ear. It's down tonight, and I love that it's down. As adorable as her messy buns are, I like her hair best like this. Easier to wrap around my fist as I'm fucking her. "We met on a flight this summer."

"That so?" Lawson's brows shoot up as his eyes slide my way. "Going to or from the wedding?"

"From."

The single word is clipped, mostly because I really don't like this line of questioning. I don't want them to know how I know Auden because I don't want them to piece anything together. There's too much on the line for both of us to allow them to get suspicious. It's bad enough that Locke knows. I don't need any of these other nosy fuckers picking up on things.

"Our flight got caught in a storm and Hutch here helped calm me down when things started to go south. We managed to land safely in Chicago, but it was a rough go for a while." She smiles up at me sweetly. It's that same damn smile I can't seem to get enough of. "I'm not sure I would have made it through without him. He's kind of my hero."

"Good man," Fox says, clapping me on the back. "Right, Keller?"

He just grunts in response, his arms folded across his chest, looking like he wants to be anywhere but here.

"You never hold my hand during bumpy flights." Lawson pouts.

"And I never will," I promise.

He juts his lip out at my answer, but his defiance is short-lived because soon he's clapping his hands. "Goody, more beer!"

Hayes reappears with a tray full of hoppy goodness and a wine for Auden.

"I said white," I remind him.

He shrugs, flopping back down in the booth. "They were out."

"It's fine. I'll drink anything."

Auden pats my arm twice in a soothing gesture, but

it has the exact opposite effect. It ignites me, lights me up from the inside out because *holy hell* have I missed her touch. I knew before I was missing her, but I didn't realize it was this bad, didn't realize I *ache* for her.

"Yeah, it's fine. Quit being all overprotective bigbrothery," Lawson says, snatching his beer from the tray and gulping half of it down.

Oh, I'm overprotective all right, but there is nothing remotely brotherly about what I feel toward Auden, and based on the way her hand lands on my leg underneath the table and gives me a gentle squeeze, the feeling is mutual. She traces a pattern against my jeans. What it is, I'm not sure, but it makes me want to haul her into my lap and show her the pattern I can trace with my tongue all over her body.

If only we weren't surrounded by these morons.

"To a better game tomorrow!" Hayes says, lifting his glass and looking around the table.

We all stare blankly back at him until he slowly lowers his beer.

"Are we not…" He chuckles nervously, reaching up and squeezing the back of his neck. "Do we not drink to that? I'm not quite sure on the club rules just yet."

"Club?" Auden questions.

Shit.

"Oh, did Hutchy here not tell you? We're the

Serpents Singles." Lawson grins proudly, feeling a little too damn confident spouting off that stupid name.

"That's not our name."

"Then you come up with a better one, Keller," Lawson snaps back.

Round and round they go, even Hayes and Fox joining in.

Auden leans into me with a wicked grin. "So, what's this club about?"

I roll my eyes. "It's nothing. It's not even a real club. We just happen to be the only single guys left on the team."

"And we're damn determined to stay single too," Lawson tells her. "We don't want anything distracting us from the team or winning the Cup." He leans across the table, his green eyes cutting right to me, his words heated, laced with venom. "Right, Hutch?"

Oh, he definitely knows Auden isn't just some woman I met on an airplane. He knows she's more than that and this meeting here isn't accidental.

"Right," I tell him, ignoring the way Auden's stare burns into the side of my head as I drain the rest of my beer.

The conversation picks back up, and we sit around for another half hour or so, mostly listening to Fox and Lawson go at it with the occasional interjection from

Keller about what a bunch of idiots they are. I'm on his side with that.

"Well," Auden says, her fingers playing with the stem of her glass, which is still full. "I think I'm going to head up to bed. It was so nice meeting all of you."

"You should come to our game tomorrow night if you're in town," Fox offers, ever the gentleman.

She smiles warmly at him. "I just might."

She'll be there all right. Even if I have to drag her onto the bus and stow her in the luggage compartment to hide her from Coach, she's coming. I won't be able to play knowing she's in town and not at the game. I've proven time and time again that I play better when she's there. The team needs the win.

Yeah, that's it, I tell myself, even though I know that's not true. I don't want her there for the team. I want her there for me.

She rises from her chair, and I follow, pulling it out so she can step away from the table.

She turns her hazel eyes on me. "Thank you. It was so great seeing you again. What a weird coincidence running into you here, huh?"

"The weirdest." I roll my lips together, knowing full well she doesn't believe in coincidences.

She believes in fate.

Keller coughs in a poor attempt to cover up a muttered, "Coincidence my ass."

I think it's Locke who smacks him for it, but I can't be sure. My eyes are still trained on Auden when I hear the telltale *thwack.*

We stand there for far too long, trapped in a staring contest neither of us is interested in losing. I wish I could close the distance between us. I wish I could pull her into my arms, wish I could slant my mouth over hers, throw her on this table, show her just how damn much I missed her.

But I can't.

A throat clears, pulling us from the daze.

"Good night, boys," she tells the table, then she sashays away in a rush.

I watch her go, trying with everything I have in me to convince myself not to run after her.

Don't do it. Don't do it. Don't do it.

"I'm going to bed," I hear myself say.

"Yeah, I bet you are." Keller snickers. "*Her* bed, maybe."

I march through the bar and almost make it through the doors before a hand lands on my shoulder, stopping me in my tracks. I'm not surprised when I turn to find Locke staring down at me, his dark brows pulled tightly together.

He doesn't say anything. He doesn't have to; the frown on his lips speaks loud enough.

"What." It's not a question that leaves me. It's pure

annoyance because I loathe the look he's giving me, the one that tells me this is a bad idea.

"Those other guys might not be aware of who she is because I doubt they're ever on the internet for anything more than porn, but I do. That's Auden Sinclair."

He knows. He knows about the contract with the team. He knows I shouldn't be doing this.

Just like he knows I'm going to anyway.

"Just be careful, man. There's a lot riding on this season to risk for some pussy."

The Cup. The C on my sweater. Everything I've worked so damn hard for.

I nod once. "I will."

His brows pull together tighter, but he doesn't say anything else. He just nods, squeezing my shoulder twice before letting me go, and like the fucking fool I am, I never make it to my room. I go to Auden's and show her just how damn badly I missed her.

Chapter 14

I'm starting to think there's something to Hutch's theory of me being his good luck charm.

After getting decimated by Anaheim 6–0, they come back the next night and flip the script, winning 4–0 and making it look like it's an everyday occurrence for them. When Hutch comes to my room after the game, he's in great spirits.

"Ahh!" A loud squeak leaves me when he hauls me into his arms the second he walks through the door I was admittedly waiting right next to. "You're a madman."

"Maybe." He presses a kiss to my lips. "But you like it."

"Maybe," I counter, kissing his stubbled cheek. He's let his beard grow out since he's been on the road, and I won't lie, I'm really liking it, especially when his face is buried between my legs.

He carries me through the room, and I expect us to head straight for the bed, but that's not the case. He lowers us to the couch, my legs draped on either side of him as I straddle his lap. Since I'm wearing nothing but a t-shirt, his already hard cock feels delightful between my legs, and I can't help but grind my hips down, craving the friction he's providing.

"Now who's the mean one?" he says between kisses.

"Sucks, doesn't it?" I grind on him harder, loving the hiss that leaves his lips.

"Nah. It would only suck if I thought we wouldn't end the night naked."

I'd laugh at his cockiness, but we both know that's exactly what's going to happen.

"Congrats on the win, Hutchinson. You played amazing."

"Had nothing to do with my playing. It was all my good luck charm." He sucks on my neck lightly.

"No. It was all you."

He pulls back. "Are you kidding? You saw how I played before you showed up last night. There's no way it wasn't you."

I shake my head. "You don't give yourself enough

credit. Did you ever stop to think it's a confidence problem and not me?"

"I have plenty of confidence."

"Sure, in the bedroom, but not out on the ice."

He stares up at me for a moment, his brows slanted together as he takes in what I just said.

After several moments, he nods a few times, his hands squeezing my hips. "I think you might just be onto something, Sinclair."

"Yeah?"

He nods, and it has me lifting my head a bit higher.

"Yeah, I am onto something," I say a little more confidently. "I think you just need to get out of your head is all. You're so worried you're not playing well you aren't really playing. It's just a mind game." I trail my hand down his chest, my fingers dancing over the tie that's hanging loosely around his neck. "You're in luck because I think I have an idea for how to help you relax."

He smirks. "Is that so?"

I nod, reaching for the top button of his shirt. "Yep."

I pluck the button free, but that's as far as I get before he snatches my wrist in his hand. I tip my head up at him.

"I have an idea too, if you're game for it."

I don't even think twice about nodding. Whatever it

is, I trust Hutch. He'd never do anything to hurt me or make me uncomfortable.

"Good. Take my cock out."

I obey his command, reaching for his slacks and pulling the button free. I unzip him, then reach inside his pants and underwear, freeing his impressive cock. I can't help it—I give him a few pumps before he grabs my wrist once more.

It's only then that I realize he's holding something.

His tie.

"Do you trust me?"

"Yes." No hesitation.

"Good." He releases my wrist. "Put your hands behind your back."

I do, stretching them back behind me in the most comfortable position I can find. He leans forward and around me, and I feel the silk of his tie slip around my wrists. He wraps it a few times, tying the ends together before giving my arms a gentle tug to make sure it's secure.

"Does that feel okay?" he asks, searching my eyes.

I nod. "Yes."

There's a slight pull on my arms that burns, but I don't hate it. He runs his fingers over my arms a few times, like he knows that sting is there and he's trying to soothe it away. Then he moves from my arms to my chest and down my sides until he reaches the hem of my t-shirt. He tugs on it, and I lift up as best I can, letting him pull it out from under me.

He raises it just enough to get a glimpse of me, and heat sparks in his eyes when he sees how wet for him I am. He reaches a single finger out, running it through my exposed pussy before bringing it to his lips and licking away the evidence of my arousal.

It's so hot seeing him do it I physically squirm in his lap. He chuckles darkly, and I love the vibration it sends through me. God, I'm so fucking needy for him it's embarrassing, but I don't care. I didn't realize how much I'd enjoy watching him out on the ice, but every time I see him play, it does something to me, setting all my senses ablaze, and he's the only one who can extinguish the flames.

"I want you to ride my cock just like this, Auden," he tells me in that gravelly voice of his. "No touching, just your cunt wrapped around my cock. Got it?"

I nod. "Yes."

The single word sounds like a moan even to my ears, and I suppose it is because what he's saying is exactly what I want. With no effort at all, he lifts me by my hips, setting me on the tip of his hard length, slowly lowering me until I'm covering every delicious inch of him.

"Oh god." I sigh, throwing my head back when I'm fully seated on his lap.

"Mmm…just Hutch," he mutters, leaning forward to kiss me as I begin to rock my hips.

And that's what we do. I ride his cock slowly, rolling until I find a rhythm that suits us both as he presses kiss after kiss to my lips and face and neck. No hands, just our mouths and our bodies pressed together.

It's exhilarating.

I have no idea how long I bounce on his lap, but it's long enough that the burn in my arms grows and my thighs weaken from the effort.

"Come on, sweetheart. You can do it," he tells me when he sees I'm fading. "I want to feel this beautiful cunt of yours squeeze my cock until I fill you up."

I don't know what it says about me, but his dirty words are just what I need to keep going. Just a few moments later, I'm coming all over him, and he's making good on his promise to fill me. It's magical and exhausting all at once, and I slump against him the second our shudders subside. Hutch reaches behind me and undoes my wrists, and I sigh with relief once I'm free.

"You did so good, sweetheart," he tells me, kissing the side of my sweat-soaked head. "So good."

He doesn't stop whispering soothing words or kissing me as he lifts us both and carries us to the bathroom. He fires up the shower, and we step inside once the water is warm. He lathers up my loofah, then runs it over every inch of my body, paying extra attention to the spot between my legs. He takes his time running his own hands over me, massaging my arms and my thighs until the warm water begins to cool.

We towel off, then crawl into bed, where we place an order for room service. When our food arrives, I grab it to keep up pretenses, then slide right back in beside him.

"Did you make the menus for the hotels too?" Hutch asks, practically moaning when he takes a bite of his gourmet burger.

"Yep." I pop a perfectly crispy fry into my mouth on a nod. "I tried to do a nice mix of everyday food with a flair and then your usual upscale stuff like steak and caviar for those who can stomach it."

"It's good." He takes another bite, chews, and swallows. "I really like the crab on this."

"It's a good touch, right? I try to add local touches to all the menus. That way people who don't stray too far from the hotel can still get a taste of the signature dishes each city offers."

"Very smart," he declares, and I eat up his praise like he eats up his burger.

I don't know why I like Hutch's approval so much, but I do. I get compliments on my properties all the time, but it feels different coming from him. It's more personal, more...real.

"We have the next two days off," he tells me once he's done with his burger, rolling up his cloth napkin and tossing it onto the tray. He motions toward my half-eaten sandwich, silently asking if I'm done, and I nod. He lifts the tray off the bed, dropping it onto the chair in the corner of the room.

"Oh?" I ask.

"Yep," he says, returning to his spot next to me. He doesn't get under the covers, just sits on top of them in nothing. We're both still naked from the shower, and I'm not complaining about the view. "We have to travel, of course, but it's a short trip since we're playing Arizona. But we have two days off because of Thanksgiving."

That's the second time he's said that, and I'm not sure what to make of it. It almost sounds like...like he wants me to come with him, like he wants me to spend Thanksgiving with him.

He clears his throat. "Do you, uh, have any plans?"

I roll my head his way, a soft smile on my lips. "Why, Reed Hutchinson, are you asking me to come with you to Arizona?"

He finally peeks over at me, then looks away just as fast, but not before I see his own smile taking over his face. He shrugs like it's no big deal. "Maybe. You are my good luck charm, after all, and I can't go too far without it."

Even though we've already established that's not true, I let him have it anyway. Mostly because I know what he's asking me: to follow him, and it's not a small ask, not for either of us. Also, I *want* to be his good luck charm, especially if that means I have an excuse to say yes.

"I'd have to check my schedule, but I think I could swing it."

I don't even get the full sentence out before he pounces, rolling me over until I'm tucked underneath him, just where I wanted to be anyway. I giggle when he drags my hands up and over my head, but the sound dies out when he rolls his hips against me, his hard cock sliding along my already slick center.

"Come with me to Arizona, Auden."

"I will," I promise.

"Best good luck charm ever," he murmurs before crashing his mouth to mine.

As he slides into me with ease, I hope for the first time that the luck never wears off. Because this thing with Hutch? It might just be real.

Chapter 15

HUTCH

We lost.

For the first time since Auden's been at one of my games, we fucking lost. The whole thing sours the good mood I've been in over the last few days.

After we left California, we had two days to do nothing but relax, and it was just what I needed. Sure, I spent the entire time locked inside Auden's room so nobody would notice that she followed the team, but even if we didn't have to hide, it would have been my ideal time off anyway.

Now we're on the plane back from Arizona, and judging from the mountains I can see out of my window, we're nearing Seattle. Most of the guys are completely passed out, a few of them playing cards in the back quietly, but not me. I'm too busy rewatching the game we just played.

It's amazing all the little mistakes you can see when you go back over something, like when Keller passes to Lawson and it's picked off by the defenseman on Arizona because they passed too close to his reach. Or when I try to check one of their forwards and miss, giving him the perfect opportunity to break away and speed up the ice, where he zips the puck right past Fox's shoulder. They're the kind of mistakes that cost you games, and tonight, we definitely paid the price for them.

"Stop watching that shit," Locke grumbles beside me. "You'll drive yourself crazy trying to figure out what went wrong."

"I already know what happened—we suck."

He scratches the long beard on his face, shaking his head. "We don't suck. It was one game, Hutch. We'll be better next time."

He doesn't get it. He just doesn't get it. He doesn't understand that this wasn't just *one game*. It was a game Auden was at and we lost. That means something.

Doesn't it?

"If I were you, I'd be a little less worried about one game where we lost because their goalie was on some other shit and a little more focused on how you're breaking a lot of damn rules by sleeping with Auden Sinclair."

"Dude," I snap, looking around to make sure

nobody heard him. It's pointless since I know no one is paying us any attention. Still, being a little more discreet would be nice.

He shrugs. "Maybe if you don't want anyone to know, don't be so obvious about it."

"What do you mean?"

He chuckles. "Do you even check the group chat, man?"

"I try not to," I mutter, swapping my tablet for my phone and pulling it up.

> Lawson: I'm not imagining shit, right? Hutch is totally sleeping with that chick from Anaheim, isn't he?

> Fox: Oh, big-time.

> Hayes: Like alllll-night-long kind of big-time.

> Keller: It was obvious as shit, too.

> Lawson: Fucking knew it. That's why that dick bailed on Thanksgiving dinner. He didn't need to stuff a turkey. He was stuffing her.

> Lawson: HOLY SHIT.

> Lawson: I Googled her.

Lawson: GO GOOGLE HER.

Fox: *whistles* Damn. Go, Hutchy!

Hayes: How do I get a sugar mama like that?

Keller: Fucking knew she looked familiar.

Lawson: I can't believe it. That little snake.

Lawson: Wait. Does this mean we're allowed to sleep with the hotel staff? Because I totally hit it off with that bartender last night. She offered to blow me, and it killed me to turn her down. I mean, it's fucking Thanksgiving and she wanted my baby gravy in her mouth. How could I say no to that?

Keller: You're disgusting.

Lawson: You're just jealous I'm getting more offers than you.

Keller: Trust me, if I wanted to, I could have any woman I wanted.

Lawson: Yet you don't. Maybe not the hotshot you think you are, huh?

Keller: Shut the fuck up, Lawsy.

Fox: Come on, guys. Don't fight.

Hayes: No, please do. I was just grabbing some popcorn for the show.

Locke: Do you really think any of this is appropriate? You shouldn't be talking about Hutch behind his back. You don't know what's going on. Stop spreading rumors.

Lawson: For starters, I'm not talking about him behind his back. He's literally in the group chat. He can see this.

Lawson: Secondly, it's not a rumor if it's true. And it's totally true, isn't it, Locke?

Locke: I'm not talking about this with you.

Lawson: That's grandpa talk for yes.

Locke: Dude, I'm like 5 years older than you. Give it a rest with the grandpa stuff.

Lawson: 5 years in hockey years is like 10 years in real life. Face it: You're a grandpa in this league.

Keller: Shut up, Lawsy.

Lawson: *middle finger emoji*

Fox: Can't we all just get along?

Hayes: Group hug?

Fucking Christ.

I toss my phone back into my backpack that's sitting open at my feet, then drag my hands through my hair. I wish I had my Yankees cap. I could use it right now to keep my hands busy, but I don't have it. Auden does. I gave it to her for her flight home because I know she gets anxiety.

"You good?" Locke asks.

"No," I reply honestly. "I didn't…" But I don't finish my sentence because whatever I'm about to say wouldn't be true.

I didn't know who she was. Partially true, sure, but also a lie.

I didn't mean to. I did. I really, really fucking did.

I didn't realize it would matter. I knew it would.

No matter what I say, it's not going to be good because I knew the risks from the start.

"It's not going to be good if the front office finds out. You do know that, right?"

I nod.

"She could lose the contract and it would tarnish her reputation."

I nod.

"You'd be kissing the captaincy goodbye."

Another nod.

"And she'd probably never forgive you for it."

I grimace because that might be the worst of it all. Auden's worked too damn hard for everything she has for this to ruin her in any way. Hell, *I've* worked too damn hard too.

I have to stop it. I *need* to stop it.

But I don't want to. Maybe if we just explain to everyone that we didn't know, that it happened before the season started and we didn't mean to let it go so far.

Even as I hear the words in my head, I know they're all a lie. It sounds a bit too much like playing the fate card, and I don't believe in fate.

"You have to break it off," Locke tells me, like I don't already know.

"I know. I will." Though as the words leave my lips, I know they're a lie…a big, messy lie, just like me and Auden.

What the hell have I gotten myself into?

"It's not that I don't love The Sinclair," I say, rubbing my hand over the silk sheets I've spent so many nights on now. "But don't you have a house or an apartment you should be spending your nights at?"

"I am at home."

I roll my head to the side, lifting my brows. "Huh?"

Auden laughs, waving her hand around the room. "I live here."

"You do not."

She lifts her chin. "I do too. Why do you think I'm here all the time? Did you think I was just obsessed with work?"

Honestly, yes.

"How does that work? Living in a hotel?"

"I don't know. It just does. I'm kind of used to the nomad life."

"Because of all your travel for work?"

"That and because I grew up living on the road."

"I…" I shake away my shock. "How did I not know that?"

She shrugs. "I don't talk about it a lot because most people think it's weird, but I spent the first ten years of my life doing it. We lived in an RV and sometimes hotels. We traveled all over the United States and Canada. My mother homeschooled me and Rory for several years until we finally settled in Washington."

Someone must have left that tidbit out of her Wikipedia page, because I didn't expect that.

"You look surprised," she comments when I don't say anything.

"I am. I can't imagine that. I had a stable home life growing up. Hell, my mother still lives in the same small town I grew up in. I can't imagine not having those roots."

She shrugs again. "And I can't imagine having roots at all. It's just not something I ever experienced."

"You might not have roots, but you have something else that's equally as good."

She gives me a confused look.

"The Sinclairs," I say. "They're all over the country, little pieces of home scattered here and there."

"That's true. I do have those." A slow smile brightens her face as she thinks about her life's work. "And what about you?" she asks, peeking over at me. "Besides your roots in New York, do you have a place here?"

I nod. "I do. I have a condo I pay an arm and a leg for because damn is this city expensive."

She laughs. "It is, but it's so beautiful it's worth it."

It really is. I wasn't sure at first I could like it here, but I've fallen hard for Washington. I just hope I'm able to pull my head out of my ass and keep playing here, give this city a modern-day Cup and parade.

"I have a question," Auden says.

"Shoot."

"If you hate flying so much, why'd you go into a career that requires so much travel?"

"I could ask you the same thing, Little Miss Jet-setter."

She narrows her eyes playfully. "I asked you first."

I laugh, stretching my arms up and folding them under my head. "I don't know. I guess when I was little I didn't quite realize how much travel was actually involved in playing. I just knew I wanted to play. Then as I got older and played more, I saw the other side of it. By then, it was too late. I was already in love with the game. I wasn't going to let anything stop me from enjoying it, not even flying."

"Have you gotten better at it? Flying, I mean?"

"Oh yeah. You should have seen me my first year playing pro. I was the king of the barf bag. Couldn't hold anything down for the longest time." I shake my head thinking about it. "But after working with the team therapist on some techniques, I was able to get out of my head and managed to get through the flights without puking or having a panic attack." I roll over onto my side, propping my head on my hand. "What about you? Why do you do it if you don't like flying?"

Auden lifts a naked shoulder. We've been lounging in bed all day. We got back to Seattle late last night, and even though I told Locke I was going to end it, I found myself coming here anyway. It's like Auden's a lighthouse and I'm just a lost boat out at sea looking for a beacon of hope.

"I didn't choose this life. It chose me."

"Come on," I say. "Give me a real answer."

She laughs, then shrugs again. "I don't know. I actually used to love flying, loved being up in the clouds. But the further I got in my career, the more I grew to hate it. I'm not sure if it's because I associated it with all the stress that came with building a company or what, but now my stomach turns at just the thought of stepping foot on a plane."

"Do you have to keep traveling all the time? I mean, don't you have a whole team of people who can do that stuff for you?"

Her lips twist and she nods, but it's reluctant, like she doesn't want to admit it. "I do, and they could. But…"

"The company is your baby," I guess.

"Exactly."

She's not looking at me when she says it, though. It's like she's somewhere else completely, lost in thought. I reach over, pushing a loose strand of hair behind her ear, and she startles a bit at the contact, then gives me a cunning grin.

"Want to go swimming?"

"What?" I laugh. "Are you crazy?"

"Nope." She shoves up and off the bed, not even bothering to try to cover her naked body. "Come on. There's a pool on the roof."

"Auden, it's the first of December—and in Seattle, no less. We can't go swimming."

"We can too." She pads into the bathroom and disappears for a moment, reappearing with two robes in hand. She tosses one to me, then slides the other on. "The Sinclair has heated pools."

I stare at her.

"What?" she asks. "Haven't you always wanted to have sex in a rooftop pool?"

That has me crawling from the bed. I slip on the stupid robe, then motion toward the door.

"Lead the way," I tell her.

She laughs, shaking her head. "Really? That was all I had to say to convince you?"

"Are you really so surprised the offer of sex got me moving? Have you forgotten what we're doing here, sweetheart?"

She stumbles, and I reach out to catch her, grabbing her by the waist.

"Whoa. You okay?" I ask.

"Yep," she says with a smile, but there's something off with it. It's not her usual grin. I just can't pinpoint what it is.

I don't have a chance to push for an answer because she's grabbing me by the hand and dragging me the rest of the way through the room and out the door to the elevator. We file in when it arrives, and she presses the button for the pool. It feels weird being in nothing but a robe heading up to the rooftop, but Auden doesn't seem fazed by it, like she does this all the time. I ask if she does.

"No," she says on a laugh. "Not all the time, but I definitely have before. Skinny-dipping is fun." She bounces her brows up and down.

"I've never done it before."

"What?" Her mouth drops open. "I'm shocked Mr. Hotshot Hockey Player hasn't gone nude in a pool before. Not even for a dare in high school or something?"

"Nope. Never. I followed all the rules all the time."

"I usually do too, but not when it comes to skinny-dipping."

That other rule she's breaking hangs between us, but we don't dare bring it up. When the elevator doors slide open, I'm relieved to find the doors to the outside access locked.

"I thought you said we could be up here…" I say when she pulls a keycard from her pocket.

"We can."

"Then…"

"What?" She grins at me over her shoulder as she pushes open the door. "Did you really think people would be up here now? It's December—in Seattle, no less."

I shake my head at her as she throws my words back at me. Then I charge forward, scooping her into my arms and jumping into the pool—robe and all. When we emerge, she's sputtering, shoving her hair out of her face and spitting water everywhere.

"Oh, you are *so* dead, Reed Hutchinson," she growls, splashing water in my direction.

"Bring it on, Sinclair," I tell her, throwing it right back.

We don't end up having pool sex, but the night is just as good as if we had.

Chapter 16

AUDEN

"You're a dirty, dirty liar."

I whip my head up, surprised to find a glaring Lilah standing in the doorway to my office.

"What'd I do?"

"Oh, you know…" She folds her arms over her chest as she marches into the room and takes a seat in the chair across from me. "You lied to me."

I rack my brain, trying to figure out when I lied to her, but I'm coming up blank—except for Hutch, of course, but that's only a lie by omission. Does it really count?

When I can't figure it out, I ask, "What'd I lie about?"

She huffs. "You don't have a goldfish."

A loud laugh bubbles out of me, and I sit back in my chair. "How long did it take?"

She glowers at me. "Too long. It didn't hit me until I was at the pet store with Carlos for our date last night."

"You went to a pet store as your date?"

"Well, no. But we ended up there because he needed to pick up food for his dog, and then I saw the fish and it came rushing back to me." She shakes her head. "Where'd you go that night?"

"That was over a month ago, Lilah. Do you really expect me to remember where I was?"

"I do expect you to know. I expect you to know because you're *still* lying to me."

"How do you figure?"

"Well, for starters, there's the fact that I've known you for almost twenty years, and I know when you're full of shit."

"Li—"

"*And,*" she continues, "you went on vacation over Thanksgiving."

"What? I don't deserve a vacation?"

"Oh, you do, just not over Thanksgiving. You *love* Thanksgiving. You live for the carbs, especially the ones I make—but not this year. This year you bailed on the delicious Maddison dinner, and dammit, I want to know why."

I grimace because I totally did do what she's accusing me of. I hadn't planned on it, not really. I just went to California to see Hutch for a night. I didn't intend to spend nearly a week with him, but man am I glad I did it. It was a spectacular few days of sex, and Rory was right—I did need a vacation. I'm happy I took it.

"Auden?" Lilah prompts.

I sigh, then meet my best friend's murderous stare. "I saw him again."

She furrows her brows, not following.

Then, it hits her all at once.

"*Him* him?" When I nod, her eyes look like they're about two seconds from popping out of her head. "How? Where? When?"

I rise from my chair and walk to the door, closing it with a soft *click* before taking my chair again. I roll it as close to the desk as I can get and lean toward Lilah. She matches my movements until we're both practically lying on top of the expansive desk.

"This does not leave this room," I tell her seriously.

"Did you kill him?" she whispers.

"What?!"

She shrugs. "What? You're being all weird and secretive about it. I assumed you murdered him."

"God, Lilah." I laugh. "No. I didn't kill him."

"Oh." She looks disappointed for a second, then shakes her head. "I meant good. That's good. You'd do awful in prison. They'd send you to the big-girl prison, not the fancy one where the tax evaders go."

"Rude."

"It's true." She shrugs unapologetically. "So, if you didn't kill him, then what?"

I twist my hands together, nervous as hell to confess what I've been hiding from her.

"I'm not getting any younger, Auden."

I ignore her, trying to gather my courage. She's going to be mad, and I'm not going to blame her. We never hide things from each other, especially not important things like this.

"Ticktock," she sings.

I glare at her. "Keep it up, and I won't tell you a thing."

"That's a lie."

Dammit. It is.

"All right," I say. "All right. I, uh, I've been seeing someone."

I wait for her to explode on me. To yell at me. To do something other than stare at me stoically like she is.

"Did you hear me?"

"Oh, I heard you," she says. "I'm not surprised. I guessed that myself when you disappeared for a week."

"You did?"

"Once again, I've known you forever—I know

when you're getting dicked down on the regular. You carry yourself differently, and I don't just mean the way you walk."

I laugh when she winks.

"But seriously," she says, "I just kind of figured it out. You've been gone a lot lately, and it's not like you to check out on the business so much."

She's right about me checking out, but she's wrong about the timeline. The truth is, I realized eight months ago that my company doesn't really need me anymore. As much as I love working and as much as I love my properties, they don't need me like they once did, and I'm not sure *I* need them either. I used to hide behind my work, but now…now I'm not sure that was the right call.

I sigh. "It's Hutch."

"What's hutch?"

"*Him*…it's Hutch. Or, as you might know him, Reed Hutchinson. As in—"

"The points leader of the Seattle Serpents?!"

I grimace and nod. "Yes."

"HOLY SHIT, AUDEN!" Her outburst is so damn loud there's no way someone didn't hear her.

"Shh!" I admonish. "Be quiet, dammit."

"Sorry, sorry." She blows out a breath, shaking her hands out. "I'm good. I'm fine. I'm good." Another slow breath, then she meets my eyes. "Are you serious?"

"Unfortunately, yes."

"Unfortunately? What's so unfortunate about that? That man is *hot*. Like the hot you read about or see on the red carpet. He's otherworldly attractive. How is that a bad thing?"

"Because he's a hockey player."

"And?" She waves her hand. "What's the big deal? That means he has lots of stamina. He's—oh."

I nod as realization dawns on her. "Yeah. *Oh.*"

She chews on her bottom lip. "That's…that's not good. Your contract with them."

"I know."

"You're not supposed to…not with the players. I saw that clause in there, right under the *Professionalism in the Workplace* section."

"I know."

"But you…"

"*I know, Lilah.*"

She settles back in her chair, shaking her head. "Crap."

"Big crap."

We let the weight of all this wash over the room. It's obvious I'm in hot water. I just don't know how damn hot.

"You're the CEO, though. You make the rules. Shouldn't this be okay?"

"Uh, no. Definitely not. CEO or not, the rules apply to me too."

She frowns. "Crap."

"Big crap," I repeat.

Another few beats of silence.

"Quit."

"What?!" Now it's me who is yelling. "You're nuts!"

"Not at all. I mean, you have your pick of board members who could easily step into the CEO role. You could stay on but take a massive step back. Hand over the reins to someone else."

I laugh dryly. "Why would I do that?"

"Because of him."

"Hutch? I'd quit because of Hutch?"

"Well, yeah. You like him, don't you?"

"I guess."

"You guess?" She gives me a knowing smile. "Please, Auden. You wouldn't risk doing something like this if you didn't like him. In fact, you wouldn't be doing this if…"

She doesn't finish her sentence, but she doesn't have to. I know exactly what she's going to say.

You wouldn't be doing this if you didn't love him.

We both burst into laughter. It's so loud and obnoxious, bouncing off the windows of my office and echoing. We do it for seconds, minutes—maybe even hours.

I'm not sure how long passes until we finally calm down, both of us swiping at our eyes.

"Good one," I tell her.

"I know, right?" She shakes her head on a chuckle.

But when our laughter fades and it's quiet again, it doesn't sound so ridiculous anymore.

Do I... Do I love Hutch?

No. *No.*

It's not possible...is it?

I mean, I like him. Probably a lot more than I should, if I'm being honest. We started this thing because we were two strangers who needed comfort for a night, but it's grown beyond that. Now I'm going to his games and he's coming to the hotel every night and we're spending my favorite holiday and all our spare time together. It's almost like... Well, it's almost like we're dating. It *feels* like we are, that's for sure.

But how could that be? How did that happen?

"Auden..." Lilah says softly. When I shift my eyes to her, she gives me a soft, sad smile, a knowing smile. "You love him, don't you?" she asks quietly.

I don't answer. I can't. Because deep down...

Deep down, I know she's right. I'm in love with Reed Hutchinson.

"Oh god," I mutter, dropping my head into my hands. "How? Why?"

I hear the creak of the chair, then feel Lilah's hand

on my back. She rubs small circles, comforting me as a big mistake turns into an even bigger one. I had a one-night stand with a guy who was off-limits, and then I went and fell in love with him.

"What is wrong with me?"

"Nothing," Lilah answers, squatting down to be eye level with me. "Nothing is wrong with you. I know you don't like the idea of it, and I don't blame you after watching what your parents went through, but you're not them, Auden. Just because their relationship was tumultuous at best, it doesn't mean yours will be too."

I uncover my face. "But don't you see that it already is? I have a contract with his team, Lilah. If I can't sleep with him, I damn sure can't fall in love with him."

She smiles weakly. "I'm sorry. I don't know what to say about that other than…"

"Quitting. But I can't quit. This company is my whole life."

"Maybe it's time to build a better life."

I scoff. "You're joking, right?"

She's not though. I know she's not. Lilah knows better than anyone how hard I've worked over the years. My entire twenties have been spent running myself into the ground to build this empire, and for what? Money? I already had that thanks to my trust fund. Fame? I don't care about that.

I did it because I *love* creating things. I love tearing down a building, designing a new one, and watching it be built from the ground up. I love filling it with all my favorite things and then watching other people fall in love with it too. I love giving people a home away from home. I've done that ten times over now.

But maybe…maybe I did it because I'm searching for something I never really had myself before—a home.

"Oh god, Lilah. You're right." I look over into her bright blue eyes. "I think I need to quit."

"Wait, wait, wait. You're telling me *you* knew before *I* did? But I'm her best friend!" Lilah whines.

"And I'm her twin." Rory rolls her eyes. "Of course I knew before you. I knew before Auden even told me."

"Stupid Twin Thing," my best friend grumbles.

I laugh because I find myself cursing the Twin Thing often.

"Another round, ladies?" Hilda asks, appearing in front of us.

We all nod, and she fills our wineglasses for the… well, I don't know how many-eth time. We're gathered in the bar at The Sinclair for happy hour. Sure, it's only one in the afternoon, but who cares? After my talk with Lilah, I was in desperate need of a drink.

I was shocked when I called Rory and she agreed to come out. I figured she'd blow us off like she always does, but she must have heard in my voice that I could really use my sister for moral support. Maybe the Twin Thing isn't so bad after all.

"Well, did you know she totally let him stick it in her butt?"

"Lilah Jane!" I scold. I grab the wineglass from her. "You, my friend, are officially cut off."

"Oh, boo." She sticks her tongue out and gives me a thumbs-down. "You're no fun." She glances around, then leans in. "Really though…did you do anal?"

"Jesus, Lilah. Shut up," Rory tells her, turning about ten different shades of red.

She shrugs, lifting her hands in the air. "Don't knock it until you try it."

I shake my head at my very drunk best friend. I should have known better than to feed her drinks in the middle of the day, the little lush, but I get it. We don't take much time to unwind, so why not take advantage of it while we can? I'm about to rock the boat at my company, so might as well have fun while things are still stable.

"I feel like I walked into this conversation at the wrong time."

Everything in me lights up as I spin toward the voice that's quickly becoming my favorite sound in the entire world.

"Hey, Sinclair," he says with a confident smile.

"Hutch," I respond, my grin just as big. I try to hop off my stool, but instead I just flop. I'm about point three seconds away from smacking face-first into the ground when two strong arms curl around me and haul me to my feet.

Then I'm staring into the most gorgeous blue-gray eyes I've ever seen.

"Oops," I whisper, and those full lips I know taste so sweet but say the dirtiest things part on a laugh.

"Oh, sweetheart." He sets me back on the stool but doesn't let go. "You're drunk."

I frown at him. "I am not."

"You are too."

"Am not," I argue like a child. "I'm just buzzed." I point my thumb toward Lilah. "She's drunk."

"Yep," Lilah declares proudly before letting out the smallest hiccup, which sends her into a fit of giggles.

Hutch steps into me, cupping my face with his big, rough hands. I lean into the touch, loving the rough pads of his fingers on my cheeks as he rubs them.

"How many glasses of wine have you had, Sinclair?"

"At least two."

He laughs. "Only two? You little lightweight."

I just grin up at him, and I love the way he looks back at me. There's no judgment. No annoyance. Just pure happiness.

I love happy Hutch.

Hell, I love grumpy Hutch too.

Aw, screw it. I just plain love Hutch.

I giggle, and his brows pull tight, probably wondering why I'm giggling, but I don't have the chance to tell him before my sister steps in.

"She really is." Rory climbs off her stool with zero hesitation and without almost faceplanting. She sticks her hand out, right between Hutch and me. "Hi. I'm—"

"The crazy cat lady," Hutch says. He moves one hand to my neck, cupping the back of it possessively, and gives his other to my sister. "I've heard about you."

My sister's gaze narrows on him. "Then you also must have heard my name is Rory, not Crazy Cat Lady."

"Uh-oh," I sing. "Someone's in trouble."

Hutch laughs, not looking the least bit fazed by this.

"My bad. It's just when I first met our little drunk here, she was wearing the crazy cat lady sweater you got her for her birthday. It kind of stuck in my head."

He remembers what I was wearing when we met?

"Kind of hard to forget," he says, looking right at me.

Did I say that out loud? Oops.

"Hi! I'm Lilah!" my best friend yells. Literally *yells*.

Once again, Hutch isn't bothered by it at all. He gives her an amused smile. "It's nice to meet you, Lilah. I'm Hutch."

"Oh, we know." Lilah waggles her brows at him before sliding her eyes toward his crotch, then back to his face. "We. Know."

"All right." Rory grabs Lilah's arm, tugging her off the stool. "Let's go."

"But...but...I didn't even get a chance to ask him about the ana—"

Rory slaps her hand over my best friend's mouth. "Don't. You. Dare."

I try to stifle my laugh, but it's pointless. It bubbles out of me anyway.

"What was she going to ask me about?"

"Nothing." I wave off his question as I try to stand again. This time, I make it all the way to my feet before swaying a bit. Yeah, I've definitely had too much to drink. I don't usually drink like this, but today I wanted to. It's not every day you decide to make a life-altering decision like I did, right?

Hutch's grip tightens on me as he tugs me to his side, holding me to him and propping me up. He's warm and feels damn good. I wish I could stay attached to his side like this forever. He can play hockey this way, right?

"I'm going to get this one home," Rory says, hooking Lilah's arm over her shoulder. "She'll thank me for it later."

"I'll do no such thing," Lilah mutters, but I know Rory is right. There's no way Lilah would ever show her face to Hutch again if she asked him inappropriate questions.

"Do you need help with her?" Hutch asks, nodding toward an already dozing Lilah.

"Nah. We've been here before. You should have seen her in college." Rory hitches her up higher. "Come on, wine-o. It's bed and a Tylenol for you."

Lilah makes a noncommittal noise.

"Just have Betty call Jerry," I say to Rory.

She nods. "Was planning on it."

"It was nice meeting you, Not Crazy Cat Lady Rory," Hutch tells her.

Her eyes scan up and down, inspecting him with those damn sharp green eyes, studying him like he's a slide under a microscope. "Yep." It's all my twin says before she hauls my best friend away.

Hutch watches as they exit the bar, then turns back to me. "I don't think your sister likes me very much."

"What? No! She does. That was just Rory speak

for, *It was nice to meet you, too. Take care of my sister or I'll bury you in a shallow grave.*"

His lips pull upward. "You got all that from a single word?"

I shrug as he leads us from the bar and to the elevators. "Twin Thing."

He nods like he understands, though I know he doesn't. Not until we're stepping out onto the twenty-seventh floor do I realize something.

"Hey, wait—what are you doing here? It's the middle of the day."

"Oh, I'm aware, my little day drinker. I have a game tonight."

"Ah. You want a little pre-game bumping and grinding before you go off and do some other, less fun bumping and grinding." I nod, everything clicking into place. "All right. Let's go do it. Let's have S-E-X."

He laughs, shaking his head as he slips his hand into my back pocket and pulls my key free. I like that he knows it was there.

"You're drunk, Auden," he states as he pushes open the door and walks us inside the room I call home. "How about we cuddle instead?"

"Cuddling. That sounds nice," I say, sliding into the silk sheets I love so much. I run my hand over the spot next to me, patting the bed. "You can sex me up later."

He slides in next to me, dragging me until I'm sprawled across him.

"Shh. Sleep, Sinclair."

"Sleep, then sex. Got it."

My body shakes with the rumble in his chest, and it's the last thing I hear before I fall asleep and dream about something I've never let myself dream of before.

A future with Hutch.

Chapter 17

HUTCH

Whatever fluke happened in Arizona was just that—a fluke. We've been on a hot streak since we got back from that trip, getting at least one point in every game. We've already almost won more games this season than we did all last year.

I'm trying not to let it get my hopes up about anything, but with how we're doing, it could mean good things for everyone. More fans in the stands. More revenue for the team. More opportunities for other players to get good contracts.

The captain spot.

We're on a roll, and I don't want to do anything to mess that up.

"Someone's in a good mood," Lawson says, coming up next to me as we do a quick morning skate before taking on Vegas tonight. The boys are already buzzing, especially after our last game against them. We know they're going to come out checking hard, so we have to be prepared.

We've been on the road for a few days now, and after tonight, we're back in Seattle until after the Christmas break. I already can't wait to be back on the West Coast, and it one hundred percent has to do with a certain brunette I can't get enough of.

Last week, after I found her drunk during the day, I took her upstairs and cuddled her until she fell asleep. When she assumed I was there for sex, I just let her believe it. The truth was, I wasn't. I just wanted to be next to her.

I'm still not sure how I feel about that.

"So, tell me," Lawson continues, because the guy apparently can't stand a few seconds of silence. "How's it going with the hot little billionaire? Has she offered to be your sugar mama yet?"

"Shut up, Lawsy."

"What? I'm curious how that whole thing works. I know we all poked our fingers with a needle and made a blood pact not to settle down until we win the Cup, but—"

"That never happened," I say.

"Hockey isn't forever." He keeps going like I never spoke. "Which means this sweet, sweet cash we're making isn't forever. Are you going to tie her down so you have someone to take care of your old ass whenever this all dries up?"

I shake my head, refusing to answer him, but he doesn't take the hint that I want him to get lost and jabs his elbow into me.

"Come on," he says. "You can tell me the truth. You're totally into her, aren't you?"

"Shut. Up. Lawsy." I emphasize each word, but he doesn't care.

He just keeps smiling and running his elbow into my side. I'm about two seconds away from slamming my glove into his face when Locke appears, snatching him by the back of his jersey and pulling him away.

"What the—"

"Get lost, Lawsy," Locke growls at him.

The smartass skates off, that obnoxious smirk of his still there, and I know that's not the last I've heard of his line of bullshit.

"Thanks," I mutter to Locke.

He shrugs. "Kid's fucking annoying sometimes."

"Only sometimes?"

Locke chuckles, never once taking his eyes off the scene in front of us. Fox is currently defending his net as player after player fires pucks at him from all different angles. I'd say his save percentage is about ninety-one percent if I had to guess. Not bad.

"You're still seeing her."

It's not a question. It's a statement.

One I don't deny.

"I am."

"I kind of figured." Locke sighs. "Coach wants to see you."

"Me? What the hell for?"

He shrugs dismissively, but I know he knows. He always fucking knows. I roll my eyes at him and slide toward the benches, hopping off the ice and heading down the tunnel toward the back offices.

"In here," I hear when I pass a room, and I walk backward, expecting to see Coach sitting in a chair waiting for me.

He is, but he isn't the only one in the room. Our general manager is here.

What the fuck is our GM doing here? He doesn't have a reason to be here unless something big has happened, and nothing big *has* happened. Unless...

No. There's no way Coach knows about Auden. It's not possible. We've been careful. He couldn't know.

"Have a seat," he says as I enter the office.

But I don't take a seat. I can't, not with the hard looks they're both giving me right now.

They know. That's the only reason the general manager would be here too, right?

Fuck, fuck, fuck. I am so damn screwed. Why

couldn't I just walk away? Why did I have to keep this going?

When I don't move to sit, Coach points to the empty chair. Only then do I heed his instruction and plop down in the cool, hard leather chair.

"I'm sure you're aware of why we called you in here today," the GM says.

I shake my head. "No, sir. Not really."

"Of course you are," Coach says, already sounding bored of this conversation that's just begun.

I swallow thickly but don't say anything. I'm too fucking scared if I open my mouth right now, I'll confess to everything. I'll tell them all about Auden and how even though I knew it was wrong, even when I found out who she was, I couldn't stay away.

"The vacant captain spot, son," the GM says.

I jerk my head back. The captain spot? That's what this is about? So they don't know about me and Auden?

"Oh."

The GM laughs, then comes around the desk to my side, propping himself against it and folding his arms across his chest. Coach sits on the other side, looking like he'd rather be anywhere else.

"We knew Hall was retiring last year and we'd need to fill his captain spot. We've been watching you since last season, Reed, and we like what we see in you."

"You…do?"

"Of course we do. What's not to like? You've got a good head on your shoulders. Excellent hockey sense, and you're a great player. It's clear you put the work in and you're willing to push through the tough times. And the guys on the team look up to you. They turn to you for advice and for inspiration. Hell, most of the young guys have been watching you play since your early years in Nashville when you won the Calder."

I remember those days, being called up to the NHL and playing my heart out. I had a rookie season for the records. I never had my eyes set on the Calder Memorial Trophy, but it was mine anyway.

"That feels like a lifetime ago, sir."

He laughs. "Tell me about it. I remember playing way back before you were ever even a thought. Talk about a lifetime ago." He smiles fondly, then clears his throat. "Anyway, Vick and I…" He looks back at Coach, who still looks annoyed we're in his office. "Well, we want you to be the next captain of the Seattle Serpents."

My jaw slackens. "Are you serious?"

The GM nods. "Very. We think you'd be a great fit for the role."

Holy shit. It's happening. Everything I've worked so damn hard for…it's happening. *I can't wait to tell Auden.*

The thought slams through me, and I wait…wait

for fear to hit me, for it to completely wig me out and send my heart racing.

But it never happens, and I'm not sure how I feel about that.

"Reed?"

I lift my head. "Yes?"

"We want you to be the next captain of the Seattle Serpents…" He sucks in a deep breath. "But we need you to break things off with Auden Sinclair."

All the air whooshes out of my lungs and my ears begin to ring, the room turning black around me.

We need you to break things off with Auden Sinclair.

Did I hear him right? Did he really just say that? They…know?

Oh fuck. Fuck, fuck, fuckity fuck.

My stomach rolls with nausea and I feel just like I used to when getting on a plane, like I'm going to lose all the contents of my stomach. I clutch the chair, hoping maybe that will help keep me together, but it doesn't work. I still feel absolutely sick.

"Son?"

I open my eyes, not even having realized I'd closed them.

So that's why the room was dark.

"Did you hear me?"

I nod.

"Do you have anything to say?"

I open my mouth to speak, but nothing comes out. What *can* I say? Deny it? Try to convince them it's nothing? I can't, and I don't want to lie to them.

I clear my throat, then meet the eyes of the man who is in charge of my future. "How?"

The GM looks back at Coach, who looks like he's checked out of the conversation completely, then back to me. "How what, son?"

I swallow roughly. "How did you know?"

He sighs heavily, looking down. "I was hoping the rumor of this transgression wasn't true." He shakes his head a few times before lifting it, disappointment clouding his eyes. "We had someone come forward with the information last night."

Last night? Last night I was up in my room—at The Sinclair, of course—video-chatting with Auden. She fingered her cunt while I stroked my cock, then I went to bed with a smile on my face.

Oh god...Auden.

Auden. Auden. Auden.

My chest tightens and I reach up to rub at it, worry flowing through me at the possibility of what this means for her, the contract, and her company. She'll never forgive me if this gets out.

But that's what I can't figure out—*how* did it get out?

"Who?"

"Pardon?" the GM says.

"Who told you?"

"I did."

I whirl around in my chair to find the asshole who just wrecked everything standing in the doorway. Fuck black—I'm seeing red. I'm out of the chair in an instant, ready to pummel the dick smirking at me, but I stop short when I hear my name.

"Sit down, Hutchinson."

I stop, but I don't sit. I can't when Rogers is still standing so tall, his chin tipped up, feeling victorious.

"How." I force the word out through gritted teeth.

That fucking smirk grows. "You should really be more careful about what you're doing at the hotel other teams stay at."

Fuck. The Sinclair.

It always comes back to The Sinclair.

I thought we were careful, thought we weren't at risk there, but I didn't fully think about what it could look like with me sneaking in and out when the other teams were in town. I hoped they'd chalk it up to me just visiting, but I should have known that wouldn't be the case, not with pissant little shits like Rogers walking around.

I try to think back to a time when he could have seen us, but nothing comes up. Unless…

No. He couldn't have seen us that night we went down to the kitchen. Nobody was around, right?

"You can go now, Rogers," the Serpents GM tells the Vegas player.

The fucker gives me one last cocky grin before he walks away. If I were him, I wouldn't be looking so damn smug. He forgets we're going to be on the ice together tonight.

The GM clears his throat. "Reed?"

I turn back around, not at all ready to face the consequences of my actions but knowing I have to buck up and get it over with. I settle back down into the chair, hating how he's looking at me, like I'm a failure.

I am, though. I failed. I failed to keep my promise to myself to focus on nothing but hockey this year. And for what?

For Auden.

Auden. Auden. Auden.

I pat that tight spot on my chest and close my eyes against all thoughts of her, as if I'm trying to brush and will them away as the GM begins to speak.

"We understand this relationship of yours began before the season started and you two were unaware of your connection."

I can't believe what I'm hearing. How do they know so much about me and Auden? Someone had to have told them, and it couldn't have been Rogers. Sure, he may have seen us together, but there's no way he knew all those details. It was someone else.

A teammate.

It had to be. But who? Who would betray me like that?

"We get it," the GM continues. "Things happen. And while we're not pleased that this relationship continued, we're willing to look the other way because we still believe you're the best fit to lead this team to a championship, a championship your teammates deserve, that this city deserves—that *you* deserve."

I whip my head up. Are they joking? After everything, they still want me to be captain?

But I can see it in his eyes. He means it.

How can he mean it?

"You're a good guy, Reed. One of the best. You've dedicated your life to the game, and we've taken notice of it. Not only that, you've dedicated what's likely the rest of your career to this team. What better person than you to lead us to victory?"

I could name about five other players on the roster who would be just as good in the role, but they aren't the ones sitting in this office right now. I am.

"Why now? Why are you telling me this now?"

The GM and Coach exchange a look.

"We want to ring in the New Year with some good

news. We want to announce the new captain of the Seattle Serpents on January first, and we'd really like it to be your name we call out."

I want that too. So damn badly. More than I've ever wanted anything before.

Well, almost anything.

"We just need to know you're on board...*all* the way on board."

They don't spell out what that means because they don't have to.

Auden. Auden. Auden.

I try not to think about the face that flashes through my mind, her long chestnut hair or her hazel eyes or those lips I love kissing so damn much. I try not to think about her husky laugh or the way she always swirls her wine before every drink. I try not to think about how she made me skinny-dip in December or how cute she is when she's drunk. I try not to think about the way she talks and snores when she sleeps, and I try really, really fucking hard not to think about how perfect she looks when she falls apart at my hands and my tongue and my cock.

I try not to think about that at all.

I've known Auden for three months, but I've been playing hockey my whole life. I know exactly the decision I need to make. I *know* what the right one is.

Another squeeze, this one slightly above my heart. I

tamp down the pain, knowing it's just the stress of this whole situation. It'll pass, just like my feelings for Auden.

"Reed?"

I lift my head to meet the eyes of my coach, then the GM, and I say two words I know will change everything.

"I'm in."

The rest of the meeting with Coach and the GM was a total blur. We went over everything they expect of me and what my role is going to be and even when and how they'll announce their decision, but I don't retain any of it. When they finally dismiss me, I'm on a mission to find one person: Rogers.

"Whoa, man."

I glance up to find Keller standing in front of me. I almost barreled right into him, never even saw him coming.

"You good?" he asks, his steel eyes bouncing back and forth between my own. "What's up?"

"I got captain."

A smile—or at least Keller's twisted version of one

—spreads across his lips. "That's great, man. They made a good choice."

I grunt.

"You're not happy about it?"

"I am," I bark, which earns me a raised brow. I shake my head. "Sorry. It's not you. It's not the captain spot. It's… Well, no. It is the captain spot. They know."

His brows tug together. "Know?"

"Me and Auden. They know."

"Oh. I see." He nods a few times. "I see."

He doesn't look surprised. Why doesn't he look surprised? Was it him? Did Keller fill Coach and the GM in on everything?

The thoughts disappear as quickly as they arose. He wouldn't. He doesn't give a shit about this kind of thing. That's not his style. He keeps his mouth shut, always has and probably always will.

"How'd they find out?"

"Rogers," I tell him, but I leave out the rest of it, that other part that's bothering me because I *know* it had to be someone on the team.

His lips pull into a sneer. "Fucking Rogers. I hate that prick."

"Heard that."

He shakes his head, looking just as pissed as I am. "What are you going to do about it?"

"Nothing."

And it's the truth. As much as I *want* to do something about it, I can't. I might not have the C on my sweater just yet, but for all intents and purposes, I'm the captain now. I can't go out there and pummel someone, no matter how badly they deserve it. I have a whole fucking team looking up to me. I have to be the example.

"You know…" Keller says, that sick grin of his I've seen too many times before popping out. "I think I feel like fighting tonight."

It's after midnight by the time we land in Seattle, and I'm more than happy to be back home after the long night we just had.

Keller wasn't kidding when he said he was feeling a fight. He fought so hard he took a match penalty and was ejected within the first six minutes of the game. He looked right at me after the altercation with Rogers and winked. It felt good to know he has my back at least, though I can't say the same for everyone else.

Even with Keller, our biggest checker, leaving the game early, we managed to stay in it. It was a mess, trading chances and goals with Vegas all night long,

sending us into OT and then a shootout, but we came
out the victors.

Now it's late and all I want to do is get some rest,
which is why I can't figure out how I ended up here,
staring at The Sinclair. I mean, I know *why* I'm here,
but I shouldn't be. This isn't where I belong anymore.
Hell, I *never* belonged here, not really. I should get back
in my car, should fire the engine right up and drive
home, then tuck myself away in my own bed.

But…I don't.

I can't.

I have to see her one last time.

The familiar rotating doors welcome me as I step
in, enveloping me between two panes of glass like a
welcome-home hug. The elevator wraps me in its
warmth as the doors slide shut and take me up to the
floor I've spent more time on lately than I have in my
own home. When I press my keycard against the
reader, it pings, turning green like it's yelling *GO*, and I
do it. I put my foot right on the gas and I push open
the door.

Auden's waiting up for me, just like I knew she
would be. She sends me a soft smile, then rises from the
couch, pressing her lips to mine. I sigh against her,
savoring her touch as she slides her hands into my hair
and I slip mine around her waist.

I lift her in my arms and carry her to the bedroom,

where I set her on the mattress. She strips off her t-shirt—*my* t-shirt—and I undo my pants, shoving them down just enough. I press her onto her back and sink inside of her, fitting like she was made for me and I was made for her. We're a mess of grunts and moans, taking and giving and taking again.

When we're finished and she's fast asleep beside me, I know what I have to do, even though I don't want to. I rise from the bed and dress, then press one last kiss to her forehead.

"Hutch?" she mumbles before turning her head and burying her face into the pillow, her soft snores filling the air once more.

As I leave the room I've grown so damn used to, I take and I give once more.

My hat and my heart.

Chapter 18

AUDEN

"How are you holding up, kiddo?"

I smile over at my father. "I'm okay."

"Are you sure?" he asks in that same old sweet fatherly tone he always uses.

"I'm sure."

It's not completely a lie. I *am* okay, or at least I will be.

Today, I sold my company. It was a crazy move, a risky one, but it was what needed to be done. Lilah was right—it's time to build a better life. I've spent so many years building and building for other people, giving over little pieces of myself each time. Now, it's time to take what's left of me and build something better, something bigger.

A home.

A life.

Love.

"For what it's worth," my twin says from the other side of me, reaching over to squeeze my hand in a rare, sweet gesture, "I think you did the right thing."

I return her squeeze. "Thanks, Rory."

She bumps her shoulder against mine but doesn't release my hand as we walk through the crowd, like she knows I need this comfort right now. Rory is right; I did make the right decision. I know I did. I can feel it in my bones, but it doesn't mean I'm not sad about it.

Everything I worked so hard for is gone. I'm entering a new chapter, and new chapters are always scary. Staring at a blank page with a blinking cursor that's just waiting for you to make your move is terrifying because the story can turn into anything, even something you're not expecting.

But that's the beauty of it, too, isn't it? Starting from nothing. A clean slate. A new chance to make everything right. That's why tonight, after the game, I'm going to come clean to Hutch about how I feel about him. I'm going to tell him I broke the rules, did the unthinkable, and I, Auden Sinclair, am irrevocably in love with him.

I just hope he feels the same.

I wasn't surprised when he slipped out of my bed in the wee hours of the morning yesterday. It's not unlike him to do so, but I was shocked when I saw his hat was missing from its usual spot on the dresser. I dismissed the worry quickly, though. I'm sure he just needed it for tonight as the Serpents play their second-to-last home game before the Christmas break.

Still, it feels weird walking through the arena without it. I've grown so used to it over the months that it's become as much a comfort of mine as it is Hutch's. Maybe I can bargain with him for it tonight.

I grin to myself, thinking of all the dirty ways I plan to get it back.

"Wow." My dad lets out a low whistle when we reach our rink-side seats. "These are damn nice, kiddo. I'm honored you brought me along."

"Of course. It's your early Christmas present."

It's a lie and we both know it. The second I decided to sell my company, I knew I was going to need my father by my side as I made this huge transition. He dropped everything and came running to Seattle, so I had to pay him back in the only way I could think of: a free hockey game.

"That sweater looks good on you, old man," Rory tells him, earning herself a glare from our father. She's unfazed by it, even going so far as to wink at him, which only further annoys him.

I shake my head at their antics, my eyes falling to the tunnel I know the Serpents are going to come skating out of in just a few moments. Excitement swims through me, not just because I now love coming to games, but because I can't wait to catch a glimpse of Hutch.

He didn't come by last night, and I find myself needing a fix like some addict. Yeah, I guess I am addicted, but I've made peace with that.

"Nachos?" Rory asks, and I shake my head. "Dad?"

"Like I'd ever pass up nachos. Need me to come with?"

"Nah." My sister shrugs him off. "I know my way around."

To my surprise, Rory's come to several games with me since that first one. Even more shocking, I've never once had to beg her to come; she's done it all on her own. I get the feeling she's grown as obsessed with the game as I have.

She scurries off up the stairs, leaving just me and my father.

"Tell me, kiddo," he starts after a few beats of silence. "How are you *really* feeling?"

"Good."

He lifts his bushy, graying brows, not believing me, and I laugh.

"Good," I repeat. "I promise, Dad. I'm feeling good."

"That company was your whole life…"

I lift a shoulder. "I know. But…it's time for something different."

"And you're good with that? With something different?"

"I am. I think I have been for a while. I just wasn't sure how to approach it, but now…I don't know. It just feels like it's time."

"Hmm."

I think that's all he's going to say until…

"And what about the guy you're seeing? Does it have anything to do with him?"

I freeze. He…knows?

He laughs heartily. "Oh, you should see the look on your face right now." He jostles me with his elbow. "What? Did you really think I'm so blind I wouldn't pick up on things between you and Reed Hutchinson at breakfast back in Colorado?"

"I…" I don't know what to say. I hadn't thought Dad was paying any attention to the two of us, just Reed and talking hockey.

"Is he the reason you sold the company?"

I wring my hands in my lap. "Part of it, yes."

It's the first time I've said it out loud. Yes, I sold the company because I wanted something more, but I sold it for him too, for what we could have, especially if we didn't have the contract holding us back.

"You love him, then?" my father asks.

I nod slowly, and a smile overtakes his face, even bigger than the one he gave me when he saw our seats.

I poke his cheek where it dimples. "What's that look for?"

"I'm just happy for you is all. I was worried after what you girls saw with your mother and me... Well, I was just worried. I wasn't sure you'd ever accept that love doesn't have to be like that. It doesn't have to be so chaotic. It can be peaceful, and it can be real. A part of me will always love your mother because she gave me you two beautiful girls, but what we had..." He clears his throat of the emotion building, blinking away the tears filling his eyes. "It wasn't the example I wanted to set for you, and I'm just so glad I didn't mess you girls up."

"Aw, Dad."

I wrap him in my arms the best I can with us both sitting. I'm sure we look silly right now, but I don't care. My dad has never been one to shy away from showing his emotions, but this? It feels different, and maybe that's because *I* feel different.

When we part, it's not only him with shining eyes; I'm teary too, and my dad takes notice.

"I'm sorry, kiddo. I didn't mean to get you all emotional. Who cries at a hockey game?"

He laughs, but that warmth he's known for isn't quite there.

"You didn't mess us up, okay? You gave us the best life you could. So you and Mom didn't work out." I shrug. "It happens. I'd rather you be apart and happy than together and miserable. Even without a traditional home life, I think Rory and I turned out all right, wouldn't you say?"

"I'd say. Between you and your company and her clinics…your old man couldn't have asked for better kiddos, that's for sure." He slings his arm over the chair, tugging me close to him and pressing a kiss to the side of my head. "I love you, Auden Grace."

"I love you too, Dad."

That's how we sit, him with his arm wrapped around me and me delighting in his warmth as we take in the people coming and going in the stands. If this is what I have to look forward to not being tied down to my company, spending more time with my father, I'll take it.

"Nachos incoming!" Rory calls, and we turn to find her carrying not one, not two, but *three* giant helmets full of cheesy goodness. She stops at the end of the aisle and wrinkles her nose when she catches wind of the emotional cloud hanging over us. "Ew. Are you two sharing *feelings*?"

Dad and I laugh, standing to grab the food from her hands as she shuffles farther into the row.

"I love you, Aurora Rose," Dad tells her, but he

skips the hug and kiss he gave me, and judging by the look on Rory's face at his outpouring of love, she's grateful for it.

"Wuvyatuf," she says as she stuffs a handful of nachos into her mouth.

I shake my head at her, ready to tell her how ridiculous she is, but the sudden eruption over the speakers drowns out my words.

"Alllllll right, Serpents fans!" comes the voice of the in-arena announcer. It's a call I've grown all too familiar with over the last few months. "Are you ready to cheer on your hometown? Let's give a big, warm welcome to your Seattle Serpents!"

As usual, the arena explodes with excitement, and all the buzz has even my father on his feet, his face pressed up against the glass like it wasn't once him out there listening to thousands of people cheer for him.

Fox barrels onto the ice, the rest of the players filing out behind him one by one. Lawson smacks a stack of pucks, unleashing them and firing one toward the net. He hits it right in the center, and everyone cheers.

Then there he is—Hutch. My breath catches in my throat and my stomach does that same little flip it always does whenever I see him.

"There's your man," Rory says into my ear, and I grin.

I watch as Hutch takes one lap, then another, firing a few pucks at the net. One hits the crossbar and the other goes soaring beyond, smacking into the boards loudly. Anticipation zings through me. This is when he comes over to me and taps his stick against the glass, sending me a wink and calling me *sweetheart*, and I'm eager for it—desperate even.

He does skate over to my side, but he doesn't stop. In fact, he doesn't even look my way. I'm not the only one who takes notice.

"What's up with that?" Rory asks between mouthfuls of chips and cheese.

"I'm not sure," I tell her.

Whatever it is, it has the distinct feeling of dread settling into my stomach. Something's wrong with Hutch, but more than that…something is wrong with *us*.

And I have no idea how to fix it.

Chapter 19

SERPENTS SINGLES GROUP CHAT

Lawson: Anyone else notice what an asshole Hutch has been over the last few days?

Lawson: Anyone? Just me?

Hayes: I don't know him all that well yet, but something does seem off.

Lawson: Fox?

Fox: He's off. He yelled at me last night after showers. Said I used too much cologne.

Lawson: To be fair, you do. You smell like the inside of a Bath & Body Works.

Fox: So, delicious?

Lawson: No. Sickening.

Keller: At least he wears cologne and doesn't smell like Walking Talking Asshole.

Lawson: Nah, it's called You're Just Jealous I'm Better Than You.

Fox: Boys...

Hayes: Do you think it has anything to do with that chick from the hotel? The rich one?

Lawson: Oooh. The new kid might be onto something.

Hayes: Kid? I'm pretty sure we're the same age.

Lawson: Yeah, but you're new to the club, so you're a kid.

Fox: That is not at all how it works, and you know it, Lawsy.

Lawson: I don't make the club rules.

Keller: Because there aren't any rules, dickweed.

Lawson: But there should be. Like what to do when someone is a perpetual asshole and we need to vote them out.

Lawson: Don't worry, I'm not talking about you this time, Keller.

Keller: *middle finger emoji*

Lawson: Is the captain not getting laid anymore? Is that why he's being a royal dick?

Locke: Need I remind you all he's in this group chat?

Lawson: So? Let him see. Maybe he'll change his tune.

Locke: Don't you ever get tired of running your mouth, Lawson?

Lawson: Nope.

Keller: Like you're one to talk, Locke.

Locke: The fuck is that supposed to mean.

Keller: You know.

Lawson: I want to know.

Hayes: Me too. Spill the beans.

Fox: Even my interest is piqued.

Keller: What? Nothing to say now, Locke?

Lawson: Aww. He's gone quiet. No gossip for us tonight.

Hayes: Boo!

Fox: Yeah, boo! Boo this man!

Keller: All of you just shut up.

Lawson: Speaking of getting laid, you might need to, Keller. Work on that over holiday break, yeah?

Keller: Always gotta have the last word, don't you, Lawsy?

Lawson: Of course I do.

Keller: Blow me.

Lawson: Nah.

Lawson: But if your mom's available later, maybe she could blow me.

Keller: That's fucking it.

Lawson: What are you going to do? Silently stare at me? Ooooh, I'm shaking.

Fox: I thought we agreed no more mom jokes.

Fox: But if not...hey, Lawson? Wanna know what your mom told me last night?

Locke: All right, all right. You're all done.

Hayes: No fun. I want to know what she said. We could compare notes, Fox.

Lawson: HEY.

Keller: Once again, you walked right into it, Lawson.

Lawson: I did, huh?

Lawson: Still can't believe Hutch hasn't checked in. We have to be blowing up his phone.

Locke: He's back in the office with Coach. He's busy.

Keller: Probably busy avoiding Lawson. Wish I could do that.

Lawson: Don't lie. You love me.

Keller: I only love two things, and you're not one of them.

Lawson: Lefty and righty?

Hayes: Dang, Keller. Switch-hitter. Nice.

Fox: Boys...come on. Let's get a grip.

Lawson: Keller's trying, but it's just too small.

Keller: Hate you.

Lawson: Whatever you gotta tell yourself. *kissy face emoji*

Chapter 20

HUTCH

One more game. Just one more game.

I can't remember the last time I was so glad to have a break from hockey. Usually, I love being at the rink, but these five days we have off are calling to me more than the ice for the first time in a long damn time.

You'd think being told I'll be named captain in the new year would have the exact opposite effect. You'd think I'd be excited to show the team I can be the captain they need me to be, but I just don't have it in me right now.

I feel…off. Nothing's been right for days, not the food I'm eating, not my sleep, not my game…none of it. I fucking hate it and just want shit to get back to normal.

"Hey."

I glance to my right to see Locke. Like me, he has a

plate in his hand. Unlike me, he's loading his up with chicken and steak and pasta. I currently have about six carrots rolling around that I doubt I'll even eat.

"You, uh, looked at the group chat lately?"

"Not really interested in watching Lawson and Keller bicker."

"Hmm." He nods, then leans in closer to me. "Maybe not, but you should probably check out what your teammates are saying about you."

"Don't give a shit," I tell him, returning my attention to the food I have zero interest in eating.

I really don't care. Maybe once upon a time I'd have picked up my phone and scrolled through their bullshit, but I just don't care about anything they have to say.

"You should, *Captain*."

I turn my head up toward him. "How do you know about that?"

As far as I know, the decision to make me captain hasn't been shared with the rest of the team yet. I have a few more meetings with the staff today, and we plan to announce it before we hit the ice tonight. So how in the hell does Locke know?

He shrugs. "I had a little chat with Coach. He came to me wanting my opinion."

"Your opinion? On what?"

"Whether you'd make a good captain or not," he

says, walking around me and scooping a heaping pile of peas onto his plate.

That's not the whole story. I don't know how I know, but I do.

I grab Locke by the shoulder, spinning him around. "What the fuck aren't you telling me?"

He darts his eyes around the room, and I follow his gaze. We aren't alone and are definitely drawing attention from the other players, but I don't fucking care. He's hiding something from me, and I want answers—audience be damned.

He sighs, and somehow in that one breath, I know.

I know.

"It was you," I say.

He doesn't even bother denying it. He just shrugs and goes to grab another spoon to get more fucking food, but I yank it from his hands, not caring when it clatters to the floor.

Oh, we definitely have the whole room's attention now.

"You really want to do this here?" he says in a hushed tone.

"I really do."

He shakes his head, then steps closer to me. "Yeah, it was me. Coach and the GM came to me after Rogers ratted you out. I wasn't going to lie to them, especially not when they had it all wrong."

"Had what all wrong?" I seethe.

"The timeline. They thought you started seeing her *after* the season started, but I had to correct them. They had to know it wasn't like that."

"So, what? You're saying you told them to protect me?"

"Uh, yeah, pretty much. And it worked, didn't it? They offered you the C."

I want to hit him. Fuck do I want to hit him. Or something. *Anything.* Of all the people I thought would disclose information about Auden and me, Locke was the last one I expected it to be.

"How could you do that to me?"

"Look, man," he says quietly. "I did it *for* you, not *to* you. You were in hot water, and I wanted to cool it down a bit. Besides, I'm not *really* the one to blame for all this, am I?"

That's all it takes. I snatch Locke up, fisting his shirt in my hands, sending our plates crashing to the floor. Chairs squeak over the tile and I hear footsteps drawing near, but Locke holds his hand up.

"It's fine," he tells whoever is approaching us. "I got it." He looks me right in the eyes. "How about we take this out in the hallway, Hutch."

It's not really a question, more like an order. While I may be the captain, Locke still has several years on me, and you don't disrespect your veteran guys like I am now. I also thought you didn't disrespect your teammates like he did me, but here we are.

Even so, I release him from my grasp and brush by, making sure to knock my shoulder against his as I stride out into the hallway. He follows closely behind, and we walk until we find a more private spot. Then I whirl back around on him.

I shove a finger in his face. "I trusted you, man. I thought...fuck, I thought we were friends."

"We are friends."

"Then why?" I throw my hands in the air, pacing back and forth so I don't do something crazy like punch my *friend*. "Why?"

"Because I didn't know."

His words stop me in my tracks. "You didn't know what?"

"That you love her."

I stumble backward. What the...

"I'm..." I shake my head at him and his ridiculous statement.

Then, I laugh. *Hard.* Love? Me? Not a fucking chance.

I don't *do* love. I gave that up a long time ago when I realized the only thing that could ever love me back was hockey, and it has. It's been good to me over the years. It's given me the chance to travel the world. It's given me stability. It's given me friends and family and community. It's given me everything I could ever want. Sure, I've had to work my ass off on it, but that's what a marriage is, isn't it? It's work, and that's what I am—married to the game.

Being in love with Auden? It's not possible. My heart is already taken.

"No," I tell him with confidence. "I don't."

He laughs like he doesn't believe me, and it just pisses me off even more.

"What's so fucking funny?"

"You and your inability to see what's right in front of your face."

"Because it's not there. You're just imagining shit."

"Oh, I am?"

"Yep."

He pushes on my shoulder, sending me stumbling backward once more. "Then tell me something, Hutch —if I'm imagining shit, why is she the person you look forward to seeing the most every day?"

"She's not," I counter, but the words taste bitter on my tongue.

"Why is she the first person you run to after we're gone for days on end?"

"She's not," I mutter through gritted teeth, and that bitter taste gets worse.

"And why is she the person you want to share all your highs and lows with, huh?"

He pokes my chest, right above the spot that's been aching for days.

"Why is she the one you go to after you play a hard game and come up empty-handed?"

Another poke, another stumble.

"Why is she the one you can't wait to see after you've decimated the opposing team?"

Poke.

"Or after you've been annoyed by Lawson for too fucking long and need someone to ground you?"

Poke.

"Why is she the person you can't seem to stop fucking thinking about?"

"She's not. She's…" I gnash my teeth so firmly I guarantee the team dentist will yell at me for it. "You're wrong."

He laughs sardonically. "Am I, Hutch?" Another poke, this one right above my heart. "If I'm so wrong, why have you changed in the months since you've known her, huh? Why is even Lawson commenting about how much you were smiling until a few days ago? Why have you been playing so well? Why is everything in your life looking a whole hell of a lot brighter since her? And why are you such a miserable fuck now that she's gone?" Locke steps closer to me, our noses nearly brushing. "Why is your life so much better with her in it?"

"It's not. It's—"

He ignores my feeble attempt at a protest, pressing harder against that now-familiar ache in my chest. "She's in here, man. Right fucking here. She's wormed her way in. She's filled that black hole you've been walking around with. She fucking fixed you, Hutch, and you're too damn worried about denying it to accept it."

I want to refute his words. I want to tell him he's wrong and he has no fucking clue what he's talking about…but the objection never comes.

Are there rational answers to the questions he's asking me? I'm sure there are, but I can't seem to find them because suddenly all the logical answers seem *illogical*. Irrelevant. Abso-fucking-lutely pointless. Because he's right.

He's fucking right.

When did she become all those things Locke said? When did she become the most important person in my life? I kept telling myself it was all just part of the routine. I'm a hockey player, for fuck's sake—I thrive on routines. They're my whole damn life.

But being with Auden…none of it felt like autopilot. It felt like a need, a *necessity*. Like I was going to completely break without her. Like she was the glue holding it all together, holding me together.

No, not holding me together—fixing me. Repairing what was broken. Making me whole again.

New.

I rub my chest, the same spot Locke touched, and I don't feel it anymore, the darkness that was there, slowly eating at me, turning me into a machine and not a man.

That darkness is now fixed, filled. It's gone, and I know. *I fucking know.* I'm in love with Auden Sinclair, and I have no clue how I got here.

I stumble again at the revelation, and Locke reaches out to stabilize me.

"Hey, easy, man," he says, helping me stay upright.

I want to shrug off his touch, but I'm too damn stunned to do it. We stand there for several moments, me with my back against the wall, Locke holding on to my shoulder for support. I'm still pissed at him, but I don't have it in me to keep yelling. I'm too damn tired, tired of fighting him, fighting what I feel.

Fighting fate.

"I didn't know," Locke says again, squeezing my shoulder. "I swear, man."

I nod.

"I just thought…" he continues. "I thought she was just a piece of ass—"

I growl at his words, and he holds his hands up, taking a step away from me.

Smart man.

"Sorry." He lowers his hands. "I wouldn't have said shit. If I had known how you feel, I wouldn't have said anything. I thought I was helping. I thought I was doing the right thing."

"I know," I tell him. "I know."

I *do* know. Locke isn't that guy. It's not his style to sell his friends out if he doesn't really think it's helping them. I'm sure if he'd realized what she means to me, he would have kept his mouth shut.

"Did they really make you break it off with her?"

I nod. "Yeah. I had to choose—captain or her."

"That's fucked, man."

I nod; it's true, but I also understand. They can't make exceptions to the rules like that, even if we didn't know who the other was. It doesn't matter; we shouldn't have continued it when we found out. That was our mistake, our *transgression* as they called it.

And now… Well, now we have to live with the consequences, no matter how damn badly they suck.

Just for a brief moment, I wish we had ended it, wish I had walked away from her in Chicago and that was it. I wish when I saw her again, we had just shared a knowing smile and gone our separate ways.

Then just as quickly as the wish came, it fades. If we had done that, I would never know everything I had been missing. I would never know just how empty and broken I was, and now that I've been woken up to reality, I want it again.

"I saw her at the game the other night. She looked…well, like you, man."

I know what he's saying without saying it—she looked like crap. I saw her too, and at first, she was excited. That smile of hers I crave so damn much was plastered across her face and she was happy.

Then when I skated out and didn't go to her like I always do—which about fucking killed me—all that happiness and excitement and light she was exuding vanished. She spent the rest of the game looking like she was about to cry.

I ached to go to her last night, to march into The Sinclair and wrap her in my arms and tell her I'm sorry, to give her back my hat and kiss her and say damn it all to hell.

But I didn't because I couldn't. I *still* can't.

"What are you going to do?" Locke asks.

That's the million-dollar question, isn't it? What am I going to do?

The sad reality is that I know the answer. I've *known* the answer. Auden has her company, her contract. I have hockey and the captain spot. We *can't* do anything about it, and that's just what we have to live with.

"Nothing," I tell Locke. "I'm going to do nothing."

Chapter 21

AUDEN

"So, it's over?"

"Just like that?"

"I wish I could rip his dick off."

"Then beat him with it."

That one earns a chuckle. Leave it to Rory to always make me laugh.

She pokes a finger into my side. "I saw that. You smiled."

I did smile, and even though it's been just four days since Hutch took back his hat and only two since he ignored me at the game, it feels like I haven't smiled in a lifetime.

"It was *my* joke," Lilah declares. "I set it up."

"And I finished it, so who's the real winner?" Rory sticks her tongue out at my best friend, and Lilah reaches forward, trying to grab it, which of course turns into a slapping match.

They're ridiculous and I love them for it. They're just what I need, especially now that I'm out of a company *and* my love life is in shambles.

Love life. Ha. Like I ever had one in the first place.

I mean, sure, we fucked, but that was it. There were no feelings attached, at least not from Hutch's end, something he made perfectly clear when he turned a cold shoulder to me like I was nothing to him.

I guess that's my fault, though. I knew. He was upfront. He said he doesn't do commitment, and I said it too. I meant it then. I really did.

But that was *before*. Now, everything's changed.

I miss him, so fucking badly. As much as I love Rory and Lilah for being here, I wish it were Hutch sitting next to me and not them.

"What the hell are they doing here?"

Rory flies off her stool, and I turn to see where she's headed. Imagine my surprise when I see not one or two or three Serpents players but five of them walking our way.

"No," my twin says, shaking her head and holding her palms up to them. "Nope. Stop right there. You're not welcome here."

"Holy shit. There are two of them," Hayes says, his

eyes darting back and forth between me and Rory. "Which one are you?"

"Not Auden," Lawson speaks up. "This one's hair is dark, and her eyes are different."

"*This one* has a name." Rory crosses her arms over her chest, and I wish I could see her face because I'd bet my entire fortune it's scrunched up like she just ate something sour.

"Why don't you tell me what it is, sweetheart?"

Just hearing the moniker roll off Lawson's lips has my stomach rolling. I've never been one for pet names, though every time Hutch called me sweetheart, I swear I fell a little harder for him.

Rory laughs, like literally laughs in his face, and man do I wish I could capture Lawson's expression. His jaw is slackened, his eyes wide. It's like he can't believe someone could dare reject him.

But he doesn't know Rory, does he?

"I—I—I..."

"I—I—I..." Rory mocks, no doubt rolling those intense emerald eyes of hers. "Go away."

Several of the guys tuck their lips together, trying not to laugh as Lawson gets knocked down several pegs.

"Fucking roasted," Keller says, and...is that a smile I see? It looks strange on him. Not forced, but not natural either. It's gone as quickly as it appears, and he's back to frowning.

Much better.

"We're just here to talk to Auden," Locke says, stepping to the front of the group. He peeks around Rory and sends me a soft smile with a small wave. "Hey."

I lift my hand. "Hi."

"Can we talk?"

"All of you?"

"Well, no." He looks back at his teammates. "I have no clue why these idiots are here. They insisted on coming."

"I missed my flight for this shit. My mom's gonna kill me."

"Aww, someone going home to mommy for Christmas?" Lawson smirks over at Keller.

"Aww, someone upset their mommy didn't love him enough to invite him home for Christmas?" my twin throws at the cocky hockey player.

"I like her," Fox says.

"Me too," Hayes agrees.

"Fuck you both," Lawson mutters, looking shaken once again.

Man, Rory's really knocked him off his game, and I can't say I'm hating it. Even after spending just an hour or so with him in California, I could understand why Hutch was always saying he's exhausting. The guy never, ever stops flirting, not even with me. I thought Hutch was going to fly over the table at him at least five different times and I'd have to hold him back.

I guess that's not something I have to worry about now, is it? A frown tugs at my lips at the reminder of the future I didn't know I wanted so badly now being so far out of my reach.

"Auden?"

I look over at Lilah, who has been awfully quiet through this whole thing.

"Hmm?"

"I, uh, I may have called them here."

"You what?"

She winces. "I just… Well, I wanted some answers. So I made Sadie do some digging and get Locke's number."

"Lilah!"

She shrugs sheepishly. "Sorry? In my defense, I didn't realize they would *all* come."

"I didn't either," Locke says. "They just followed me."

"Because we're a team," Fox says, stepping forward and placing his hand on the older man's shoulder with a wide smile. "We have each other's backs."

"We're not a team." Hayes steps up, his hand landing on Locke's other shoulder. "We're a club."

"Serpents Singles, baby!" Lawson yells, placing his hand on Locke's head. He looks back at Keller, then jerks his head toward Locke, like he's trying to get his teammate to join in on the…well, whatever the hell is happening.

Keller just stares at him like he's a moron, which he is.

"Get the fuck off me," Locke grumbles, shaking the guys off. He sighs, then looks back over at me. "So can we talk?"

I look at Lilah, who is giving me a look that says, *Do it*, then at Rory, who—to my surprise—is saying the same thing.

So, I nod.

My sister steps aside, and Locke walks past her, muttering a quick *thank you*. I'm unsurprised when the rest of the guys follow closely behind him, just like I'm unsurprised when, the second Lawson shoots a seductive grin Rory's way, she sneers at him. He shrinks back, and it earns her a second laugh from me tonight.

Locke takes a seat on the stool next to me, the rest of the guys grabbing a nearby table and pulling it closer, then plopping down in their chairs. Rory returns to her spot next to me, placing a comforting hand on my back. That's when you know I'm in bad shape—

when Rory's willingly touching me. She must know this one, whatever it is, really hurts.

Locke clears his throat. "First, I want to say I'm sorry."

I tilt my head, drawing my brows together. "For what?"

"Well, for ratting you out."

"For...ratting me out?"

"To Coach and the GM. I was the one who told them about you and Hutch."

I rear back, my eyes wide because, um, what?

"You did what?" I ask incredulously.

He reaches up and scratches his long beard. "Did Hutch not tell you?"

I scoff at his question, grabbing my wineglass—which is still full because not even that sounds good right now—and twirl the stem between my fingers. "*Hutchinson* hasn't said a word to me since he snuck out of my room four nights ago."

"He..." Locke sighs, and I swear I hear him call Hutch an asshole under his breath.

It makes me grin because I agree—he *is* an asshole. Just as quickly as it came on, the grin fades, because yeah, as much as Hutch is an asshole, he's *my* asshole, and I miss him. The sadness sets in all over again.

"I didn't know he never told you."

I push my shoulders back, lifting my chin. "Well, he

didn't. He didn't say anything to me. He just left, took that damn Yankees hat with him and disappeared, then ignored me at his game."

Yeah, I'm bitter about that too.

Locke frowns. "I'm sorry he did that. That was a dick move."

"It was."

"But he did it for a good reason."

I meet his serious, soulful brown eyes. "And what reason could that possibly be?"

"They offered him the captain spot."

I gasp. "They did?"

Locke nods. "They did."

My stomach rolls once more. He got captain and he didn't tell me? The thing he's been working so damn hard for? The thing he wanted so badly? He got it and he didn't say a word?

Hutch is an asshole.

"But," Locke continues, "in order for him to become captain, he had to break it off with you."

"Something they only knew about thanks to you." I glower. Maybe if I glare hard enough, I can transfer all my anger toward Hutch to Locke because screw him for telling.

"No. It wasn't me."

My glare transforms into confusion, my brows pulling together. "But you said…"

"I didn't tell them until *after*. I wasn't the one who broke the news. It was Rogers."

"Rogers? Who is…"

Oh god. It all comes flashing back to me—that guy going over the red line and knocking Hutch down, the fights that ensued afterward. Hutch punching the guy out and embarrassing him in front of a sold-out arena, the Vegas player promising revenge.

Well, I guess he got his revenge, huh?

"How did he know?" I ask.

Locke waves his hand around the bar I've spent entirely too much of my time in over the years. "The Sinclair. He must have seen you guys together when Vegas stayed here, and he bided his time."

Crap. I…I didn't even think about Hutch sneaking around here when other teams were in town. It's not like my face is plastered all over the place, so I never worried about someone knowing who I was. They'd know Hutch, of course, but I didn't think it would matter if he was here. I guess it did, though, at least to Rogers.

"That guy," Locke says, referring to the jerk who ruined everything, "he's a dirty player, one of the worst in the league. He's been suspended I don't even know how many times for terrible plays. He's out for blood and he doesn't care who it is he's hurting. When Hutch knocked him out… Well, he didn't appreciate that, even though he definitely deserved it. You were just an unfortunate victim of his revenge."

"Yeah, but what's it matter?" Hayes speaks up. "Hutch is still going to be named captain, so what did Rogers really get out of this in the end?"

"Well, Hutch is super fucking depressed, so there is that," Fox says.

"And playing like trash," Lawson adds.

"Heartbreak." Everyone's eyes snap to Keller, who is sitting with his arms crossed. He shrugs. "That was Rogers' reward: Hutch's heartbreak."

I laugh, but there's no humor in the sound. "What heartbreak? He seemed fine to me the other night. Besides, it's not like he was in love with me or anything. How could his heart be broken?"

All the guys exchange a look.

"What?" I ask. "What was that look for?"

"Tell her," Fox whispers not so quietly.

Lawson nods. "She's got a right to know."

"Know what?"

"Look, I'm super against love," Keller says, "but even *I* think she should know."

"I'm team bros before hoes, but, yeah, what they said." Hayes tips his chair back on two legs as he offers his two cents, and I want to yell that if he breaks my chair, I'll break his face, but I don't have it in me. I'm too damn curious about what it is I need to know.

"Locke?"

"Dammit," he mutters, then he sighs heavily before leveling me with a stare. "Hutch is in love with you."

"Bullshit."

The word falls out of my mouth so quickly I don't think anyone was expecting it, especially not me.

Locke chuckles softly. "Sorry, Auden, but it's true. He told me himself just yesterday."

"He did not," I insist, but even as the words pass my lips, I know they're pointless, just like I know Locke isn't lying—Hutch is in love with me.

"But…but…how?"

He lifts a shoulder. "That's for him to tell you, if you'll give him the chance."

Give him the chance? I'd *love* to give him the chance, but that's not up to me. He's the one who walked away.

"Uh, not to be a total Debbie Downer or anything," Lawson says, putting his hand in the air like he's asking the teacher a question. "But how exactly is him confessing his love—which, ew—going to fix anything? Isn't there still the issue of the contract Auden has with the team?"

Fox and Hayes nod, muttering a "Yeah" and "Good point."

"She quit."

We all turn toward Lilah.

"What was that, sugar?" Fox asks in a thick Southern drawl.

Lilah's eyes jump to him and…is that a blush I see stealing up her cheeks?

"She quit." She shrugs. "She doesn't own the hotel anymore, and that contract isn't hers. It was transferred with the company to the new owner."

Now *I'm* the one everyone's looking at.

"Is that true?" Locke asks. "Did you sell your company?"

I slide a loose strand of hair behind my ear and nod. "It's true. I started working on it a couple of weeks ago, and we just finalized everything a few days ago. Actually, it was…"

I trail off, choking back the emotion rising in my throat when I think about the day I finalized the biggest deal of my life, when I changed everything for the man I love, only to have him ignore me.

I give myself a shake, pulling myself back to the present. "I'm no longer the owner of Sinclair Properties."

"Christ," Locke mutters, pinching the bridge of his nose. "I didn't know. *He* doesn't know, Auden."

And how could he? He refused to talk to me. Hell, he refused to even look at me. He just walked away from it all—from *us*.

"If he had known, he wouldn't have walked away,"

Locke says like he's inside my head. "He wouldn't have. He's too damn crazy about you for that to happen."

"But he *did* walk away. He did. What am I supposed to do with that? Just show up and tell him I quit and we confess our love and live happily ever after?"

"Yes!"

The outburst startles me, not because of the volume at which it's yelled but because of *who* yelled it.

"Excuse me?" I say, turning on my stool. "*You* think that's what I should do?"

Rory blows out a breath, rolling her eyes at the same time. "Yes, Auden. God. Don't make me repeat all that sappy crap, but yes. It's so damn obvious you're head over heels for this guy, and if what these guys are saying is true, Hutch loves you too. No matter how revolting that is, are you *really* going to let true love pass you by because of one little misunderstanding?"

My mouth is hanging open because...huh? This is Rory talking—*my* Rory. The woman who hates, hates, hates love. Who hates everyone, actually. *She's* the voice of reason? She's the one telling me to chase after Hutch?

I blink up at her. Have we entered an alternate universe and I just wasn't aware of it?

"Don't give me that look like we're in some sort of

alternate universe where you're the love-hating fool and I'm the hopeless romantic," she says. *Damn Twin Thing.* "I'm just saying…if you love him, tell him. Maybe it'll work out." She points a finger at me. "But if it doesn't, no crying. I hate crying."

I laugh because *of course* she had to ruin her beautiful speech in the most Rory way. I look at her hard, studying those eyes of hers that have studied me so hard over the years. Then I look at Lilah, then Locke, and then all the rest of the guys. Hayes, Fox, and Lawson are all on board.

All except Keller. Not until I lift my brows in his direction does he sigh, tossing his hands into the air.

"Fine. But he's out of the club."

"What club?" Lilah questions, but nobody answers her. They're all too busy waiting for *my* answer.

I blow out a heavy breath, then look at Locke. "All right. I'll tell him. But…how?"

A slow grin spreads across his lips. It's mischievous, maybe even a little devious, and I have a feeling I'm going to regret asking when he says, "I think I have that covered."

Chapter 22

HUTCH

When my mother called and asked me if I would consider flying home for Christmas to help lift the spirits of my soon-to-be-divorced evil stepsister, I was shocked when I found myself saying yes without any hesitation.

When I was gunning for the position of captain, I thought I was ready for what the job entails, thought I could handle it with ease. I felt sure I would be the best damn captain who ever captained.

Boy, was I fucking wrong. I'm not even officially wearing the C and I've already screwed up more times than I can count, first with Locke and almost fist-fighting him at the lunch buffet, then taking not one or two or three but *four* penalties in our last game, effectively throwing it for the entire team.

It was terrible. *I* was terrible.

Mix all that with the fact that I fucking miss Auden? Yeah, I was more than ready to leave Seattle and escape for a few days.

I reach up on my head, adjusting the Serpents hat I'm wearing. I have no fucking clue what happened to my Yankees cap. I could have sworn I tossed it in my bag my last day in the locker room, but I must have left it behind. Sure, I could have swung by the arena and grabbed it, but by the time I realized it was missing, I was already running late for my flight.

That's another thing going wrong—I got bumped. *Me!* Fucking bumped.

I was livid with the guy at the ticket counter when he told me I wouldn't be making my 6:00 flight and instead would be on the 8:00 one. How fucking dare they. I even tried playing the hockey player card—one I never, ever play—but it was pointless. They wouldn't budge.

So, I waited. I waited for *two damn hours* in the first-class lounge, where I had to sit and listen to *Sports Desk* go on and on and fucking on about how badly the Serpents suck and how we're just trying to tank our season all thanks to me. It was torture, especially since I slipped the bartender a hundred bucks to change the channel and then he couldn't find the remote. Convenient, huh?

But that's all behind me. Now I'm sat safely in my

very large and mildly comfortable first-class seat. We're only moments away from takeoff, and I'm already feeling better. I'm going home and getting away from all this bullshit. This break is going to be good for me, even if I am going to be forced to listen to my evil stepsister cry. It'll give me time to refocus on what's most important: hockey. It's all I need, right? That's what I said at the beginning of the season and that's what I need to stick to. I let myself get distracted, and I won't do that again.

It doesn't matter how badly I miss Auden, how badly I itch to touch her soft skin again, how much I want to push a strand of her hair behind her ear just one more time. It doesn't matter how much I'm dying to hear her laugh or how I'd give anything—*anything*—to smell that orange-honey perfume of hers tickle my nose.

I pull my headphones over my ears and close my eyes, resting my head against the window. Someone sits down next to me, but I ignore them, pretending to be asleep, pretending to dream. Maybe…just maybe…if I pretend hard enough, I can conjure all those things I miss about Auden so much.

Just one last time, I tell myself. *For old times' sake.*

I picture her lying on top of the silk sheets at The Sinclair. She's smiling up at me after I've just come home after a game. Her long brown hair is fanned out around her shoulders, and she looks like a fucking goddess, especially when she parts her legs, giving me a glimpse of those curls I love to run my nose against so much. She giggles at me, then crooks her finger, calling me closer, and I go. I walk right over to her, and I kiss her, taking her soft lips with mine until neither of us can breathe. Then I trail my lips over her chin and down her neck, burying my face right in the crook of it and inhaling that scent I associate with only her.

I inhale sharply and swear I can actually smell it. It's like she's right here next to me it's so strong. I suppress my groan, frustrated that this little fantasy of mine can't be true. I wish it were. So fucking badly. I wish, for the first time ever, I didn't have hockey, didn't have a contractual obligation and she didn't have one either. I wish we could just *be*.

God, I sound like a lovesick fool. I shake my head at myself, shifting in my chair, but I don't shake hard enough because I swear I can still smell her perfume. It's not possible, I know that, but man do I wish it were.

"Excuse me, ma'am, but we're going to need you to put your tray up for takeoff," I hear faintly through the headphones.

"Oh, um…I can't," a soft voice says. "It's broken."

The other woman sighs. "Can you hold it, then?"

"I guess, but then what am I supposed to do with my Fritos?"

My eyes pop open and I rip off my headphones, my hat flying off my head and landing who knows where. I look over to see a woman holding up her tray with one hand while she folds in half and sticks her head down between the seats. Slowly, she sits back up, and all the air leaves me as time stands completely still. A sweet grin curves her lips, and she extends her hand to me.

"You dropped this."

I glance down, down, down, right at the navy hat with the faded Yankees logo in the center of it. Everything snaps back into place and time returns to normal. I take the hat, running my finger over the logo. I peek back up at her, finding her watching me expectantly.

"Sinclair," I say, and she giggles.

She fucking giggles.

"Mr. Grumbles."

And everything that has felt so wrong for far too many days feels perfectly right again.

"Uh, ma'am?"

Auden looks up at the stewardess, then back at the tray that's hanging in her lap. She picks it up and latches it with ease.

"Oh, look at that—I guess I fixed it."

The attendant gives her a tight smile. "I guess you did." She sticks her nose in the air, then carries on to the next row, clearly annoyed by the woman sitting next to me.

Auden turns back to me, and I'm fighting the urge to ask her what the hell she's doing here, resisting the desire to haul her into my lap to kiss her. I settle on something in the middle.

"Hi."

That same giggle as before bubbles out of her. "Hi? That's all I get?"

"Fancy meeting you here?"

She rolls her lips together. "A little better. Try again."

"I miss you."

She sighs, closing her eyes for a moment. When she turns her hazel gaze back to me, I feel like the only person on this sold-out flight.

"I miss you, too."

I reach for her, but at the last moment I remember she's not mine to reach for, not anymore. She never even really was. I pull my hand back, tucking it into my lap so I don't accidentally do it again. And then, I stare.

And stare and stare.

I can't look away from her because I can't believe she's here. She shouldn't be. She should be at The

Sinclair because she's still her and I'm still me and we still can't be together. I wish I could go back in time and refuse the captain spot, tell them their rules and contracts are bullshit, tell them they can't hold this over me because it was never my decision to love Auden. It just happened.

She just happened.

"Aren't you going to ask me what I'm doing here?" she finally asks.

I swallow, my throat dry and scratchy when I say, "What are you doing here?"

"Well, see, the weirdest thing happened. I was trying to get a flight out tonight—I'm heading to New York, you see. Anyway, I was trying and trying and trying and finally I said to the guy at the ticket counter, 'Don't you know who I am?' And he looked at me like I was crazy, the word no written clear as day on his face. So, I pressed my shoulders back"—she does just that—"and I lifted my chin." Up her chin goes. "Then I said to him, 'I'm Auden Sinclair, billionaire hotel owner, and I demand to be on this flight.'"

She shakes her head, grinning as she relaxes back into her seat.

"You want to know what that jerk said? He said, 'Ma'am, no you're not.' Can you believe it?" She huffs. "So I told him, 'Google it. Get your phone out right now and tell me I'm a liar.' And he did. He pulled his phone from under the desk and tapped his fingers along the screen and waited for the results to load, then he laughed." She tosses her hands into the air. "Laughed!" She crosses her arms over her chest, and I roll my lips together, trying not to laugh at her theatrics. "Then, just to rub some dirt in my wound, he turns his phone my way and points at the screen and he says, 'See? Auden Sinclair is not the owner of Sinclair Properties. She sold the company last week.'"

She sits back in her seat, shaking her head with a grunt of dissatisfaction.

"I told him he was nuts, said there was no way she'd do that. She loves that company. She wouldn't sell. Not unless there was something..." She rolls her head my way. "*Someone* she loved more."

She stares at me.

And stares some more.

When I don't say anything, she shrugs.

"Anyway, I Googled it myself and he was right. She sold it. That little lovesick fool."

When several seconds pass and I *still* don't say anything, she peeks over at me. I try not to laugh. Damn do I try, but it's so hard not to when she's looking at me like she is, her bottom lip snug between her teeth as she chews on it with worry.

"Are you done?" I ask.

She nods. "I'm done."

"Good."

Finally, I do what I wanted to do before—I haul her into my lap and I kiss her. I kiss her hard. I kiss her soft. I kiss her and kiss her and kiss her until that damn flight attendant is back and yelling at us to get into our own seats.

Only then do I pull away, tucking Auden safely back into her spot and buckling her belt for her. She giggles when I latch it and settle back into my chair.

She looks over at me with a grin. "So?"

"So…you sold your company?"

She nods. "I did."

"For me?"

"No." Her words surprise me. "I did it for me. I did it because it was time."

"Time for what?"

"To put down roots." She fiddles with the belt across her lap. "Do you think I'm crazy?"

"I could never think you're crazy."

She smiles. "Somehow I doubt that."

The plane lurches as it begins making its way down to the runway for takeoff. I wait for her to grab my hand, but she doesn't.

"I heard you got captain," she tells me.

"I did. I…" I sigh. "Fuck, Auden. I'm so sorry. The way I walked away…the way I treated you at the game…" I shake my head, disgusted with myself. "You didn't deserve that."

"You're right, I didn't, but I understand it. I know why you did it. You had to. You thought we couldn't be together, and you did what you had to do to protect your heart." She lifts a shoulder, her gray sweater slipping down to reveal her pale skin. "I would have done the same thing."

I nod because she would have. I know she would. We're the same like that—two broken people who guarded our hearts and put everything else in front of us to keep anyone from penetrating the walls we put up.

"Can I ask you something?"

"Anything," she tells me.

"Did you mean what you said earlier?"

"Which part? I said kind of a lot."

"About loving me."

"Oh. That." She gulps, then slowly nods. "I meant it, Hutch. I meant it a whole lot. I love you. So much. I didn't mean to. I know that wasn't the deal, but it happened. It happened and I'm not sorry about it, okay? I just can't be sorry about it."

I try not to laugh at her rambling.

"Is that so?"

She tilts her chin up. "That's so."

"Well, that's good," I say as the plane picks up speed, takeoff just seconds away.

Her eyes widen. "It is?"

"Yeah." I nod. "Because I love you too, Sinclair."

"You do?"

"Yep, and I'm not sorry about it. I just can't be sorry about it."

She grins, and as the wheels of the plane leave the ground, I wait. I wait for her to reach over and wrap her hand around mine, but she doesn't.

"You good?" I ask.

"Hmm?" She looks completely unfazed.

"Flight anxiety—are you good?"

"Oh, that." She shrugs. "I'm good. No nerves."

"Why is that?"

"Because I have you, Hutch. Are *you* okay?"

"Me? Oh, yeah. I'm good."

"Why is that?" she echoes.

"Because I have you, Auden, and with you, I know I'll always be okay."

She smiles, then winks. "What a weird coincidence."

But it's not a coincidence. Not at all.

It's fate.

Chapter 23

AUDEN

Meeting Hutch's family wasn't exactly what I had in mind for Christmas. We just made this thing between us official and it feels entirely too soon, but that didn't stop me from getting off the plane with him in New York and immediately agreeing to stay.

"You can go or stay. I know which one I'd like, but it's up to you, Auden. You're calling the shots."

"I'll stay."

He was looking at me like I was his entire world, and I couldn't have said no if I tried. It wasn't until we'd picked up our bags and stepped outside to find his mother and stepfather standing there with a sign that said *My Little NHLer* that I realized what I'd gotten myself into: spending several days inside a strange house with strange people and my new boyfriend.

But, despite all the initial awkwardness from

everyone—because, hello, surprise guest!—it's been drama-free...mostly. His mother is sweet and caring and almost a little too doting, but she's also warm and inviting and everything I always pictured a mother would be. His stepfather is polite, albeit a little quiet, but I don't mind it.

His stepsister, though? She's a whole different beast, which is why I'm currently standing outside despite the below-freezing temp. The yard is completely covered in snow so deep it comes up above my knees, and it looks like a Hallmark movie out here, especially with the lights strung over the wraparound porch and the snowman in the front yard. It's beautiful, and I'm going to be sad to leave in a few days.

"There you are."

I spin at the intrusion and grin over at the man who brought me here. "Hey."

He saunters toward me in that effortless way of his, not stopping until I'm crowded against the porch railing I was just leaning on.

"My mother was wondering if you want any milk and cookies. You know, before Santa comes tonight and steals them all."

I lift a brow. "Santa, or you?"

"I'll have you know I've only had five cookies."

"Since dinner."

He wants to deny it, but we both know there's no point. I've learned something new about Hutch on this trip: he's a Christmas cookie fiend, and his mother is more than willing to feed his addiction.

"Guilty," he murmurs, pressing a soft kiss to my forehead. "What are you doing hiding out here? It's freezing."

"I have a coat on," I tell him, though despite the thickness of it, I'm still chilled to the bone. "And I'm not hiding. Just getting some fresh air."

"You mean you're hiding from my evil stepsister?"

"Stop," I hiss, peeking around to make sure she's not lurking like she has been this entire trip.

It's safe to say Hutch's sister isn't fond of me, or even of Hutch himself. Hell, I'm not even sure she likes her own father, who has spent most of this trip holed up in his office "working." I may have totally caught him watching football on his laptop, but that's our little secret.

"What?" He shrugs. "She terrible, and you know it."

"She's not that bad."

But we both know I'm not being honest. She really is that bad. I thought for sure Hutch was just exaggerating, but that's not the case. She's mean and vindictive. Just hearing all the payback she's cooking up for her soon-to-be-ex makes the hairs on my body stand up. I don't know how someone could be so evil.

"She's pure evil, and you know it, Auden."

I chuckle, shaking my head. "You're mean, and you know it, Hutch."

"Mean or not, you still like me. In fact, I have it on good authority you might even *love* me."

"People are always spreading rumors." I roll my eyes playfully.

"They are. Did you hear the one about how I'm in love with you?"

I smile slowly. "You know, I think I did. Couldn't possibly be true, though. The Reed Hutchinson I know doesn't do love or relationships. He took a blood oath to stay a member of the Serpents Singles forever."

Hutch groans, tossing his head back. "We didn't take a blood oath. Fucking Lawson."

I laugh. "He's something, huh?"

"Exhausting, that's what he is. He needs someone to knock him down a few pegs."

"Oh, you should have seen Rory yesterday. She was more than willing to do so."

"I knew I liked her." Hutch presses another kiss to my forehead, running his hands up and down my arms when I begin to shiver. "Come inside, sweetheart."

What he doesn't know is it's not the cold making

me tremble. It's him. It's always him, and I have a feeling it's always going to be him.

"I love you, Reed."

His eyes widen at my words like he's surprised to hear them again. I don't blame him. I'm still surprised I'm saying them, but I'm even more surprised by how natural they feel, how right it is. Everything with Hutch feels like what I've been missing for so long.

He closes his eyes, sighing contentedly as he rests his forehead against mine. "I love you, Auden. So fucking much. I can't..." He shakes his head. "What you did...selling your company..." He pulls away, peering down into my eyes, into my *soul*. "I'm so glad I didn't have to lose you, but I'm so sorry that's what it came down to."

"Don't be sorry. I'm not. I'm totally at peace with my decision. In fact, I feel lighter than I have in years. The stress of it all...I think it was affecting me more than I ever let on. I've never been happier than I am now that I've sold the company, though I think that might have something to do with you, too."

"It's the orgasms." He shrugs, giving me a proud smirk.

I don't refute his claim, because I'm almost certain that *does* have something to do with it. They certainly don't hurt.

"But seriously…" His grin slips, his lips pressing into a thin line. "Thank you, Auden."

"For what?"

"For loving me enough to put down roots with me. I promise…" He swallows. "I promise to make it all worth it. To give you a life you'll never regret. To love you unconditionally. To make you the happiest I can possibly make you every single day."

"You already make me happy, Hutch. This…*us*… it's enough for me, and it always will be."

"You're enough for me, too."

I sigh softly, rising up on my tiptoes and resting my lips against his. It's supposed to be a chaste kiss, something quick…but that's not the actual case, not with us.

Hutch presses his lips against mine harder, taking control as he angles my head where he wants it and slips his tongue into my mouth. I have no clue how long we stand here kissing like teens on a Friday night about to be late for curfew. All I know is I never want it to end.

When we finally part, I'm truly trembling, and not just because of Hutch's touch. It's growing colder by the minute, and it's starting to snow again.

"Are you ready to stop being stubborn and come inside now?" Hutch asks, back to rubbing my arms to warm me up.

"I-I-I s-s-suppose."

He laughs, grabbing my hand and tugging me toward the door. "Come on. I think I know just the right way to warm you up, Sinclair."

"Are you trying to woo me with orgasms again, Mr. Grumbles?"

"Always."

I laugh, following him into the house. We're about halfway up the stairs when a voice stops us in our tracks.

"Reed? Auden? Is that you?" his mother calls from the kitchen. "Come join us for cookies and milk!"

His stepsister sighs like she's never been more annoyed, and I know in that instant that Hutch and I will not be sneaking upstairs together. We have to go rescue his mother.

"Do you mind?" Hutch whispers to me.

I shake my head. "Not one bit. Besides, why should Santa get to have all the fun?"

He smiles then kisses me quickly. "Come on. I promise to make it up to you later."

I know without a doubt he'll keep that promise, again and again and again. Because this thing with Hutch? It's not a fling. It's not just fun.

It's fate...and I think it might just be forever.

Epilogue

HUTCH

"Let's move it! Give me hustle!"

I press my hands to my knees, sucking in gulps of air and trying to catch my breath as I stare over at our new hire.

Just before the All-Star break, after we lost five games in a row, Coach was let go. The losing streak coupled with the GM not being happy about how he handled the shit that went down with Auden and me meant it was over for him. I liked Coach. He was a good guy, but his behind-the-bench presence left something to be desired.

With the ups and downs of this team since its beginning, I'm not surprised by this big move. I thought maybe it would happen during the offseason, but I guess they felt they couldn't wait. They needed to make a change and shake things up if we wanted to have any chance of getting to the postseason.

We've only had two practices with the new guy who was previously working with the Comets—*those fucking Comets again*—then did a short stint at the AHL level, and I'm already feeling more confident in this team.

"Can't believe I'm stuck with this old man again," Hayes complains, glaring over at the head coach. "Thought I was done with the Comets when I got sent out here."

"Don't worry, Hayes, I can't escape them either," Lawson says, clapping him on the shoulder, referring to his older brother who plays for Carolina.

"This is his first coaching gig, right?" Fox questions, eying the new guy warily.

"Second." Keller skids to a stop in front of us. "Ish. He did video before this for the Comets and the AHL."

"He was an incredible player. I have no doubts in his coaching ability," Locke adds, always the voice of reason.

I nod, agreeing. "What Locke said."

Surprise flashes in his eyes for only a moment, gone just as quickly as it appeared.

Things were a bit awkward for a few days after

Christmas break, but we fell back into our usual groove easily. I'm still a little pissed, but thanks to Auden telling me how Locke was the one who helped facilitate a way to fix everything between us, I've mostly forgiven him. After all, we're still teammates. It's not like we can stay mad at each other forever, not if we're hoping for a chance of winning the Cup.

"Well, if you two are on board, I'm in too," Fox says, flashing that same smile he's always sporting.

"Hmm," Keller grunts.

Hayes and Lawson nod, agreeing to being all in on the new coach. I'm glad. I'd hate to have to beat a teammate's ass during my first few months as captain.

"Dude, whoa." Lawson smacks Hayes, then points toward the bleachers. "Who is that?"

Hayes looks at him like he's stupid. "Um, Auden?"

"No, the woman next to her."

"Rory."

Lawson glares at the young player. "No, you idiot. The bombshell redhead that just walked in."

"Ah, her. She's—"

"*Mine.*"

We all turn to find our new coach standing behind us, arms crossed over his chest, brows pulled in tight together.

"She's mine," he reiterates, his eyes drifting from us to the bleachers where the newcomer sits. As if she can feel all our eyes on her, she lifts her head, then sends our head coach a wave.

I turn just in time to catch the twitch of his lips. It's the most I've seen him smile since he was hired.

"Duly noted," Lawson mutters, turning his attention elsewhere. Guess he can be smart sometimes after all.

"Back to skating, boys," Coach instructs.

"Yes, Coach Smith," we all say in unison then get to moving.

Practice runs another fifteen minutes before we're cut loose. After hitting the showers and grabbing my bag, I head for the lobby where I know Auden is waiting.

Now that she's no longer working an insane number of hours, she's spending more of her time at the rink. I'm not complaining or anything, but I swear I saw her picking up trash from the bleachers the other day. While she's definitely happy and still okay with having given up her business, I think not having anything to do is slowly starting to drive her mad.

"Hey, you." Auden pushes off the wall and presses her puckered lips to my waiting ones.

"Gross." Rory makes a gagging sound, but we ignore her, extending the kiss far beyond what we originally planned.

"You're all sweaty and gross," Auden says when we finally part.

"You like me sweaty and gross."

She lifts her eyes skyward, but there's no malice behind the gesture. She knows I'm right. "You guys looked good out there. Better."

"Yeah?" She nods. "Good. I thought so too."

"Coach Smith seems to be fitting in," she remarks. "And his fiancée is really nice."

"And totally smoking hot," Lawson says as he waltzes up, his hair still wet from the shower. His eyes find Auden's twin, and his entire demeanor changes. A slow smirk inches across his lips, and I swear he puffs his chest out some. "Is this what you do now? Stalk our practices? Because if so, I'm going to have to talk the new coach into doing a shirts vs skins game. I call skins." He bounces his brows up and down.

"Really? You'll take your shirt off? Dreams really do come true," Rory says, all the fake excitement in the world in her voice. "I'd especially love to see you dragged across the ice with no gear." She bats her lashes sweetly despite her dark words then rolls her eyes. "I'll be in the car, Auden."

Rory takes off down the hallway without another word, leaving Lawson standing behind with his tongue practically hanging out as he stares after her in wonder.

I shudder just thinking about falling on the ice with nothing on. That's a pain I never want to feel.

"She's so mean," he mutters, then he grins. "And she so wants me."

I laugh, patting his back. "Keep dreaming, buddy. Keep dreaming."

"Sorry, Lawsy, but I'm with Hutch. Rory doesn't want anyone. She's probably more committed to staying single than you are."

"Who said anything about not staying single?"

He goes to waggle his brows once more, but all it takes is my taking a step toward him to have him holding his hands up and backing away.

"What's that, Hayes? You need me? Coming!" He spins on his heel and darts away down the hall to where absolutely nobody called for him.

"Either she's going to strangle him, or he'll wear her down eventually. I can't decide which."

Auden laughs. "Oh, strangle for sure. I know my sister too well—she'd never get involved with Lawson."

I hope to hell she's right. I need him focused for the rest of the season, not prancing around the locker room doing victory laps, which I can totally see him doing.

"So," I start, pressing another quick kiss to her cheek. "Lunch?"

"Please. I'm starving. I skipped breakfast."

I want to lecture her on that, but don't. I've learned my lesson when it comes to hungry Auden—leave her be and feed her as quickly as you can.

"Where to? The Sinclair?"

She shakes her head, slipping her arm through mine as we begin walking toward the parking lot. "Nah. I have somewhere else in mind."

"Really? Where?"

"There is this place I've been wanting to give a try…"

"Name it. I'll take you anywhere you want to go."

She grins up at me, fully knowing the truth behind my words. She recently mentioned she's always wanted to go to Greece but has never found time to make it happen, so I surprised her last week with tickets for this July.

"It's local, so no need to go spending a fortune." She gives me a pointed look.

I shrug. "It was worth it."

"And I love you for it."

I try not to let how much her words mean to me show. I never thought I'd be in love and I definitely never thought I'd be so casual about it either, but it's easy to do both with Auden.

"So where is this place? I'll pull it up on the GPS." I pluck my phone from my back pocket.

"Here, I'll type in the address."

I hand over my phone without a care in the world, and she starts pressing her fingers against the screen, typing in the destination like she's done it a thousand times before.

When she hands it back, I'm confused.

I peek over at her. "This is where you want to go?"

She bobs her head up and down. "Yes."

"For lunch?"

"And dinner. Breakfast too," she adds, then she sighs. "I was even thinking Easter, Halloween, Thanksgiving, and Christmas. And New Year's, of course. Maybe a little repeat of this last one." She bumps her shoulder against me then tries to walk ahead, but I don't let her.

I grab her hand, pulling her to a stop, and she spins toward me, a grin etched across her face.

"Yes?" She says it so innocently I almost believe her.

"Auden…" I roll my tongue over my lips, running my thumb over the back of her hand where it's entwined with mine. "Are you saying what I think you are?"

She tucks her lips together, piercing me with those hazel eyes of hers I love so much and nodding several times. "I am."

"And you're sure?"

"Surer than I've ever been."

I drag her the last remaining inches toward me, not stopping until she's flush against my body, hers pressing on mine in that familiar way I'm not sure I'll ever tire of.

"You moving in with me, Sinclair?"

Her lips twitch. "I'm moving in, Hutch."

"Fucking finally." I capture her lips with my own, showing her with my mouth just how happy I am with her decision.

I mentioned it to her not long after we got back from Christmas with my family. I didn't want to put any pressure on her because, hell, we were moving kind of fast, but it also just felt so damn right, like it was the natural next step. She told me she'd think about it, and I let it go.

Now...now she's moving in with me, and I can't fucking wait.

We stand pressed together—our bodies and our lips—for what feels like forever and not long enough all at once. Not until a throat clears do we finally break apart.

"Oh, good. You're done mauling my sister." Rory lifts her brows. "Can we go now?"

Auden laughs, pulling away from me and shooing her sister forward. "We can go now." She peeks back at me over her shoulder. "See you at *home*, Mr. Grumbles."

For the first time in my existence, I get a speeding ticket on the way home, and I'd do it all over again… for Auden.

Bonus Scene

AUDEN

"I'm coming!"

Unfortunately, it's not in the way I *want to* be coming right now.

It's the doorbell going off for what feels like the millionth time already today, which means the knot in my shoulder is growing bigger and bigger by the minute.

I worried whenever I gave up my company, I would grow bored and feel like I had nothing to do.

That was before Hutch and I decided that building a house would be a good idea. Now, all my days are filled with rounding up construction workers, picking tile, and deciding if I truly cook pasta enough to warrant a pot filler faucet over the stove.

Since Hutch is currently on a "must eat pasta

before every game" kick, I think the answer to my latest dilemma has been decided for me.

I push off the counter I've been leaning over for the last hour, then close my laptop I've been staring at for just as long.

It's already been a tiring day, and it's not even time for lunch yet.

Another knock sounds at the door as I make my way to the entrance of the house that's still wrapped in chaos.

"Coming!" I call out, picking up my speed and trying my absolute best to ignore the mess around me. There are tools strung about, canvas sheets to help collect dust, and a few water bottles here and there because those damn workers *never* clean up after themselves.

I put blinders on as I stride closer to the door. I wrap my hand around the massive handle, which some might consider gaudy, and tug it open.

"You're late. You were supposed to—"

The words die on my tongue as I take in the sight before me.

It's not the landscaper who was supposed to be here an hour ago so we could go over the final design for the backyard.

No. Not even close.

"Hutch," I whisper, my eyes sliding over him. "You look ridiculous."

He chuckles. "I'm sure you meant to say *hot* instead of ridiculous."

I shake my head, trying my best to hold back the grin threatening my lips. "Definitely not."

He waves his hand over his frame. "What? Is this look not doing it for you?"

I take in his attire. He's wearing jeans that mold to his legs, making his thick and perfectly sculpted thighs look ten times better than they already do. A simple white t-shirt clings to him, showcasing the abs I know he's hiding beneath it. There's a toolbelt filled with tools I've never seen him wield slung loose around his waist. And finally, a bright yellow hard hat sits atop his head.

"What are you doing here?"

"Why, I'm here to work, ma'am. I think we had an appointment scheduled today."

I fold my arms over my chest, leaning against the doorframe. "I had an appointment with the *landscaper* today."

"Knew I should have gone the shirtless route," he mutters under his breath as he pulls the hard hat off, tossing it onto a stray chair sitting on the porch. He runs his hand through his hair, then gives me a wide grin. "I'm sure you can make some time to squeeze me in. Emphasis on the *in* part." He bounces his brows up and down a few times.

I roll my eyes on a laugh. "As fun as that sounds, I have meetings all day. The landscaper is an hour late. Then the tile guy *again* because he found something he swears we're going to love. After that, I have a meeting with the decorator to finalize everything. And *you* are supposed to be doing that thing with Rory and—"

He holds up his hand, halting my words. "It's all taken care of. I rescheduled your meetings to tomorrow, and Rory has been looped in, given specific instructions not to bother us unless someone is dying."

"Hutch…"

He shakes his head, stepping into me and sliding his hands over my face, his thumbs brushing over the apples of my cheek. "No. No arguing. You need a break. You've been working too damn hard lately."

"Because we're on a time crunch. We're trying to build a house before the season starts, and that's coming up *quick*."

"I know that, Auden, but you need a break. You—"

"I don't have time for a break," I whine.

Hutch's lips pull into a soft smile. "Sweetheart, you do. And I have a feeling I know just the way to convince you to take one."

Without warning, he bends, hooking his hands under my ass and lifting me into his arms.

"Hutch!" I call out on a squeal as he carries me through the house in rushed steps. He doesn't stop until we're in the kitchen, where he drops me onto our new marble countertop.

"What are you doing?" I ask, but it's pointless. He's clearly a man on a mission, dropping his lips to my neck in an instant, kissing me and nipping at me so eagerly it has me squirming against the counter in seconds flat.

He peppers kisses across every inch of my jaw, down my throat, and as far south as he can go with my shirt in the way. Then he retraces his steps, kissing me until I'm a panting mess, *needing* to be touched in any other way.

He must read my mind because suddenly he pulls away, a cool air hitting me the second I lose his touch, and Hutch is dropping to his knees, that ridiculous tool belt he's wearing clanking as he does so.

He slides his hands around my calves, running them higher and higher and higher, taking the knee-length skirt I'm wearing right along with him and not stopping until it's bunch around my thighs.

"Up," he instructs, and I know instantly what he means.

I lift myself off the counter just enough to allow him to push the material up. I gasp when my bare legs hit the cold counter, and he chuckles, leaning forward to torture me with his mouth more as he begins to kiss my inner thighs.

For hours...*days*...he kisses me. Soft and sweet and right up to just where I want him, only for him to retreat and start over. He torments me repeatedly until I know there is no way he doesn't see the wet spot on my gray panties.

"You're being mean."

"You like it," he counters, yet doesn't give in.

Instead, he continues kissing me for several more agonizing minutes until finally—*fucking finally*—he presses a soft kiss to my still panty-covered pussy.

And barrier or not, I swear I feel it down to my soul.

"Reed," I moan out his name. "More."

He laughs against me, the vibrations zinging through me and to my toes, dragging my orgasm closer and closer.

It's incredible how he can still bring me to the brink of combustion so easily after two years together.

And wildly unfair because he knows *exactly* what he's doing.

He drags his hand up my leg, pushing my thighs farther apart to the point it's almost painful, then uses a single finger to push back my panties, exposing me to him.

He sits back, his eyes never leaving the place he

loves to spend his time. He drags his tongue over his bottom lip, taking me in with hungry eyes, and I love every second of it.

He looks like he wants to devour me, and it just so happens that's exactly what I want too.

"Please…" I beg on a whisper.

He tears his gaze from my drenched pussy and up, up, up until he's staring right into my eyes.

"Ask."

"I did."

He shakes his head slowly, brushing his thumb gently over my clit. "Not properly."

"Please…" I whimper. "I need…"

"What, sweetheart? What do you need?" His voice is gruff as if he hasn't talked in days instead of only seconds.

"Taste me, Reed. *Please.*"

He heeds my request, running his tongue over me with such slow, delicious precision I could cry.

And that's exactly what I feel like doing when suddenly he shoves to his feet.

"No, no, no. What are—"

My words are cut off when he captures my mouth in a rough kiss. He wrenches his lips from mine only seconds later, peering down at me with a hard and heated stare.

"Turn over. Hands on the counter, Auden."

I don't hesitate to listen, dropping from my perch and spinning around, loving when he pushes me down until the cool countertop rests against my cheek.

Hutch is behind me, already pulling my underwear down my ass and exposing every inch of me to him.

"So fucking beautiful," he murmurs before landing a hard smack on my exposed cheeks.

"Oh god." I groan, shoving back because I want more. I *need* more. "Hutch…"

"Going to fuck you so good," he tells me, and I have no doubt he means the words.

I hear him moving behind me, and then that ridiculous toolbelt hits the floor, and all I can think about is how good he's going to feel sliding inside of me.

I don't have to wait much longer because the next thing I hear is his zipper being tugged down, and suddenly, he's right there, pressing against my pussy and begging for entrance.

I push back, searching for him, and he laughs at my impatience.

"So needy."

"Your fault," I bite out.

"I'm not hearing any complaints."

"The only complaint I have is that your cock isn't inside me right now."

Another rumbling laugh. "I think we can fix that."

Then slowly—so fucking slowly—he pushes inside me inch by torturous inch. I hate it because it's not enough, and I love it because it's just how I want it.

I'm such a conflicted mess of emotions as he finally bottoms out inside of me.

"Fucking hell," he mutters. "This never gets old."

"Never," I echo. "Now fuck me, Hutch. *Please.*"

This time, there's no teasing. He pulls out until just the head of cock sits inside me, then slams back in with full force, and it's everything I didn't know I'd been missing.

Hutch is right. I needed this more than I realized.

He finds a rhythm that works for us both and doesn't stop, thrusting into me over and over until we're sweaty messes. Our grunts and groans echo off the still-empty walls, and it's the most beautiful sound I've ever heard.

"God, I wish you could see this," he tells me, still pumping into me. "Wish you could see how you look taking my cock right now. So fucking good."

"I'm so close," I tell him.

"Me too," he says, then slides his hand around my waist, dipping his fingers between my legs. He strokes over my clit with a deftness he's perfected in the time we've been together, playing me like his favorite instrument until my orgasm slams into me with such force that tears spring to my eyes.

"Holy mother of... Yes, yes, yes," I chant as he slams into me, my orgasm still rocking through me with every punishing thrust.

Less than a minute later, Hutch comes with a shout, spilling himself inside me and filling me up with his cum.

When he finally stills, he's breathing hard, folding himself over me and kissing a path down my back.

It's only then I realize I'm still fully dressed, and so is he, and it makes this mid-morning tryst all that more exciting.

I have no clue how much time passes before he slowly slides out of me, then steps away, pulling my skirt back down to cover me like his cum isn't currently running down the inside of my thighs.

My body is achy as I push off the counter and turn into Hutch's embrace, loving how he captures my lips with his instantly. He kisses me softly and sweetly, like he didn't just fuck me hard and harsh.

He grins down at me when he finally drags his mouth from mine.

"Now tell me that break wasn't worth it."

I lift a shoulder. "It was fine."

"Fine?" he practically growls, and I laugh.

"Maybe a little more than fine."

"Auden…" he warns, his eyes darkening.

But I'm not scared. Not with Hutch. *Never* with Hutch.

Because not only has he kept his promise to give me a life I won't regret, to love me unconditionally, and to make me the happiest he can every day, but he's done so much more than that.

He's given me a new family, new friends, and a renewed sense of adventure. He's given me endless laughter and much more fun than I could have imagined.

He's given me roots.

And most important, he's given me *him*—fully and forever.

Hutch grabs my left hand, lifts it to his lips, and presses a soft kiss against the simple gold band that circles my finger.

"I love you, Auden."

"I love you more, Reed."

He shakes his head. "Impossible."

And maybe…just maybe…he's right about that.

THE END

Other Titles by Teagan Hunter

SLICE SERIES

A Pizza My Heart

I Knead You Tonight

Doughn't Let Me Go

A Slice of Love

Cheesy on the Eyes

TEXTING SERIES

Let's Get Textual

I Wanna Text You Up

Can't Text This

Text Me Baby One More Time

INTERCONNECTED STANDALONES

We Are the Stars

If You Say So

Want to be part of a fun reader group, gain access to exclusive content and giveaways, and get to know me more?

Join Teagan's Tidbits on Facebook

Stay on top of my new releases, cover reveals, sales, and more by visiting:

www.teaganhunterwrites.com

Thank You

My husband, Henry. YOU are my roots.

Laurie. Sometimes we find people in life who just make sense for us. You're that person for me. An incredible, loyal friend, and an amazing assistant. Couldn't do this without you.

My editing team. Caitlin, Julia, Judy… Seriously couldn't make these books happen without your expertise. Thank you for always being so amazing.

Kim and Nina and the VPR team. You took me in when I was feeling lost in my career. You gave me purpose and direction and I am forever grateful for all your wisdom.

Shannon, Katie, and Emily. You ladies create stunning covers and take the best photos. Thank you for bringing my visions to life.

Tidbits. You're my favorite group of people. Thanks for letting me be ME and always having my back.

Washington/PNW. One of the very first adult books I ever read was *Watch Them Die* by Kevin O'Brien. It was set in Seattle and I immediately fell in love with the city. There was just something about it I loved. Something that called to me. Then Twilight happened not long after that and I fell even more in love with Washington. I promised myself that one day, no matter what, I would visit it. Being from a small town, I never, ever thought that dream was really possible. Then my life took a weird turn and suddenly, it was *very* possible. So we hopped into our converted van and drove from South Carolina to Washington and I finally made my dream come true. I fell even more in love with the state. We sold our house during out three week trip, went back to South Carolina and packed up our lives, then moved to Washington on a whim. It's been almost a year, and it's the best decision I've ever made. So, thanks Washington, for allowing me to fall in love with you.

You. Thank you for taking a chance on this book. There are millions of stories out there to read, and I am so, so thankful you picked up mine.

With love and unwavering gratitude,

Teagan

TEAGAN HUNTER writes steamy romantic comedies with lots of sarcasm and a side of heart. She loves pizza, hockey, and romance novels, though not in that order. When not writing, you can find her watching entirely too many hours of *Supernatural, One Tree Hill,* or *New Girl*. She's mildly obsessed with Halloween and prefers cooler weather. She married her high school sweetheart, and they currently live in the PNW.

www.teaganhunterwrites.com

Printed in the USA
CPSIA information can be obtained
at www.ICGtesting.com
LVHW040828230124
769571LV00084B/871